Merritt and her CHILDHOOD CRUSH

Merritt
and her
CHILDHOOD CRUSH

EMMA ST. CLAIR **JENNY PROCTOR**

Copyright © 2023 by Emma St. Clair

All rights reserved.

No part of this book may be reproduced in any form or by any electronic or mechanical means, including information storage and retrieval systems, without written permission from the author, except for the use of brief quotations in a book review.

To all the fans of Steve the pelican.
We see you, and we raise you a Banjo the raccoon.

AUTHOR NOTE

This is book two in a series. If you jumped in here, that's okay! These are standalones, which means you don't HAVE to read book one, *Eloise and the Grump Next Door*. I'd recommend it, but you can totally keep on reading.

If you DID read book one, this book takes place days after Eloise has left for grad school. This book's timeline overlaps a little with book one. (Which has Jake even grumpier than usual.)

Carry on and enjoy Oakley Island!

Quick content warning: We write happy romcoms. HAPPY. That said, this book touches lightly on divorce, teen pregnancy, family estrangement, and cheating. AGAIN—lightly touches on.

ONE

MERRITT

I AM A FRAUD.

The words loop in my head as I run mile after mile down the beach. I can't go fast enough to escape their refrain. Or the truth behind the words.

I am a fraud. I'm a fraud.

Hello! Nice to meet you. Just call me Ima Fraud.

I haven't committed the kind of fraud that could land me in the clink—*do people really call jail that?*—but more the personal kind. I haven't defrauded investors or committed mail fraud or any of the other kinds of fraud out there. No—I've just been pretending to be someone else for, oh, I don't know … almost ten years of my life.

With absolutely no warning, I stumble, my ankle turning sharply as I pitch forward onto the sand.

I lie there for a few seconds, panting, ankle throbbing, pride stinging mightily.

Even the universe—not that I believe in woo-woo stuff like that—is judging, finding me in need of punishment for being such a little liar. What other explanation is there for what seemed like a picture-perfect life on the outside—successful career, relationship on the path I thought would lead to a ring and beyond—becoming a dumpster fire?

No—a dumpster fire isn't big enough. My life is more like a whole landfill engulfed in flames. Stinky. Disgusting. Burning out of control.

Even worse: at its core, my life was trash to begin with. Just trash.

Drama much?

Yeah, normally I leave the theatrics to my sisters. Eloise and Sadie aren't drama queens by any stretch, but comparatively, I'm the last one people would expect to throw a pity party lying facedown on the beach.

And yet, here I am.

Groaning, I sit up.

Unwilling to deal with my ankle yet, I focus instead on all the sand. It's on my chin, my palms, down the minimal cleavage inside my sports bra.

Is it in my teeth?

Yes. Yes, it is.

I squeeze my eyes closed and try to focus on my breathing, matching it up with the sound of the surf pounding a few feet away. I want to laugh at the enormous one-eighty I've done in the past month. More specifically, in the last week.

Before, on a normal day, I looked like the kind of woman who would walk into a conference room and cut you with my stiletto if it meant getting a contract signed.

A woman who had accomplished more by twenty-six than most.

Who could run for ten miles at a seven-minute pace and still finish with enough energy to hit up a cycling class later.

But I don't know what a normal day is anymore.

Because right now, I do not recognize the sandy, sweaty woman in a panting heap on the beach in front of my recently deceased grandmother's beach house.

Maybe this is the new normal. Maybe THIS is the real you.

I snort. I'm not sure where this snarky inner voice is coming from, telling me I'm dramatic and directionless. That this messy failure of a person with sand in her molars is the "real me." Let's hope not.

Something tickles my cheek, and I reach up, expecting to brush away sand. When my fingertips come away wet, I'm horrified.

TEARS?!??

Oh, no. Nope. We are not CRYING over this.

It's okay to cry.

I swallow. Hard. That's not my inner snark. It's a memory of my grandma's voice, and it's all too easy to close my eyes and lose myself in the comfort of her words.

"It's okay to cry," she says, squeezing my hand.

I clench my jaw, tight enough that it aches with the effort.

I can still feel her soft, wrinkled hand on my cheek, the ghost of her touch. On what was arguably the worst day of my life, it was amazing anyone could offer comfort at all. But she did. That was Gran's way.

"You don't need to be a turtle, Merritt Isabelle Markham."

"A turtle?"

"Wearing a hard shell you can retreat into when you're scared or hurt. Don't let this moment make you draw into yourself even more."

Her gentle smile in my memory almost undoes me. But then—aren't I already undone?

"Need help?"

A hand flutters in front of my view. A *large* one, encased in a worn suede work glove.

I know that hand. I know that voice. Even if it's been years since I've seen Hunter Williams.

Think of the devil—or, just the worst day of my life—and he appears.

I swat his hand away without touching it at all. Because even if there's a glove to protect me from the heat of his skin, the familiarity of it, I'm not sure what a touch from this man will do.

"I'm fine, Hunter."

"Doesn't look like it."

I surge to my feet, a huge mistake given the throbbing ankle I forgot about. With an undignified cry, I pitch forward —right into a hard, flannel-covered chest. I immediately try to wiggle away, but it's a challenge when I can't put weight on my ankle.

Hunter smells different. Not like the boy I knew with his drugstore cologne and teen boy aroma. Now he smells like a MAN. Spicy and woodsy and so, so, so, so good.

No! NOT good. Not at all good.

Hunter's arms come around me. It's less of a hug (which I wish I weren't desperate for) and more like a mall security officer restraining an irate customer. I struggle harder.

"Stop fighting me," he says, sounding exasperated. "Let me help you."

"I can't."

I really, really can't.

Already, I feel the tickle on my cheeks and the stinging in my eyes. Ugh—more tears. I cannot cry in front of Hunter Williams. Of all the people in the world, NOT HIM.

It only takes a few seconds of silent struggle for me to

give up. Because the truth is, for once in my life, I can't solve this problem by myself. I can't put weight on my foot any easier than I can shove the tears back in my eyeballs. I am a crying mess who more than likely just sprained my ankle, and my only rescuer is the man version of the boy I used to love.

To use my most hated phrase in the entire world, *it is what it is*. But I certainly wish it *wasn't*.

"You're hurt," Hunter says when I finally look into his face (after discreetly drying my tears on his absorbent flannel shirt).

He's more handsome than he was at eighteen when I last saw him on That Day. The beard is also new. It's a bit long and unkempt, but it suits the hard planes of his face.

I wonder how it would feel under my fingertips. Or on my cheek…

My heart does some kind of heavy flop, landing with a thud somewhere in the vicinity of my belly button.

It's dead now. DOHA—dead on Hunter's arrival.

Here lies Merritt's heart. Stopped by the sight of the man she swore she'd never see again.

"Who wears flannel at the beach?" I demand, sounding more like my fraud self, the one who feared nothing, felt nothing. The one who wore the hard turtle shell with pride— a woman with all hard edges and zero vulnerability.

Ever.

Most especially not in front of the man who makes me feel more vulnerable than anyone in the whole world.

He grunts, then says, "Let's get you back home."

I'm about to scoff because this island isn't home. My grandmother's beach house, in the process of being renovated into a bed and breakfast, is not home. The carriage house where I'm staying after my little sister flew off to grad school is not home.

But then, after everything blew up at work and with my relationship, New York isn't home either.

I guess I don't really *have* a home.

"I'm fine."

The words are still in my mouth when Hunter's strong arms sweep me up, bridal style.

Oh, no he DIDN'T.

The moment I begin fighting, he shifts, tossing me over his shoulder in a fireman's carry. Having briefly dated a fireman, I know this is *never* a hold they use in a burning building. They actually drag people because it keeps them low and out of the smoke.

Funny that given the flaming state of my life, a fireman's carry feels completely appropriate here.

"Put me down!"

Hunter ignores me. I stop just short of pounding on his back because that would make me feel even more childish and out of control.

"I'm covered in sweat and sand," I protest.

"The flannel will protect me."

I grin, then bite down on my lip—*hard*—to stop the smile.

There he is—the quiet man with the surprisingly quick humor that makes rare and perfectly timed appearances. Most people never get to see it. Only the few whom Hunter allows to get close to him.

Maybe he's a turtle, too.

I stay limply draped over his shoulder the rest of the way, over the wooden crosswalk and up the crushed oyster path to the carriage house.

I do my very best NOT to take deep inhales of Hunter's spicy scent. I try—really, I do—NOT to watch his denim-clad butt as he walks. This man is *married*. Even if we didn't have a complicated history, he would still be entirely off-limits.

But it's *right there*. Unless I close my eyes, there is nowhere else to look. This feels like the perfect excuse for a free pass. Observation only, of course, but he IS the one who threw me over his shoulder with my head facing his butt in the first place. It's like he's MAKING me look. And *oh* it is a phenomenal butt.

As though he can hear my thoughts, or maybe hear me not-so-subtly breathing him in, Hunter grunts and says, "Take a picture. It'll last longer."

"Sure. Want to hand me my phone? It's in my hip pocket," I shoot back.

I swear, his whole body stiffens at my words, and I wonder if I've pushed too far. He was speaking generally because I was staring, but I just asked him to stick his hand in my pocket.

As much as I hate to do it, I force an image of Hunter and his wife Cassidy into my head. I have to keep them—the two of them—front and center in my brain.

My body jostles as Hunter climbs the stairs, and I repeat like a mantra in my head: *married, married, married, married.*

"Uh, what's happening here?"

I squeeze my eyes closed at the sound of Jake's voice. The lawyer inhabiting the other side of the carriage house WOULD be here to witness my humiliation. Of course he would.

Why can't I just have one private moment to fall apart in peace???

"Nothing," I say just as Hunter says, "Sprained ankle."

"It's not sprained," I snap.

Hunter turns around so I can lift my head and see Jake.

Or perhaps so Jake isn't getting an eyeful of MY butt perched high on Hunter's broad shoulder.

"Morning, neighbor." I lift my hand and wave like I'm just out for a morning stroll. No big deal. Nothing to see here!

Jake is also in running clothes. He deals with things—things like missing my youngest sister, Eloise, who is currently all the way across the country—like I do: working too hard or running too long.

"Are you sure you're okay?" Jake asks, glancing between me and Hunter.

"Nothing that a little ice and rest won't fix," I answer.

And a lobotomy to scrape out the scent of Hunter, the image of his butt as he walks, and the kindness of this whole rescue.

My brain snags and catches on this for a moment. Why was Hunter down on the beach anyway? How did he see me fall? I expected to see him around the main house working on renovations, but I hoped, if I stayed close to the carriage house, I would avoid running into him.

"Well, if everything's okay here—"

"It is," Hunter and I say at the exact same time.

Jinx.

Another echo from the past floats into my head the way they've been doing ever since I set foot on Oakley Island. I see Hunter's grinning, boyish face, his wide smile, the one I used to think only I was privileged to see.

"You owe me a soda," he says.

The Coke machine whirrs, then spits my crumpled dollar back out. I use the corner of the machine to flatten the bill out. Hunter leans against the wall with his arms crossed over his chest while he watches.

"This is the only time I've ever seen you quiet. It's kind of nice," he says.

The can thuds its way down into the bottom of the machine. The Dr Pepper is cold against my palm as I hold it out. Hunter's fingers brush mine as he takes the drink. He pauses just a moment longer before saying my name to release me from the jinx. "Mer."

I haven't heard my name on his lips since we were fifteen. It hasn't gone without notice that Hunter hasn't said it now.

Hunter is on the move again, totally unaware of how my mind keeps dipping into unwanted memories. The kind that make my chest ache.

But your heart is dead, remember? It died a few minutes ago when you saw Hunter's face for the first time in so many years.

The screen door creaks as Hunter walks into my side of the carriage house. It's a duplex, two mirror-image apartments with Jake on one side and me on the other.

Until yesterday when I dropped her off at the airport, Eloise lived here, doing her sisterly duty according to our grandma's will. One of us—me, my other sister, Sadie, or Eloise—must live on the property until renovations on the main house are done. Then we're free to sell it as the B&B Gran always envisioned.

Or keep it, I guess, though we haven't discussed that complicated possibility.

Lo took the first shift since she had just graduated college when we were surprised by this inheritance. Could Sadie have stepped up? Sure. She works from home. But to do her government internet security job, she needs servers and the kind of tech stuff that always has me crossing my eyes and zoning out. Eloise had no plans and no job, which made her the perfect solution. Until she got an opportunity to start a grad school program in the Pacific Northwest.

That left me. And since my life had recently imploded with uncannily perfect timing, I came to Oakley. As of yesterday, I'm living in what was Eloise's half of the carriage house and driving her car—since I haven't owned my own vehicle in years. My sisters both think I'm working remotely. I'm not ready to discuss being jobless and boyfriendless and all the -lesses, so I left out a lot of the details.

You know. Just a few teensy things.

"Where's all your stuff?" Hunter asks, gently lowering me to the couch.

Some part of me—*is that my ovaries? Do they even exist?*—weeps as he backs away, the warmth of his strong body and the feel of his soft shirt disappearing from my cheek.

I shrug. "I didn't bring much. My apartment in the city was half this size. Plus, I'm not staying long."

"Of course. You'll be out of here the first chance you get. Back to big city life." His jaw tightens, and he spins around. "Let me get you some ice."

"I can get my own."

It's true, even if it would involve painful hobbling.

Hunter only grunts at this and roots around in the kitchen, tossing his work gloves on the counter. I think about his words, the ones he threw like spears—that I'll be gone the first chance I get. *Back to big city life.*

The problem is that I don't have a big city life anymore. I quit my job. Sublet my apartment. Ran for the hills—er, the island. And though being on Oakley feels like trying to fit into the same shoe size I wore in eighth grade, I actually have no plans to leave.

Because I have nowhere to go.

My big city life went POOF! And the whole fraud realization has me questioning everything. The truth is—I'm not sure I know what I want, much less who I am anymore.

Hence the careless running on the beach leading to an emotional breakdown and a probably sprained ankle. Even if I won't admit any of these things out loud.

I watch Hunter because I just can't help it. He's really grown into himself. Exactly who he was, just bigger. Older.

Better looking. The boy I knew never would have snapped at me, but I've given him every reason to.

Back then and again today.

I'm the only one who's changed into this hard, unrecognizable version of myself—striving for perfection to the point of total exhaustion. Which is something I only realized when things fell apart. If I'm being honest—and Gran's voice in my head is pretty much demanding it at this point—I hate the woman I've become.

Or … the one I've been pretending to be. The fraud. New York Merritt.

"Really, Hunter. I don't need you."

I don't realize how harsh the words sound, how much meaning they convey, until they spill out of me.

Hunter pauses, one hand scooping ice out of the freezer. His deep brown eyes meet mine and hold.

"I know you don't."

He goes back to gathering ice.

I need something to do that isn't staring at him, so I examine my ankle. I can't really tell how bad it is, and I won't until I get my sock and shoe off, but the ache seems to have subsided.

Or maybe it just feels better compared to the deep ache in my chest.

Hunter is there suddenly, kneeling by my feet. "Let me."

I should protest—I *really* should—but I know he won't let me.

And is it so wrong to want his touch as much as I want to push him away? I allow myself this one small thing even as I remind my heart that this man belongs to someone else.

I don't fight as he oh-so-gently lifts my foot. I try to focus on the pain rather than his deft fingers pulling off my shoe. I hiss as he slides the sock down my ankle.

"I'm sorry," he says. And when his eyes meet mine, his words carry much more weight. *Years* of it.

I drop my gaze, searching for some kind of appropriate answer when I realize something. The kind of something that freezes me in place.

Why isn't Hunter wearing his wedding ring?

TWO

Merritt

IF I WEREN'T HALF-HOPPING, half-wobbling on my stupid ankle, then wandering the aisles of Oakley Island's one grocery store might actually be soothing. The wide aisles (so different from the cramped corner store closest to my apartment in New York). The neatly organized options. The uniquely Southern offerings I haven't enjoyed since I was a kid—things like stone ground grits, Carolina Gold barbecue sauce, Moon Pies.

If I have to be essentially homeless and jobless, there are worse places than Oakley to be marooned, at least from a purely food-based perspective.

I snag a variety pack of Moon Pies—chocolate, vanilla, *and* banana—and toss it in the cart before slowly hobbling onward. I probably look ridiculous, but honestly, I'm past caring, a sensation that feels both utterly foreign and completely liberating at the same time.

New York Merritt never would have left her apartment looking sweaty and disheveled with no makeup on. Even while running, New York Merritt looked polished and poised. New York Merritt also wouldn't be buying Moon Pies after ogling Hunter Williams's butt.

Apparently, Oakley Island Merritt is FULL of freaking surprises.

Speaking of surprises.

Neither version of Merritt would have agreed to come at all had Eloise informed her that *Hunter Williams* was the contractor working on Gran's house. I mean, I knew before coming that I might bump into him here. Living his perfect life. Enjoying his perfect wife.

But to be working at Gran's where I have to *see* him every day?

I never would have agreed. Unfortunately, by the time Lo mentioned Hunter's name, I already *had* agreed. I was already here, even. Present. Committed.

Still, I can't blame Lo. She has no idea the kind of history Hunter and I share. She was too young the last time we were in Oakley to realize what was going on.

Now, if Sadie were involved, this would be some kind of scheme. She likes to poke the bear more than anyone I know, and she at least has some idea of how I feel about Hunter.

Oof. Felt about Hunter. Those feelings are definitely past tense.

Theoretically, past-tense feelings mean I should be able to handle this whole situation like a grownup. I try to imagine casually talking to Hunter about bathroom fixtures and wall colors and cabinets.

Nope. Can't picture it.

Especially not after suffering through the delicious torture of being thrown over his shoulder, smelling his new, manly

Hunter smell, feeling his Hunter touch as he lightly gripped my thighs. I swear, I can still feel the imprint of his big hands.

Big hands NOT wearing a wedding band.

He probably takes it off for work reasons, I tell myself before stomping on that thought like an errant spider.

Yeah ... *no.* This is all too much.

Sadie will have to come down here and figure out how to do her high-level security work from Gran's carriage house. *Sadie* can handle the renovations and dealing with Hunter.

Which would leave me ... living with Mom and the stepdad I barely know? Oh man. No thanks. That might actually be worse.

You could just be brave and stay.

Gran's voice echoes in my head, a light chuckle woven through her words like she's issuing a personal challenge to me. But Gran should know better. Even the subliminal version of Gran's voice that's taken up residence in my head since I arrived. Gran had a front-row seat to the horror show and heartbreak my last visit to Oakley turned out to be. She's the only other person who knows—*knew*—about That Day—the one where, like an enormous idiot, I drove all the way here to surprise Hunter and tell him I loved him.

Spoiler alert: never, ever decide to surprise someone you haven't talked to in a few years to confess your love. Trust me. It won't work out.

"Excuse me," an older woman in a green apron emblazoned with Gator's Groceries says, stopping next to my cart.

Her smile is blinding, and I have to remind myself that down here, it's normal for random people to speak to you. Or smile at you.

"Hi," I say.

"Y'all need help finding anything? Not to be rude, but you look a little lost."

Understatement of the year. Also, I forgot how y'all can mean one person or twenty.

"No, but thank you."

"And we do have a motorized cart if that would help."

She eyes my ankle, which screams, *Yes! Please get a motorized cart!* But the rest of me cannot imagine anything more humiliating than being a twentysomething riding on a motorized vehicle through Gator's Groceries.

"I think I'm good."

"Alrighty, then! Just holler if you need me."

She disappears and I add three different kinds of chips to my cart. This level of wallowing—which seems to keep getting deeper—demands extensive supplies. Preferably the kind loaded with carbs and calories.

My brain is still trying to come up with a solution for the Hunter problem.

Maybe I can leave him notes about the beach house renovation. Texts. Emails. Post-it notes left on the front door or in random places around the property. Honestly, I'd be willing to learn how to send smoke signals if it will keep me from having to see and talk to him face-to-face.

I push my shopping cart around the corner—my ankle still yelling about the motorized cart—and freeze.

Because a few yards away and looking as sweet and pretty and soft and all the things I'm not is Hunter's wife, Cassidy.

She is inspecting the eggs, one hand thumbing through the carton. Then she lifts it to her nose and smells it. Who DOES that? Why?

I have so many questions, but they disappear the moment I see her rounded belly. Though I know you're not supposed to make assumptions about women being pregnant, there is no doubt. Especially when Cassidy sets down the eggs and rubs a hand over her abdomen. She's even got the glow and, as she takes a few steps forward toward the milk, I see she's also got the waddle.

Okay. So, Hunter is having another baby. Fine. Whatever. I decided a few years ago I would never want kids anyway. Further proof our lives diverged, and he's better off with Cassidy.

I'm debating how to make my exit since it will mean walking right by Cassidy when I see the little girl beside her. She so obviously belongs to Hunter, it steals the air right out of my lungs. She has his mouth. The same shape to her eyes. Same dusting of freckles and dirty blond hair. When she touches Cassidy's belly and smiles up at her mom, the sweet moment makes my stomach cramp.

Scratch my earlier thought—there is no WORSE place to be marooned than Oakley Island. And there is no way I'm going to be able to handle this.

I need to escape.

RIGHT NOW.

I can't just stand here and stare. Eventually, they'll notice me, and then. . .

Oh. And then nothing. Cassidy probably doesn't even remember me.

I can't forget *her* because I could tell even way back when that she liked Hunter. It was in her not-so-subtle disappointment whenever she tried to hang out with him only to find out he was with me. Hunter missed her hints completely, but it made jealousy rage inside me like an inferno.

It still does.

Because once upon a time, her husband was *mine*. I was *in love* with him—even if I didn't fully realize it in the moment—and looking back, I think he maybe loved me too. But not anymore. Now, he belongs to Cassidy. And she probably hasn't given me a second thought. Why would she? It's been years since my last summer on Oakley Island.

I suddenly have an intense urge to yell my name into the dairy section of Gator's Groceries just to see if it matters.

To her. *To anyone.*

I grip the handle of my cart a little tighter, shifting my weight more fully onto my good foot. I've already been on my feet too long, and my ankle is throbbing and angry. It'll probably be black and blue with bruises by tomorrow. I really should get home. Get it elevated and iced. Eat the entire box of Krispy Kreme donuts I just dropped into my cart.

To do that, I just need to wheel past Hunter's wife and child like a normal, emotionally stable human, which I can absolutely do because I AM an emotionally stable human.

Mostly.

Mostly-ish.

One foot in front of . . . the same foot, Mer. You can do it. Channel the fearless New York Merritt for a minute.

I hop forward, then freeze AGAIN, this time nearly gasping out loud when a man approaches Cassidy and drops an arm around her shoulder.

A man who is definitely not Hunter.

The embrace could *almost* be brotherly, but then he kisses her RIGHT ON THE LIPS.

At first, I am enraged on Hunter's behalf. But it only takes a moment for puzzle pieces to fall into place in my brain.

Hunter wasn't wearing a wedding ring this morning.

Hunter's wife is kissing another man in a very public grocery store on a very small island where residents drink gossip like water.

Which means Hunter's wife can only be his *ex-wife.*

Huh.

My heart flutters.

NO. NO HEART. STOP IT RIGHT NOW. THIS CHANGES NOTHING!

DO YOU HEAR ME? NOTHING!

But my heart does *not* hear me. The realization that Hunter and Cassidy split up already sets the ball rolling in what feels like a Rube Goldberg machine inside my body. One reaction leading to another to another until I'm left a quivering mess.

My thoughts go to the gentle way Hunter handled me earlier—even his fireman's carry felt careful—and then to the concern in his dark eyes when he apologized as he gently removed my shoe and sock.

More flutters in the heart region. More thoughts racing, memories resurfacing, my pulse taking off like a sprinter at the sound of the gun.

I have GOT to get control of myself.

But how? My brain and my heart are working together now, flooding me with feelings, with memories, with the ache of a long-dormant desire waking up.

But I can resist. I have a lot of practice hiding behind very thick walls. So what if this island makes me feel like those walls are built on sand, their foundation already shifting? I can dig deeper. Fill the holes with concrete strong enough to withstand the strongest waves this island can throw at me. Upgrade my walls from pressure-treated wood to stone. Or iron.

"Hey, um, miss?"

My eyes pop open, darting around until they settle on the little girl standing beside my cart. *Hunter's* little girl.

"Hi," I manage to say, my voice cracking. I clear my throat and try again. "Hello."

She holds up a bottle of pain reliever. "This fell out of

your cart."

"Oh." I hold out my hand. "Thank you."

"Sunshine, let's go!" Cassidy calls, thankfully not looking back. Just in case she does remember me, I will not be able to handle polite conversation with her right now.

The little girl smiles and waves. "Bye!"

Cassidy calls again, "Isabelle!"

A lump takes up immediate residence where my heart is supposed to be.

Isabelle.

Hunter named his daughter *Isabelle.*

I close my eyes one more time, the memory as clear and sharp as a scalpel.

"Okay. You're going to live in a mansion," I say, tilting the notebook so Hunter can see it. "You drive a Porsche, which obviously I bought for you because you're a garbage truck driver, you're married to me, and we have two kids."

"A boy and a girl," he says easily, like it's perfectly normal for us to talk about our future like this. He reaches across the white wicker sofa on Gran's back porch and tugs at a piece of my hair. "Isabelle is the oldest."

I smile when he chooses my middle name.

"She's stubborn like her mom. But she's brilliant like her, too."

I bite my lip. "And Ashton for the boy," I say, choosing Hunter's middle name, "after his dad. He'll have your big, brown eyes. The same elusive smile."

Hunter grins, and my heart jumps just like it always does. I could be wrong, but it feels like I'm the only one who makes him smile so easily. And that smile has a direct link to my heart.

"Elusive, huh? You and your SAT words."

"Shut up. You like me for my vocabulary."

"Not *just* your vocabulary."

The way he looks at me when he says that wakes some new part of me, a part that's just beginning to stir when I'm around Hunter. I rip the page of MASH out of my notebook and fold it up before slipping it into the back pocket of my cutoffs.

"What are you doing?" he asks on a laugh.

"Evidence," I say, my expression serious. "I'm holding you to this, Hunter Ashton Williams. One day."

A spark of heat flashes in his eyes, then his expression shifts to something lighter. "Fine by me," he says. "But do I really have to drive a garbage truck?"

I am both elated that Hunter named his daughter Isabelle and *furious* that he did so when he was married to anyone else but me. How could he? *Why* would he?

More importantly, what am I supposed to do now that I know this?

My ankle throbs.

You're supposed to get yourself home to ice your ankle and stuff a dozen Krispy Kreme donuts in your face, you big baby.

I look to my right and grab the biggest bottle of wine I've ever seen, lowering it into my cart. It's a practical decision, really.

I'm going to need something to wash down all the donuts.

THREE

Hunter

"SIMMER DOWN, buddy. Having no legs doesn't mean you get a free pass to act like a monster."

I use my boot to nudge Vroom's food bowl away from the other dogs. The dachshund mix likes to be the dictator of dinnertime. Vroom doesn't actually have *no* legs—the front two work just fine, but he's missing his back two and has a wheeled mobility cart. He gets around almost as well as the other two rescue dogs I have. But pair his disability with the small-dog syndrome, and Vroom can be a little bit snappy when Sunbeam and Lilith get too close.

I can relate.

There's a tug on my jeans, and I glance down to see Banjo the raccoon waiting not so patiently for his food. "Sorry, bud," I tell him, walking a few feet away to get his bowl set up on a small table. To keep the interspecies conflict to a minimum, it's best to keep Banjo's food out of reach.

He's not the first raccoon I've taken care of since becoming licensed to rehab and foster wild animals. But Banjo is the first one I'll be sad to see go. He's a total nuisance—one I've grown accustomed to having around. He's nearly back to normal after being hit by a car a few weeks back, but if I haven't quite mentioned his quick recovery, well—I will. Eventually.

Am I running a miniature wild kingdom of rescued animals over here? Yes, yes I am.

When all the animals settle into their own food bowls, I walk inside, letting the screen door slam behind me. I need to fix the springs so it closes nice and soft the way it should. I've been saying that for three years, since I first bought the place. It's so much easier to fix things in other people's homes than attend to the broken parts of my own, which feels a bit like a metaphor.

One that's way too on the nose.

This glorified cabin may need a lot of work, but it's livable. More than that, it's peaceful. Located on the southern tip of the island, just on the edge of uninhabitable marshland, I have almost half an acre to myself, and I can't even see the next closest house.

"Mom says you live like a hermit," Isabelle told me recently.

Not untrue, but I wish Cassidy would be more careful about the things she says in front of our daughter. "I'm not a hermit," I told her. "But I do really like things quiet."

"I'm not quiet," Isabelle said, chewing her lip, and I wanted to kick myself for saying the wrong thing. Again.

Though Cassidy and I divorced amicably when Isabelle was barely two, at times I see our daughter worried about approval, anxious to know she's wanted. According to the articles I read, this is a normal part of growing up but can be harder for children of divorce, even if the parents are both still involved in their lives.

I ruffled her hair and gave her a kiss on the cheek. "I don't need you to be quiet, ladybug. I like you just the way you are." Then I challenged her to a shouting match, and we went out back and yelled at the marsh, scaring off some shore birds while the dogs barked and Banjo ran in circles.

I could use a little of Isabelle's noise right now. While I do love my quiet life, today is one of those days when the quiet feels as heavy as the humidity in July.

Or maybe it's just that the lack of sound leaves too much space for my thoughts to get loud. And ever since I saw Merritt running on the beach, my thoughts have been screaming.

Earlier this week, Lo oh-so-casually mentioned Merritt would be taking her place overseeing the renovations. I had about forty-eight hours to prepare. Not nearly enough time to know how I feel about her return. About her.

I'm still not sure.

What's strange to me is that Lo clearly had no idea what happened between her sister and me. I don't know how to feel about that.

I mean, on the one hand, Lo is a good five years younger, at least. Which doesn't matter so much now, but back when Merritt and I were *whatever* we were, Lo was close to Isabelle's age, so not likely aware of what Merritt was thinking or feeling. But to think that Merritt *never* mentioned me? That I was less than a speck in her rearview mirror?

I guess it only makes sense—that's what I was.

After our last, ugly conversation, Merritt never called. Never texted. No email, no regular mail, no adding as a friend on social media. For the next year, I waited. Then another, and another. Then I decided I was an idiot for thinking Merritt would ever come back, and I tried with Cassidy. Tried being the operative word.

A sharp bark disturbs me from my thoughts, and I realize I've just been standing here at the sink, staring out over the marsh for I don't know how long.

"Coming, guys." I grab my water and head back out, where Vroom, Lilith, and Sunbeam are milling about in the yard, eager for our evening walk. Creatures of habit, just like me. Banjo has wandered off into the yard, probably looking for a place to nap.

At the fence, Sunbeam nudges the latch.

"Don't even think about it," I tell the shepherd mix, easily the smartest of the bunch. He may only have one eye, but it doesn't slow him down the least bit or keep him out of trouble. I've had to rework this latch several times to make sure he can't escape and let the others out.

As soon as the gate is open, the dogs tear off down the path toward the marsh. Only Lilith, the old Great Dane, circles back to lumber alongside me. She moves right up against my thigh, nudging her big head under my hand.

"What—you think I need a friend? You would be right. It's been kind of a day."

Talk about an understatement.

Seeing Merritt for the first time left me feeling a little woozy. Unsteady.

I've seen grown-up Merritt before, courtesy of her LinkedIn profile. And yeah, maybe I joined under a fake name just to look her up. Her profile wasn't very personal, but I still learned a lot. Namely, that Merritt became exactly what she told me she'd be back when she was breaking my heart: a big city-dweller working a high-powered job. She has the kind of accolades under her belt most people work decades to achieve.

Not to mention she looked beautiful.

Even if the polished, professional headshot of her was almost unrecognizable compared to the wild-haired, shoeless, free spirit who ran around every inch of this island with me. Her hair was the same color, at least, and the photo revealed the same stormy blue eyes that captivated me all those years ago. But the freckles that always popped out after she'd been on Oakley a few months were nowhere to be found. And her smile looked ... wrong. Fake? Or just different. Even through the smile, her expression felt stern. Closed-off.

That one professional photo made me question all my memories of her. Maybe she was never who I thought she was. Or, I don't know. Maybe it was only that she was having a bad day and hates having her picture taken like I do.

What is not up for debate is that I've spent too many hours staring at that one LinkedIn profile picture, trying to superimpose the memory of Merritt's ghost onto the woman she grew up to be.

Today, though, when I saw Merritt fall—I saw a crack in her seemingly perfect veneer. It was lucky I saw her at all. I don't typically spend time near the beach, but I'd been negotiating prices with the guy building new cabinets for the beach house and had wandered toward the water in search of a stronger breeze. Merritt crossed into my view not seconds after I hung up the phone.

Then she tumbled, her expression shifting, and I caught a glimpse of the girl who would go crabbing with me, leaning over the dock with a chicken leg tied to a string. The one who wore the same dirty cutoffs nearly every day of summer, only washing them when her grandmother forced her to take them off.

It must have been the glimpse of the old Merritt that

made me pick her up and carry her off the beach. It was stupid. Overbearing. Caveman-like.

I thought it might satisfy my craving, to get close, to test the limits of my self-control by helping her when she needed it—even if she didn't want my help.

Instead, it only woke the long-sleeping desire for more of her.

The dogs and I reach the end of the trail where the land slopes down to marsh grass. Vroom chases Lilith—a good match-up since Lilith only has three legs—and I find a stick to throw for Sunbeam.

Yesterday, this evening ritual felt like enough—the dogs, the sunset, the pop and crackle of the marsh with its briny scent. For years, this has been the *amen* to end every day.

But today, just like the quiet, this feels off. *I'm* off. And I know without needing to say it, it's because of her. I hate that even just seeing Merritt again was enough to throw off the equilibrium of my life.

Standing at the marsh's edge, watching as Banjo appears out of the brush and joins Vroom in his chase, I promise myself I won't let Merritt's presence derail me anymore. She's my past. Temporarily part of my present.

Definitely not my future.

MY PHONE BUZZES JUST as I'm stepping out of the shower. It's a number I don't recognize, an area code I don't know. A lot of people who hire me are new folks, moving down to Oakley and snatching up old homes to renovate them, so calls from unknown numbers aren't all that unusual. But they never come in this late.

Then again—this could be Isabelle's handiwork.

My daughter has recently decided that I need a new wife. It's probably because Cass is having a baby. Her mom is nesting; Izzy is matchmaking.

First, there were the dating apps that mysteriously appeared on my phone. I'm not sure how many women responded to the profiles Izzy set up with misspelled words and a photo she took while I was glaring and telling her to give my phone back. But respond they did, and let me tell you—I am ill-equipped for the dating scene. Cass was the last girlfriend I had, and considering we got married at eighteen, I've pretty much got no game. Nor do I *want* game.

Despite a long conversation about how I'm just fine on my own, my daughter's stubborn streak is about as long as mine. She is so far undeterred.

Now, based on the last strange call I got from someone named Gail, Isabelle has shifted from dating apps to handing out my business cards to random women, not-so-casually mentioning that her daddy needs a new wife.

Of all the things I *don't* need in my life, a new wife is at the top of the list.

I let the phone go to voicemail as I pull on sweatpants, but it starts ringing again almost immediately. This time, it only rings once, then stops. Then starts again.

"Hello?" It comes out a little sharper than intended, but it's late. And I'm not really in the mood.

"I have an issue with the tile choices."

"Merritt?"

"It's too expensive. And I don't like it."

I sink down on my bed, rubbing a hand over my jaw. She's been here less than a week and she's already upending things. Or trying. I don't plan to let myself be upended any more.

"It's already been ordered."

"Isn't it on back order? That will cause delays. And I—*we*—want this project done as soon as possible."

So you can run off again?

I don't say it, but it takes all my effort to bite back the reply. "Why don't we discuss this tomorrow at a more civilized time? I try to limit my conversations about tile to the hours between eight and five."

She's quiet for a moment, and I catch myself trying to analyze her silence. Which is so stupid. I need to stop pretending like I know this woman. Or like I *need* to know her.

"You got divorced." A statement. Not a question.

I don't notice until she says the word *divorced*, but Merritt sounds like she's slurring a little. Not quite a slur. More like her syllables are playing a little loose.

I guess it shouldn't shock me so much that Merritt knows I was married at all. Oakley is a small town, and small towns talk. Her grandmother probably filled her in on the whole situation. I can't imagine it painted me in a good light. It's always a scandal when you get your girlfriend pregnant during your senior year of high school. I did right by Cassidy, as best I could, though I was hardly husband—or father—material at eighteen.

So many mistakes. Why does Merritt arriving suddenly seem to highlight them all?

"Have you been drinking?" I ask.

"No." Her tone is way too defensive, and I'm not even a little surprised when she adds, "Not the *whole* bottle."

I catch myself before I can laugh. "Good."

"It was a big bottle. The biggest."

Her last word sounds like *biggesh*. So—NOT good.

"Merritt, do you need help?"

"I've got everything I need right here on the couch. My

wine, my water, aspirin, my phone ... wait—I can't find my phone!"

"You're talking on it, Mer."

The nickname slips out, and I wish I could yank it right back. Especially when I hear a sharp intake of breath on the other end of the phone. Squeezing my eyes closed, I swing my legs up into bed and settle in against the pillows. Might as well get comfortable.

I should hang up. But I know I'm not going to.

"Mer means the sea," she whispers.

"In French, yeah. It does." I used to tell her that, how she reminded me of the sea—wild and vibrant and beautiful.

The sea is also powerful and dangerous. I didn't know Merritt was those things too. Not until I'd already been carried out by her riptide and drowned.

Wow. Might as well be dressed all in black at some poetry reading with those thoughts. I shake my head.

"I saw Cassidy today."

I swallow, wondering where this is going to go. "Okay."

"And *Isabelle*."

The way she says Izzy's name—*her* name—triples the impact of Merritt's statement. I probably owe her an explanation, but I don't want to give it under these circumstances. "It's late, all right? We can talk tomorrow. Right now, I should get to bed."

"Or you should explain why you gave her our name. I mean, *my* name. My middle name, Hunter."

"I know."

There's a pause. It's the space meant for an apology. I mean, it does sound bad when you lay it all out there: I married another woman and named our daughter using Merritt's middle name. Which was also the name Merritt and I always talked about naming our kids.

Playing games like M.A.S.H., I remind myself. *Silly kids' games.*

"She's so beautiful, Hunter," Merritt says.

My heart swells. Then sinks.

"She's amazing. Best part of my life."

It's weird how silence can convey a mood just as well as music. This one is weighty but not as uncomfortable as it should be.

"Can you come over?"

Merritt's voice sparks a memory. Not her words but the tone. Soft. Pleading.

"Will you kiss me, Hunter? Please? I can't start eighth grade as the only girl who hasn't ever been kissed."

She looks up at me with such hope, such trust. It's the trust that does me in. The feeling that Merritt Markham thinks—for whatever reason—that I'm good enough to be her first kiss.

How can I say no?

"Just to talk," she adds in that same siren-sweet voice.

She has always been my weakness.

WAS. She always *was* my weakness. Not anymore.

"Unless you're injured or in some kind of trouble, I'll see you in the morning, Merritt."

Will she even remember this conversation tomorrow? I can't tell exactly how much she's been drinking. Enough to loosen her tongue. But she still seems coherent. Mostly.

"Don't be late," she says, like now the big concern is my punctuality. "And I mean it about the tile."

"Tomorrow."

I don't say goodnight before I end the call. I have too many memories of playing the goodnight game—*You hang up first. No, YOU hang up first.*

I program Merritt's number into my phone, remembering the moment I deleted her contact information from the beat-up iPhone I used through most of high school. It was the night before I married Cassidy—my final attempt to root Merritt out of my heart once and for all.

Little good it did.

For ten solid minutes, I sit there, holding my phone, willing it to buzz again in my hands.

FOUR

Merritt

UNFORTUNATELY, I only drank enough wine last night to loosen my tongue and lower my inhibitions.

I did NOT drink enough wine to forget the things I said when I called Hunter. Asking about Isabelle. Saying how my nickname means *sea*—something he told me over and over back then.

And the clincher: *Can you come over?*

New York Merritt is frowning in disapproval. Come to think of it, Oakley Island Merritt (or whoever I am now) is also disapproving. Overall—bad form. Terrible choice.

And now it's morning and I get to live with my wine mistakes. Yay!

I roll my eyes and limp around the kitchen while I wait for my coffee to brew. My ankle is better, but I can't even pace like a normal person who needs to physically work off steam. Normally I'd run, but that's definitely out for a few more days at least.

Ugh. Stupid sand. All uneven and ... sandy. In New York, I might have to sidestep a rat here or there. Maybe dodge a group of tourists taking selfies or a guy selling watches out of a suitcase in the park, but at least there, the concrete was smooth and even. I could run for miles without stumbling.

What was I thinking—asking Hunter to come over? Of *course* he couldn't come over. He *wouldn't* come over. And what conversation did I honestly think we would have if he had actually shown up?

I mean, yes—there are things I want to ask him. I have a million questions running through my brain. About Isabelle. About Cassidy. About our whispered promises, our plans to grow up and tackle life together.

But then, I know the answer to that question, don't I? I have no one to blame but myself.

Your life is too small for me, Hunter. And if you never leave Oakley, it always will be.

I cringe as the memory of my own foolish, angsty, teenage words rushes through me like an icy breeze. *Hurt people hurt people,* Gran used to say.

I hate when trite sayings are true.

I don't *really* want to go down this path of remembering, do I? What purpose will it serve to drag up old memories? To unearth old hurts?

Last night, in the dim lamplight, the edges of everything softened by wine, my mind was just hazy enough to think it was a good idea. To ... miss Hunter.

But now? In the crisp, clean morning light, I think I'd rather have a root canal than deal with the past. A double root canal. With*out* Novocaine. While being forced to watch a horror movie or golf—which has to be the most painful sport to watch.

I smooth down the front of my shirt and take a steadying breath. I can't change the fact that Hunter Williams is the contractor Eloise and Jake decided to use for the renovation. My best bet is to keep things professional. Talk about tile and backsplashes and flooring and cabinets without focusing on the fact that he was the first boy I ever loved.

And the first boy to ever break my heart.

You broke his too, Mer.

I don't know where THAT voice came from but—*rude!*

I pull a coffee mug out of the cabinet, setting it on the counter a little forcefully. A tiny piece chips off the bottom, and I don't bother putting it in the trash. It's like a tiny rebellion, leaving that broken shard. Take that!

I'm not sure who I'm rebelling against or trying to teach a lesson. Me? The universe?

I pour my coffee, then add a healthy dose of flavored creamer, for once not caring about the added calories. Oakley Island doesn't feel like the kind of place where anyone needs to worry about calories.

My phone vibrates from the counter, and I scoop it up, coffee in my other hand, and head to the front porch. I wasn't outside enough when I lived in New York. Other than running or getting to and from work.

That's at least one thing I can appreciate about Oakley Island. Maybe not the running on the beach part, but the fresh air and the lack of car horns and sirens and people elbowing you out of the way on a crowded sidewalk.

Is it weird that I sort of miss the smell of exhaust and hot pretzels?

A cool ocean breeze brushes across my face, as if in

response. *Okay.* Point taken. Trading city smells for this isn't *all* bad.

I sink down on the steps and answer Sadie's video call just in time.

"Hey-ay," she sing-songs. "How are things—oh my gosh, Mer. What happened to you? You look like the squirrel I ran over yesterday."

I frown. "What? I do not. Also, ew."

"You do," Sadie says, pointing her finger at the camera. "The circles under your eyes look like literal vortexes into purgatory."

I pull my phone a little closer, switching my view so my face fills the screen, reducing Sadie to a tiny thumbnail in the corner. *Oh dang.* The low light in the bathroom this morning was a lot more forgiving than this natural sunlight. A roadkill squirrel from purgatory is just about right.

"Are you hungover?" Sadie asks, with a little too much glee. "Did you learn nothing from your youngest sister's mistake?"

"What mistake?" *Change the subject. Good plan.*

"The one where she got tipsy on two glasses of wine —*such* a lightweight—and lawyer Jake had to carry her home from the bar?"

I *knew* I was right about my sister and Jake! "Pretty sure that mistake set them on the path to falling in love." I pause. "Or on the path to heartbreak? Know anything about that?"

Sadie scoffs. "Lo has told me very little. But I can tell she likes him. A *lot*. It's like she's got googly eyes, but in her voice. Googly voice—it's gross."

"You're too jaded to have a fair opinion," I say, glancing toward Jake's front door. I slept late enough that he's probably at work, but I definitely don't want him to overhear our conversation.

It's weird to be right here, living next to the man my baby sister might or might not be dating and not have ANY of the important details. I'm slightly hurt that Sadie knows more than me. Then again, she's always been the one who pushes her nose into everyone's business, while I … well. If I'm going to examine all my poor life choices this morning, I can admit I'm better at pushing people away. My sisters have been no exception.

They're more the rule, actually.

Maybe I should make more of an effort to keep up with my sisters.

I'll make that priority number one. Or two—right after avoiding Hunter.

"Not all of us can be like you, Mer. All happy and content. How's the long distance working?"

Maybe I'll make keeping up with my sisters priority number *three*. Or five. Or twenty-seven. Because the last thing I want to talk about with either sister is the overly dramatic end to my most recent relationship.

"I'm not done talking about our sister," I say, deflecting like the pro that I am. "Did Lo tell you anything about a breakup?" I lower my voice. "She was cagey when I drove her to the airport, but she didn't say anything specific."

"A breakup? No. We've texted about her program and how much she loves it. Though, maybe that should have given me a clue—no mention of Jake. I'll find out. Has *he* said anything?"

"Nothing. But he seems extra broody? I don't know him well enough to tell, but I swear the man runs a thousand miles a day. Maybe he's running out his angst?"

"Sounds like someone else I know. Let me see what I can needle out of Lo."

Perfect. Sadie will absolutely get info out of Eloise. And it will give her something to focus on other than me. Mission accomplished.

The sound of a saw cuts through the air, and I look toward Gran's house, wondering if it's Hunter. If he's around somewhere ... sawing things. With his new, man-sized body I couldn't help but notice when he was carrying me over his shoulder like a Costco-sized bag of flour.

"How are *you* holding up? How's taking over all the reno stuff?" Sadie asks.

"Today is the first day the contractor"—I'm very careful not to mention Hunter's name—"is working. So, we'll see. I've already identified some changes I can make to keep us more on budget and on a faster timeline."

"Poor Lo. She leaves for one day, and you swoop in and change all her plans. How very *firstborn* of you."

"Shut up with your birth order nonsense, middle child. Do you want this place sold for max profit or not?"

"Definitely max profit. Carry on demolishing whatever adorable plans Lo made."

Sadie takes a sip from a mug that says *I read because kicking people is frowned upon*. So VERY Sadie. Her eyes slide over to the left, and a slight frown makes a crease between her brows. She sets the mug down, and I hear her typing for a minute. Then, she's back.

"So, how is it being on Oakley again?" she asks, like she didn't just stop some kind of cyber-attack with a few keystrokes. "It was weird seeing it again through adult eyes."

You can say that again.

"It's definitely weird."

"Have you seen Hunter yet?"

Annnnd ... *there it is*. It's not like I didn't expect the question at some point. Even if Sadie doesn't know the whole story—only Gran did—she at least knew Hunter and I were *something*.

As a kid, her nosy nature looked more like spying, and it drove me crazy how readily she figured things out about me. She's only honed her skills as an adult, which means she'll get the truth out of me eventually, but this is not a conversation I want to have right now.

I've only had ONE cup of coffee. After a night of drinking wine and practically begging Hunter to come over, I'll need more caffeine in my system before I'm ready to tackle *this* particular subject.

"Briefly," I finally answer.

I can't bring myself to admit the details of our encounter, though Sadie would appreciate a description of the view I had while Hunter carried me back to the house. I wish I could scourge the mental image from my brain.

Or ... print it out and frame it. Can't decide.

"Then I saw his wife—well, ex-wife?—and kid at the grocery store. She was with some other guy. She's about to have a baby."

I don't mention Isabelle by name.

Sadie's eyes drift back to what I assume is her computer screen, and she talks while she types. "She and Hunter did get married really young. Statistically, odds were against them making it."

"Man. You're like the spokesperson for anti-marriage."

"*Spokesperson?*" She shrugs and wrinkles her forehead. "No. But a card-carrying member of the never-getting-married society? You know it. And proud, too. But kids—I don't know. I like them. Maybe one day."

"Really?"

I'm not sure why this shocks me. Even though I've claimed, publicly and frequently, I'll never have any, out of the three of us, I would have picked Sadie as the one who'd be childless by choice. Not me.

Because you wanted children once. You and Hunter talked about having kids, a very annoying voice reminds me. *Are you sure you didn't make this rash change because of Hunter?*

Man. I might be doing okay dodging Sadie. But this pesky internal voice—which reminds me so much of Gran—won't give me a break.

"Is that so surprising? Do you think I'd suck as a mom?" Sadie sounds shockingly vulnerable for a moment, and I'm stunned into a momentary silence.

"No. You'd be amazing." She would. Fun and creative and whip-smart, Sadie would commit every parenting book to memory just to find healthy ways to break the rules and forge her own path. Her kids would adore her.

Why am I having such a weird, emotional reaction to talking about kids?

"I just thought because you're so anti-relationship, that meant you weren't thinking about starting a family. Seriously, you'd be the best mom."

Sadie ducks off-screen for a moment—*is she crying???*

When she comes back in view, her normal sardonic smile is back in place. "Yeah, can't blame me for not wanting to get married after watching our parents."

The three of us carry deep scars from our parents' ugly divorce. Dad blindsided Mom when he left her, then spent all the money he could without leaving her *anything*. Which continued to be a theme for him. It's exactly why Gran—our dad's mom—left the three of us everything and her own son nothing.

The divorce made me harder.

Though I'd prefer to use the term sturdier or stronger. With Dad out of the picture, someone had to take care of the family while Mom hid in her bedroom and licked her wounds.

Sadie got more sarcastic and jaded.

And Eloise … I find that I don't quite know how the divorce impacted her. Her effervescent bubbly optimism is totally foreign to me.

Somehow, Lo seemed to retain a happy, starry-eyed view of the world. Of people. Bright and optimistic and romantic. If she has armor, it comes in the form of colorful dresses and a smile wide enough to disarm anyone. I've always looked down on her for that, I realize now, but maybe I should have been taking her cues instead.

"Divorce is awful for any kid," I say.

Sadie scoffs. "Honestly, I'm shocked you turned in your card to the happily single club. Out of all of us, *you* should be the most bitter. Not me."

She might be right, but despite everything, despite the way I'd love nothing more than to climb up in a tower, Rapunzel style, and never come down, I DO have hope for a happy marriage. At least, I did. Not kids, though. At least, that's been the refrain I've repeated to myself over and over for years.

Now that I'm here, in Oakley, seeing Hunter, I realize I can pinpoint the exact moment my desire to be a mom changed.

Still, with or without kids, I've always clung to my hope for a happily-ever-after romance. Maybe that hope is a little tattered right now. But it EXISTS. And its existence makes me feel sad for Sadie. But then, her hope for kids makes me feel sad for *me*.

"What's that look for?" Sadie asks, narrowing her eyes.

Now is NOT the time to tell Sadie I wish she hoped for love too. Especially given my current secretly single status after a nasty breakup. If I start talking about relationships, she will want to talk about mine, and I'm nowhere near ready to open up about my sniveling, rotten-to-the-core ex, Simon, with any measure of detail.

Instead, I find myself saying words I'll probably regret later. "I should feel sad about Hunter's marriage, right? That he and Cassidy didn't work out? I mean, they have a kid together."

Sadie's face is carefully blank. "Are you thinking maybe you *aren't* sad about it?"

"No. That's not—I don't know. It's stupid. Everything just feels really stupid right now."

Most especially, *I* feel stupid right now.

"Merritt, you *loved* him. That's not stupid."

My eyebrows go up. Maybe Sadie knew a bit more than I realized about me and Hunter. I wonder exactly how much she saw when she was spying from treetops and under bushes.

Before I can respond, she crows triumphantly. "I knew it! You loved him!"

Ugh. I just walked right into a classic Sadie trap. She isn't just nosy. No, she's *conniving* in the way she manages to wrangle information out of unwilling victims.

"I was a *child*, Sadie. I didn't even know what real love is."

She rolls her eyes. "Yes, you did. And you weren't a *child*. You were fifteen years old when we left. That's old enough to fall in love. Not for everyone. But some people do. And *you did*."

She might be right, but fifteen isn't old enough to know anything about how the real world works. You can't just love someone and expect to be with them forever, or for love to make all your problems go away. I've made that mistake twice now. Though, as I'm thinking about it, I'm not sure I *was* in love both times.

I lost a promotion to my ex right before I left New York. Right after I found out he'd been cheating—for months—with someone else in the office. The very public humiliation was horrible. But it wasn't the crushing heartbreak it should have been.

More of an embarrassed and slightly vengeful anger.

Is it possible that I haven't loved anyone except Hunter?

That is most definitely a thought to dissect on another day.

"Too bad you aren't single. You could see if there are still sparks," Sadie says in a very pot-stirring kind of voice.

Oh, there are MORE than sparks. But I'm pretty sure the lit fuse on my end was extinguished on the very wet log of Hunter's clear disinterest. He was polite when he helped me with my ankle, but he didn't seem too excited to sit around and chat. And last night, he couldn't get off the phone fast enough.

"I thought you liked Simon," I say.

I tell myself I'm not lying to my sister. I'm omitting information. Like, say, the fact that Simon and I are very much over. And that I quit my job.

"Meh," she says, wrinkling her nose. "*You* like him. *You* seem happy with him. So, I *tolerate* him. He's just such a *Simon.*"

I'd like to ask what that means. But the longer the conversation stalls here in Simon-land, the more chance I'll slip up and tell my sister that my ex cheated, got the other woman pregnant, and now I'm carrying around their wedding invitation in my purse.

But you know what—I think I get what Sadie means.

Inviting me to the wedding was a TOTALLY *Simon* thing to do. Cheating—also a very *Simon* thing to do.

Simon is now my new favorite negative adjective.

Simon. Makes a pretty good curse word too.

"So, are you gonna move into the big house at some point?" Sadie asks.

"Probably not. It isn't exactly livable. And all the furniture is in storage right now. Or at least, all the furniture Lo decided to save."

Sadie laughs. "So by that, you mean all the funkiest, weirdest stuff?"

"I haven't had time to go look, but probably. She's got a 'vision' for this place. That's for sure. I just can't decide if it's fueled by brilliance or—"

"Instagram?" Sadie asks, and I laugh.

"Yeah, that."

"Lo knows what she's doing. It might look like madness now, but she has good instincts. Trust them—if they're not too over-the-top, expense-wise. At the very least, it has to be better than what you would come up with." She laughs. "Can you imagine Gran's beach house decked out like your apartment in New York?"

The comment stings more than it should. Sadie has been to my apartment, and she's right. All the sleek, modern lines, the leather and chrome, it would look ridiculous here.

But I was an artist once. One with an eye for color and design, one who painted impressionist sunrises over the ocean or clouds over swaying marsh grass.

I wonder what happened to all those paintings. Or that version of myself.

But I realize the answer to the second question even as I ask it. New York City Merritt ate her right up, then spit her back out and stepped on her for good measure.

"Speaking of New York," Sadie continues. "I know it's tough for you to be away from the office, you adorable workaholic. I've got to get through this next project, but then I'll have some flexibility to come down and take over for you. Two weeks? Maybe three?"

"Sounds good," I hedge. "We'll firm up plans later."

Movement catches my eye, and I look up to see Hunter cutting across the backyard of the beach house.

"You have got to be kidding," I groan under my breath.

The man looks like he's posing for a calendar. He's wearing jeans torn at the knees, his toolbelt slung around his hips. His gray t-shirt stretches tightly across his back, the sleeves hugging the curve of his biceps. Which are visibly flexed as he's currently carrying a stack of two-by-fours on his shoulder.

Yesterday, that stack of wood was me. The realization and the ridiculousness of it all makes me snort out a laugh.

"What?" Sadie asks, reminding me of the unfortunate fact that I'm still on a video call with Ms. Nosypants herself. "What's funny?"

"Nothing. There's just ..." My eyes scan the expanse of grass between the house and the dunes for something else that could possibly have made me snort.

"Stop trying to come up with a lie," Sadie says. "*Show me.*"

"Ugh. Sisters are the worst. Hold on." I flip the camera view so Sadie can see Hunter as he stops by the back stoop and lowers the wood to the ground. I don't know why, but watching him while knowing Sadie is also watching makes my heart race and my cheeks heat.

"Oh, Mer. You are in so much trouble. Simon was an idiot for letting you go down there."

Simon is an idiot for so many reasons. But he let me go long before I got to Oakley.

I promise myself I'll tell Sadie. *Soon.*

Hunter stands and brushes off his hands, then sees me sitting on the steps of the carriage house.

Can't go unnoticed now.

I wave half-heartedly. It is the limp gesture of a woman with wine regrets.

"Wait, wait. Is he—are you telling me *Hunter* is the contractor? *Your* Hunter? And you didn't think that was worth mentioning?"

Sadie's voice goes shrill, and as Hunter starts this way, I flip the camera back around to show my face, wincing when I realize I still look like roadkill.

"I've gotta go. I'll call you later."

"Don't hang up! I want to see this. And for the record, Hunter is *way* better than Simon."

She *of course* says this at top volume just as Hunter reaches the porch in all his fitted jeans and tight t-shirt glory.

"Who's Simon?" he asks, and I want to throw my phone. Or my sister.

"Merritt's very boring boyfriend," Sadie says loudly. "Hey, Hunter!"

"It's Sadie," I explain with a sigh, though I'm sure he's put two and two together by now. I turn the phone around so he can see her.

"Hey," Hunter says, giving an awkward wave.

I turn the phone back around and glare at my sister, who is definitely my least favorite. "Bye, Sadie."

"Have fun you two! Don't do anything I wouldn't do," she says, and I hang up in the middle of her evil laugh.

I put my phone on the step beside me and drop my hands into my lap. I am chill. Calm. Professional. I mean, *yes.*

Minutes ago, I was ogling Hunter like I wanted to order him out of a catalog, but he isn't exactly playing fair. Walking around with all *that* going on. Maybe we can pretend like Sadie didn't just mention the boyfriend I no longer have.

Also—if Sadie disliked Simon so much, why didn't she mention this *before* he cheated and got someone else pregnant?

You wouldn't have listened anyway.

Yeah, yeah. *Shut up, inner Merritt,* I think, ignoring *again* just how much inner Merritt sounds like Gran.

"Good morning," Hunter says. I detect a trace of wariness in his tone. Not that I can blame him after last night. Or just now. A surprise Sadie phone attack is never a good way to start the day.

"Good morning." I channel New York Merritt and paste on a boardroom-professional smile. "Have you had coffee? I made a whole pot."

Did I do so *just in case* I had the opportunity to offer said coffee to *someone* who might want some, and because the list of someones *might possibly* include Hunter? Maybe.

Hunter glances at his watch. "I could probably use another cup."

His lip twitches the tiniest bit, making the bristles in his beard twitch too. I find myself transfixed by the movement. I've never dated a man with facial hair. Which means I've never *kissed* a man with facial hair.

My brain is suddenly dragged down a wanton alley. Not that alleys are a good place for the kind of kissing I'm imagining, but—

Hunter clears his throat, and I jerk my eyes away from his mouth.

"I didn't sleep all that well last night," he says pointedly. He pauses in front of me, halfway up the porch steps.

I suck in a breath but quickly mask my reaction. "No? That's too bad. Hopefully, more coffee will help."

I stand up, only remembering my ankle when pain shoots up my leg and I wince. Hunter immediately reaches forward, steadying me with a firm grip on my elbows. The touch sends warmth cascading through me.

He frowns, glancing down. "Is your ankle still bothering you?"

"It's fine." I wiggle out of his grasp and try not to limp to the door.

"Doesn't look fine. Let me help."

"I've got it."

As if to prove a point, I open the screen door and stop to hold it for Hunter. I don't realize until it's too late how difficult it is for two adult-sized humans to stand in a doorway at the same time without touching. Suddenly, Hunter is close enough for me to feel the heat radiating from his big body, to smell the slight muskiness of his sun-warmed skin.

He moves slowly, pausing long enough for me to lift my eyes to his. There's something sparking in their dark brown depths, but I can't say what. Years ago, I would have been able to read him. But this adult version of Hunter makes me off-kilter and wobbly. I swallow, about to ask him what he's doing, but then he moves inside and the tension between us snaps.

Except, maybe there isn't tension between us. It might actually be all *my* tension—the whole fuse to the wet kindling analogy, which is all too fitting. For all I know, this attraction or whatever it is I'm feeling is only building inside of *me*.

I clear my throat and move toward the kitchen where fixing coffee will give me something to do with my hands. "I guess construction hours start early."

"It's cooler in the mornings."

"Right." I pour him a mug and slide it down the counter. "Milk? Sugar?"

I bite back a joking remark about neither of us drinking coffee at fifteen. No need to rehash things. He's here for a job. I'm here to … oversee? Micromanage? Help? I'm not sure exactly how this part worked with Lo, or how it will work with us.

He nods toward the cinnamon vanilla creamer still sitting on the counter from when I made my own cup. "That works."

I hand it over and do my best not to smile. This big burly lumberjack-looking man likes frou-frou coffee. Why do I find this adorable?

He tops off his mug with a long pour of creamer, almost making the mug overflow. When he takes a sip, I *do not* notice his Adam's apple bobbing. I also don't trace my eyes across the line of his jaw or try to imagine what he might look like without the beard.

Probably more like the Hunter I used to know. Not that I'm thinking about that. Or wondering if his beard is soft, or—

"Merritt?"

"What? Yes. No."

He raises his eyebrows. "Yes and no?"

Oh my word. "Sorry. Um, I missed what you were asking?"

He lifts his coffee mug, and I swear it's to hide a smile. "We said last night we were going to, uh, discuss some things today. If I remember, you wanted to talk."

I freeze, my mug halfway to my lips. Did he *have* to bring that up? Couldn't we both pretend the whole conversation never happened?

New York Merritt comes to my rescue, clearing the

cobwebs out of my head. I set down my mug decisively. "Yes —the tile."

"The tile," he repeats, almost like he doesn't believe me.

"I wanted to talk about the tile." I give him a curt nod.

Eyeing me warily now, Hunter takes another sip of coffee, then says, "You asked me to come over close to midnight last night to discuss *tile?*"

"Yes. But I'll try to keep questions and phone calls relegated to business hours only from now on."

I cross my arms, channeling the woman who feels more like a part I played in a high-school theater production, not who I am. Or *was*. It's been long enough, surely Hunter can't tell the difference.

"I don't want delays. I'd like to find a replacement tile that's in stock."

"Shouldn't be too hard."

"Good."

"Okay."

"Fine," I say, strangely desperate to have the last word.

Hunter and I take sips of coffee at the same time, mirror images of avoidance. Or maybe not avoidance exactly. I stare into his unreadable, chocolate-brown eyes. There's a sense of anticipation here that makes me think we're more like the picture right beside the dictionary definition of *delay*.

FIVE

Hunter

"SO, what kind of tile did you have in mind?" I ask. "Travertine? Porcelain? Marble? Saltillo?"

Merritt and I have moved to the big house, where I'm taking more enjoyment than I probably should in messing with her. The woman clearly has zero knowledge of tile. But what she lacks in knowledge, she makes up for in a stubborn refusal to admit that she wanted to discuss something *else* last night. I'm not even sure Merritt knows which tile is on backorder—it's for the kitchen backsplash—or that some of the ones I'm suggesting aren't even the correct material or style.

"Porcelain," she answers decisively.

Good guess. I was hoping she would say Saltillo, which is a porous tile best suited to hacienda-style flooring. It definitely wouldn't fit with the aesthetic Lo chose. Or work for a backsplash of any kind.

Pulling the pencil from behind my ear, I scrawl down *porcelain*. I don't need the note. I just need something to do with my hands. And something to look at other than Merritt's face, which I'm finding is no less alluring to me than it was years ago.

Maybe even *more* alluring. Because now, there's mystery. There are gaps in my knowledge of the woman before me. She's familiar, yet foreign. The same, but so very different. And it feels incredibly *necessary* that I identify the differences and similarities between the girl I knew and the woman who's little more than a stranger. I am Sherlock Holmes, and she is my most beguiling case. One I feel compelled to crack.

"How about the pattern?" I ask. "Square-set? Subway? Herringbone? Basketweave? Offset vertical?"

Merritt clears her throat, glancing around the room like she's going to find a cheat sheet defining these terms printed on the wallpaper. *No help there, Merritt.* Just a funky palm leaf print Lo insisted is the next hot thing. I don't get it. But it's not my job to get it; I just install it.

"Maybe …" Merritt trails off, clearly trying to look thoughtful.

Instead, she kind of looks constipated. I bite the inside of my cheek and press the tip of the pencil so hard into my paper it makes a dent. This game shouldn't be so much fun. But in addition to figuring her out, I have a seemingly unquenchable desire to fluster this new, harder version of Merritt.

Am I trying to shake loose the younger, less rigid Merritt from my memories? Perhaps.

What if she doesn't still exist?

That question makes me swallow hard. Because some part of me desperately needs to believe that Merritt hasn't lost the qualities I love in her.

Loved, I remind myself. *Past tense. VERY past tense.*

"How about chevron?" I ask. "Diamond? Versailles?"

Her eyes narrow and laser in on me.

Okay—I might have pushed too far. Merritt is done pretending. I watch the shift in her expression like it's the morning sun cresting the horizon, chasing away the velvet night sky. There is nothing unsure about *this* Merritt, and I shouldn't find it so sexy.

She points a finger at me. The ruby red polish on her nails is just starting to chip. "I know what you're doing."

With exaggerated casualness, I lean back against the counter. I am the literal picture of innocence. Move over, newborn babies. You've got nothing on me.

"And what am I doing?"

"Teasing me. Messing with me."

I shrug. "You said you wanted to discuss tile. In fact, you were so dead-set on discussing tile that you called me late last night. So—here we are. Discussing tile."

Tile—not all the other things she brought up last night. Things that awakened a whole mess of feelings and memories I can't seem to shake.

I dreamed of Merritt last night—that's how bad it is. Her laughter, echoing through a dark cavern I stumbled through, chasing glimpses of a girl with wild, dark hair and paint smeared across her cheeks.

"Are those all even tile patterns or are you making things up?" she asks, clearly disbelieving.

"Those are all tile patterns."

She deflates. "Oh."

Her eyes drop, and I feel the slightest amount of guilt at my behavior. My instinct is to apologize, to smooth that crease of worry in her forehead away, to pull her into my arms. Which isn't happening. Which *can't* happen.

"But," I admit after a moment, "I *was* messing with you. A little bit anyway."

"I knew it!" Her eyes light up again, and she offers up the very first real smile I've seen since I picked her up off the beach yesterday.

Her smile is like the pulled pin of a grenade. I am SO done for.

I manage to respond, keeping my voice light, as though she didn't just slay me where I stand. "And I knew you didn't know anything about tile, so ..."

"Guess that was pretty obvious, huh?" Merritt shakes her head, a lock of dark hair falling across her cheek.

At one time, I wouldn't have thought twice about tucking that hair behind her ear. Now, even though the urge feels completely natural, as instinctual as hunger or thirst, I can't. I can't touch her hair or let my fingertips graze her cheek. I can't touch her at all for so many reasons. Not the least of which being: she has a boyfriend.

Simon. A perfect name for a man Sadie described just now as *boring.* I have trouble even thinking his name without sneering, which doesn't make any sense. Merritt hasn't been a part of my life in almost ten years. We were kids. Our feelings were ... well—it doesn't matter what they were. We're adults now, and she's a free woman. A grown, free woman who can date all the Simons she wants. I can't be jealous of *Simon.*

"Hunter?"

I realize I'm gripping the counter behind me so hard, my hands are cramping. I let go, stretching out my clenched fingers. "Sorry. I got lost in my thoughts."

That much is true. Even if I won't admit what thoughts are occupying my brain right now.

I run a hand over the beard I started growing when it

became clear things between Cassidy and me weren't going to work out. She never liked me with facial hair, so I never wore any, a small thing compared to all the other ways we didn't match up. Despite my best effort to be the man I needed to be for her, for Isabelle, it was never enough.

And you never stopped loving someone else.

Yeah. As much as I don't want to admit it—that too.

In the end, I kept the beard because it makes me look older. I'm twenty-six, which is young for a general contractor running his own business. I need all the help I can get.

"I'm sorry I messed with you about the tile," I say, needing to talk so I don't have to listen to my very loud thoughts. "It wasn't very professional of me."

She raises one dark brow. Slowly. She means it as a challenge, but probably not the kind my body takes it as.

"So, is that how it will be between us, Hunter?" she asks in a deceptively soft voice. *"Professional?"*

How can I answer that?

Yes—it needs to be professional because she has a boyfriend. And she made it clear years ago how she feels about living on this island. About me.

So why don't those facts seem as relevant as I want them to be? Why am I fighting back the urge to take a step closer and see if *professional* is really what *she* wants?

Simon, I remind myself.

"Professional," I agree, though the tone of my voice seems to say just the opposite.

Merritt sighs, and whatever electric tension had been hanging in the air between us disappears.

"I'm sorry I pretended to know what I'm doing," she says. "I don't. None. House stuff is not my wheelhouse. I'm a little bit … lost."

You think? But I say nothing because it's like one layer of the Merritt wallpaper has been peeled back at the corner. I'm starting to see what's underneath. Curiosity may have killed the cat, but I thrive on it. It's amazing what you can learn from people when you're comfortable being quiet.

"Considering how little I know," she continues, "how is this going to work?" Her gaze holds mine, her bottom lip tucked in between her teeth.

"This ...?"

"Like, the contracting stuff. You and me discussing things. Making decisions. I assume I'm going to have to make some, right? How will it work?"

I have *no* idea. Because right now, *work* is the last thing on my mind. With Merritt in my space, she is all I can think about. In very unprofessional, un-contractoring, and *inconvenient* ways. My heart is conflicted, two opposing desires locked in a wrestling match and fighting for dominance. One half wants to remember every wound Merritt inflicted while the other wants to drag Merritt's mouth to mine.

Yeah—this is NOT going to work. I'm about to admit as much when Merritt continues.

"How did you and Lo do things? Did you have spreadsheets or a shared folder or what?" She pulls out her phone. "Lo sent a document, but I don't know how the two of *you* communicated."

Everything was different with Lo, who buzzed around this place like a happy honeybee. It annoyed me at first, but I got used to the way she made everything brighter.

"Well," I say, then trail off. I am a man of many thoughts and stupid words this morning.

"I know she had a strong hand in picking things out, but is it your job to make recommendations as well?"

"Um." I scratch my beard, thinking.

Lo had vision and strong opinions but somehow managed

to express them without being overbearing. I can already tell Merritt will be much more like a boss.

Shouldn't I mind that more than I do? With anyone else, I probably would. Somehow, with Merritt, it works.

"No—make it lower," she says, tilting her head to look.

"This is the fourth time I've adjusted it, Mer," I tell her. But there's no irritation in my tone. I don't mind adjusting the easel I made her. Anything to have an excuse to be near.

"I'm sorry," she says. "I'm a total diva."

I frown. "You are not a diva."

Divas are the island girls who go to Savannah to get eyelash extensions. They wear complicated sandals with heels instead of flip-flops. They never say what they mean and say more than they need to.

Merritt isn't that. She is ... particular. She knows what she wants, and what she wants is usually very precise. Orderly. Exact.

Yet I see a tiny swipe of blue paint on her neck. Her hair's coming out of her ponytail even though she just tightened it. And she's wearing the ugliest shorts I've ever seen. They look like plaid pants belonging to her dad that she cut off with a kitchen knife and are held on her hips by a woven belt.

Not a diva.

"It's just ... I think I'm going to start on the giant canvas," she says.

"Are you going to do the self-portrait your gran keeps asking for?"

She makes a face. A really cute one. "I don't paint people. Just sky and sea," she says, her voice going all dreamy.

I lower the wooden canvas support, tightening the screw and testing it out before I place the largest canvas in the room on it. "All set."

Merritt walks around the easel, grinning. Pride hits with a rush. I spent all spring working on this easel in wood shop, then gave it to her the first day she arrived.

When she circles back to me, her smile makes my cheeks hot. Then she throws her arms around me, pressing close, and all of me is hot.

"I still can't believe you made this for me. And it's beautiful. You're so talented."

She didn't see my first failed attempts. Or when I got so mad I snapped a board in half and spent a day in detention.

"Thanks."

She squeezes me once more, then steps back. I can't tell if being so close has the same effect on her as it has on me. But she immediately busies herself with her paintbrushes, so... guess not.

"Want to stay? It won't be fun," she says, smirking. "I'll just boss you around and make you hand me tubes of paint."

"Do I get to fan you with palm fronds?" I ask.

She laughs, tossing her head back. Her ponytail shakes loose, the rubber band dropping to the floor of the sunroom where her grandma sets up Merritt's studio every summer. I watch her dark waves shake as she laughs.

"Will you also feed me grapes, one by one?"

I look at her mouth and for a second, I can't talk. "Yeah."

"Scratch that. No grapes—red vines."

My phone buzzes, and it's like I've been dropped from a four-story building into this kitchen. I'm here. It's now. Merritt is clearly waiting for an answer while I'm remembering things best left forgotten.

"Sorry." I blink and try to relocate myself in this room, not in the memory I just fell into. "What did you say?"

"How did you and Lo communicate?" Merritt repeats slowly, like I'm an idiot.

Can't argue there.

"Text is fine."

She keeps going, like whatever controls her tongue is malfunctioning and she can't stop spitting out words. "Text. Good. I can definitely text. Especially since we know I have your number." She winces, like she's remembering last night all over again, then she clears her throat. "And um, was it like this?" She motions between us. "You discussing things in the kitchen together? Or over meals? Drinks? Coffee? Did you argue over her choices?"

"Merritt."

Wringing her hands, she starts rocking a little. I liked seeing her control slip earlier, liked riling her up—but this isn't that. I'm suddenly seeing that the tough shell is just that. Underneath, there's something broken here. *Merritt seems broken.*

Which is shocking, given how together she clearly *wants* to be.

"Did you ever make suggestions or give her ideas or did Lo just tell you what she wanted? I know she asked people on Instagram and Sadie said—"

"Mer."

As her nickname falls from my lips, as it's wanted to do a hundred times already this morning, I lean forward and cup her cheek.

My hands aren't the gentle kind. They're big and sun-toughened, calloused and rough. But when my palm touches Merritt's soft cheek, the flood of words from her lips stops, and she sighs sweetly.

For approximately half a second, we both seem to forget ourselves, lost in the moment. Lost in memory. Lost in the connection that's always been there and never left.

I find myself leaning toward her, closing the distance between our foreheads, our noses, our *lips*. Her irises are two deep blue pools, drawing me in. My heartbeat grows louder, faster. Her gaze drops to my mouth before her eyes flutter closed.

Then—as though some hypnotist snaps his fingers and wakes us—we remember.

Her eyes fly open as I jerk away, even as she slaps at my hand.

She gasps, looking horrified, then outraged, then embarrassed. "What are you—we—"

"I'm not—you were just—"

"THE TILE!"

We shout this at the same time, like *tile* is some kind of safe word, and then we both bolt from the room faster than if it were on fire.

Thankfully we go in opposite directions because if we'd had one of those movie moments where the hero and heroine run smack dab into each other, I wouldn't have hesitated to pull Merritt into my arms and press my mouth to hers. My resistance to the woman is as thin as a piece of tissue paper.

Simon, I remind myself. *Stupid, stupid Simon.*

The boyfriend does make a compelling case for why moments like this can't happen. I won't ever be that man, cutting in on what isn't mine.

I stop in the hallway outside the kitchen and press my forehead against the wall. It smells like dust and old wallpaper glue. It calms me. As much as I *can* be calmed, anyway.

When the back door slams—evidence of Merritt's hasty retreat—I finally take a deep breath. Still, with Merritt gone, the air doesn't quite fill my lungs the same way.

SIX

Merritt

FLEEING the big house isn't enough distance. So I hop in Lo's car and put thirty minutes, a giant bridge, and an entire intercoastal waterway in between me and Hunter.

Hunter—who was totally messing with me *and I liked it.*

Hunter—whose big, callused hand cupped my cheek with impossible tenderness *and I wanted to kiss him.*

Hunter—who already broke my heart once *and I can't live through it again.*

Armed with the address for a tile store Lo put in her planning doc, I make a pit stop at Crumbl. Honestly, there isn't much that a five-hundred-calorie Kentucky butter cake cookie can't cure. Especially when it's chased by a giant cold-brew coffee.

At least once a week, my coworker bestie, Jana, and I escaped the office for Crumbl cookies. Though it's a chain, I thought it might remind me of New York or make me feel homesick for the city. Nope. Already, my life there feels like a skin I've shed.

Trouble is, Oakley doesn't fit either, which leaves me in a bit of a freefall. How am I ever supposed to feel like I'm *home* when I don't actually belong anywhere? Except, in that brief moment when Hunter's hand cupped my cheek, I *did* feel like I was home.

The thought makes my throat feel tight.

No. No, no, and a little more no for good measure. Hunter does not—CANNOT—feel like home because I will never be the same for him.

I give my head a good shake as I follow the GPS directions toward the tile store. I can't forget that everything about this situation is temporary. I just need to get a hold of myself, figure out a way to keep my composure even when Hunter is around. Then we can finish the renovation and move on with our very separate lives.

I dig deep and channel a little bit of New York Merritt. She was never flustered in stressful situations. She always kept her cool, knew exactly the right words to say.

Because I always knew the right answer. That's it. I just have to do the same thing here. Arm myself with knowledge. Know the answers. *Need Hunter less.*

"I will OWN you, tile," I say out loud as I park my car. "Subway tile. Backsplash. Grout. See? I know tile words."

Maybe not what they all mean, but vocabulary is a good start.

My new resolve, combined with the rush of sugar and caffeine in my system, has put me in a fantastic mood by the time I walk up to Hamilton's Custom Tile and Interiors. This place is so very Eloise. The shop is in a small strip center and has a bright pink and green awning with the name in a handwritten script font. Big potted palms out front complete the picture.

Inside, as I wander the aisles, making notes in my phone about various tile shapes and materials—I realize just how much Hunter was messing with me.

"Oh, you're bad, Hunter. So *very* bad."

I'm staring at Saltillo tile—one of the more memorable names Hunter mentioned. Is it appropriate for a kitchen backsplash? No. No, it is not. Does it look at all like it would fit with Lo's aesthetic for the house? Not even close.

The tile *is* pretty. I could see the pinky coral square tiles working in another beach house with a different vibe. But only on the *floor*. Because these are *floor* tiles.

"Don't think I won't give back as good as I get, mister," I mutter.

Mister? I sound like Gran. Plus, I'm talking to myself out loud, something she always used to do. Maybe living on Gran's property is rubbing off on me. Whether that's good or bad, time will tell.

What's definitely not good is whatever happened earlier between Hunter and me.

What even was that moment? We were fine. Talking about tile. And then I spiraled into a sort of babbling panic, and Hunter moved closer. Then he put his hand on my face and leaned closer and—

"Are you looking for flooring?" a voice asks.

I recognize the man with the bright smile and long dreads who is standing beside me. He was chatting with other customers when I walked in. He looks just amused enough to make me think he overheard me talking to myself.

"Backsplash, actually."

He glances at the Saltillo tile sample in front of me.

"Right. Well, these are mostly used for flooring. If you're looking for backsplash—"

"What if your contractor *suggested* Saltillo for a backsplash?"

He looks surprised. "I'd say hire a new contractor."

Now, *there's* an idea.

But already, I know this much: I need Hunter to work on the house. It would be a pain to replace him, especially when he *does* know what he's doing. But even more—I need an excuse to see him again.

"I'm Dante," the man says, and I appreciate the way his smile is friendly but not in the least flirty. Or patronizing, despite my obvious tile incompetence. "I noticed you limping. If you'd like, I have a counter where you can sit. Tell me about your project, and I'll bring over some samples that might meet your needs."

He offers his arm in a most gentlemanly way, and as he helps me to a stool in front of a counter at the back of the store, I explain the project and Lo's vision. Once seated, I pull out my phone and scroll through a few pictures I had the foresight to take this morning.

"I love it," Dante says. "I'll be back in just a few with some samples."

Several minutes later, I have a bottled water in hand (thanks, Dante!) and an array of tiles on the counter.

"Which would you pick?" I ask.

They're all similarly priced, and they're all in stock, so I can just pick any and be fine. But for some reason, the decision feels exceptionally difficult. What if I screw this up? What if I pick one that no one else likes?

I'm trying my best here, but these are all questions that are very unlike New York Merritt. She is never indecisive. Not a people pleaser.

Where is my swift (and sometimes cutting) decisiveness? Where is my confidence?

I have a sudden impulse to call Eloise and see if she can survey her Instagram followers, but that would only reveal how out of depth I feel. What I need to do instead is make a decision. Then another and another until I'm more confident about making these kinds of choices.

Dante runs a hand over the dreadlocks he pulled into a ponytail moments ago. "I'd probably go with this one," he says finally, touching the third sample spread out on the counter.

I may be struggling with decision fatigue—more like decision exhaustion—but I know the moment he says it, that's not the right one. Why is it that sometimes another person's choice helps you feel more certain about your own?

Rather than tell the man who deserves a giant tip or commission that I actually prefer the first tile, I lean my elbow on the counter, swiveling on my stool to face Dante.

"Can I ask you something else? Slight subject change."

He chuckles. "That's why I'm here."

"What would be the worst choice for the guy installing the tile?"

He scratches the side of his jaw, where dark stubble mixes with a little gray. "These tiles would all be fine for anyone installing. I'm sorry—I don't quite understand the question. Is this about the contractor who suggested floor tiles as backsplash?"

"Yes. What about grout types? Are there some that are harder to work with?"

Dante shakes his head, looking baffled. "Not really. Not for this. But I don't really see why you'd *want* to make things more difficult. Especially if you're already working with someone who isn't familiar with this type of project."

"Oh, he's familiar," I mutter.

Dante rests his elbow on the counter, mirroring my pose. His brown eyes are curious. "Don't you want the project finished faster? Isn't that why you're choosing a new tile that's in stock?"

"Yes. But say I want my tile guy to suffer—just a little," I add when Dante's expression shifts to something like shock. "How about patterns? Is there one that's trickier than another?"

When Dante hesitates, I lean forward, whispering conspiratorially. "Look. I'm not a horrible person." He looks unconvinced. "But let's say my tile guy is a real piece of work. Good at his job but ... stubborn. Proud. Kind of a know-it-all. Suggesting a floor tile as backsplash just to show me how little I know. That kind of thing."

Also: Charming when he wants to be. Deeply kind. Looks good enough to eat in a simple pair of jeans.

"You don't want to work with someone who's like that," Dante says. "Are you here in Savannah?"

"Oakley Island."

"Then I've got a guy." He pulls a business card from his back pocket, setting it on the counter in front of me. "This is my recommendation. He's the best."

I glance down, then throw my head back and laugh.

"Seriously? This," I say, jabbing my finger on the card. "*This* is the guy."

Dante rears back a little. "Seriously? Hunter's giving you trouble?"

"Not real trouble. I'm sure he'll do fine. It's personal. He's just giving me a hard time, and I want to give him a hard time right back. I probably won't *really* make him do extra work. I'll just make him *think* he'll have to do extra work."

Dante's surprise shifts right into amusement. He grins. "Then tell him you want Versailles. Hunter will hate that."

Something about the way Dante responds or maybe the way he says Hunter's name prompts me to ask, "Do you know Hunter well?"

"Oh, we're *well* acquainted. He's a great guy, but let's just say I'm not mad about this idea at all."

"Okay, then." I smile, happy to have a co-conspirator. "So, what's hard about Versailles?"

"It's complex and requires four different tile sizes. You have to do a lot more planning and measuring. Plus, Hunter recently had a client choose it for a whole house. You should have heard him complaining. Man, I never thought I'd hear the end of it."

So, tile-store Dante and Hunter sound like friends then. They must be if Hunter actually talks to the man. I want to press Dante, ask some nosy questions about Hunter, but I have the feeling Dante would be more than happy to tell his buddy all about our conversation.

I grab my phone and tap a little note into the app still open from my earlier browsing. "Thank you, Dante. This sounds perfect."

"It sounds," says a deep voice right behind me, "like the two of you are conspiring against me."

Hunter steps up to the counter, because of course he does. I left the island to escape him, and poof! Like the Ghost of Merritt's Past, he appears. Right in the middle of a conversation about him. I barely manage to stay on my stool.

Dante only grins. "Welcome in, man. What can I do for you on this fine day?"

Hunter moves closer to me, giving me a look that says I won't escape unscathed. The promise in his dark eyes makes me shiver.

He turns to Dante. "Oh, no. Don't think you're getting off that easy."

Dante's eyes widen. "Me? I'm just going the extra mile to help a customer."

"He even brought me a stool," I add, and Hunter grunts, glancing down at me. Our eyes lock and hold, and my heart takes this as a sign to start thrashing wildly in my chest. Whether it's trying to get closer to Hunter or run away, I'm unsure.

"I'll give you two a few minutes to talk about the project," Dante says. "Or any other more personal items you might need to discuss. Have fun."

He heads to the front, where the bells chime as another customer walks in. The sound makes me wonder how Hunter came in without us hearing.

"Did you sneak in here?" I accuse, like I'm in any position to do so.

"I always come in the back. Dante and I are friends."

"Friends, huh? So why was he so eager to help me torture you?"

"Friends joke with each other. It's a sign of affection."

I try not to read too much into his words because even if he is implying he teased me about tile because we're friends, he said *friends*.

But he also said affection.

Why does it sound like Gran is in my head, planting ideas where they don't belong?

Maybe they more than belong. Maybe those ideas have always been there, growing deep roots, just waiting for the right time to bloom.

Ugh!

My mouth is suddenly dry, and I have a hard time swallowing.

"Are these the choices for the backsplash?" Hunter asks.

He could move to the opposite side of the counter, where he'd be standing across from me like Dante was. Instead, Hunter stays where he is, planting one hand on the counter and leaning forward, bringing him much too close.

We aren't quite touching, but somehow that's worse, like he's a giant, bearded tease.

I adjust the sample tiles so they're in a neat row. I point. "Dante suggested this one."

Hunter grunts. "But you don't like it."

How does he, after so many years, still read me so well?

"I like it, it's just …"

Hunter turns to look at me, and with the way he's leaning in, our faces are much too close. Giving me allllll kinds of bad ideas. Waking up allllll kinds of sleeping feelings that need to go back into hibernation. Bringing allllll kinds of buried memories gasping up to the surface for air.

Like the way Hunter's hands felt wrapped around my waist. The soft, sweet, hesitant press of his mouth on mine. The warmth and weight of his body hugging me. Even though our kisses were as awkward and feverishly excited as teenage kisses can be, they stayed with me.

What would those big hands feel like now, cupping my jaw? How might his lips feel, the scratch of his beard against my skin while he kissed me?

"This one." I lean forward, putting a little more distance between Hunter and me, and tap the first tile.

I knew the minute Dante suggested a different tile that this was the right one, but it feels good to say it out loud, to own this. I hope Hunter doesn't notice the gentle shake of my hand.

He moves around me to where Dante stood a few minutes before. A professional distance. But it might as well be a million miles away. I hate it as much as I hated his closeness a moment ago.

Maybe more.

"That's the one I would have chosen too," he says. "It's perfect."

I try to hide my smile, which stems from a mix of validation in my choice and from the fact that Hunter would have picked the same one.

"Let me pull up my measurements and I'll see what Dante has in stock. Maybe I'll insist he get the boxes from the hardest-to-reach shelf first."

"Be nice. He was very helpful."

Am I wrong, or is the flash in Hunter's eyes jealousy?

"*So* nice," I add. "We had a really nice talk, bonding over how to get you back for messing with me."

Hunter's eyes narrow, sliding with a particular venom toward the front of the store where Dante is chatting with a customer.

Oh, yeah. *Definite* jealous vibes. Hunter suddenly has the look of a wolf about to close his jaws around another wolf's neck to show dominance. Based on my extensive Discovery Channel viewings. Simon never understood my fascination with animals, but I feel like there's a lot to learn about humans from studying animal behavior.

I reach over and touch Hunter's forearm. Lightly. Quickly. But enough to jerk his attention away from Dante—who is an innocent bystander in all this.

"Do you like being a contractor?" I ask.

Surprise moves across his features at my subject change, but then Hunter's expression turns more thoughtful.

"It pays the bills," he eventually says, leaning against the counter.

"I think I expected you to wind up doing something more creative. Making furniture, or building things, I guess."

"I do build things," he says, his tone prickly.

"No, I know. I just thought—I don't know. You were always so good with your hands." That doesn't sound good. "With wood," I say quickly.

Which only makes it worse. The tiniest smile lifts the corner of his mouth as my cheeks flame.

"Furniture! You made that easel for me, and it was amazing—"

His smile vanishes. "That was a long time ago, Mer."

There's my nickname again, falling off his lips so easily. It makes my breath catch and my hands tremble, especially because he sounds so angry. Or maybe it's hurt I hear. I curl my fingers into fists and tuck them under my arms, not wanting Hunter to see me react.

"You're not giving yourself enough credit. You were talented back then."

Hunter ignores my comment. "Do you still have time to paint with that big city job of yours?"

He says this like it's simply an acknowledgment, carrying no judgment, even though he has every right to judge me. After all, I was the one who told him Oakley was too small-town for me. I was the one who said I needed something bigger.

You can't get bigger than New York City.

And look where that got me. Nowhere near a paintbrush, that's for sure.

And nowhere near Hunter Williams.

What I realize as I watch Hunter NOT look at me while he flips one of the tiles over and over in his calloused fingers, is that he has no idea the depth of hurt *he* caused. Even if he didn't mean to.

Maybe you should tell him about the day you came back. That Day.

Hunter has no idea about what I think of as That Day. He couldn't know that after a few years of being miserable about my parting words, of missing him, of wishing I hadn't blocked and deleted his number so I could text or call, I decided to throw it all on the line. I came back for him.

And he most especially doesn't know that I showed up on —day of all days!—his wedding day. To a visibly pregnant Cassidy in a wedding dress, standing next to Hunter. My Hunter.

Not *my* Hunter anymore.

"I'd like to present Mr. and Mrs. Hunter Williams," the officiant says, holding out both arms. Cassidy smooths her hands over her very pregnant belly and beams up at Hunter, whose expression I can't see. But his eyes are on her.

That's all I really need to know.

The best man, one of the guys I vaguely remember as one of Hunter's football friends, leans over and whispers something to the officiant.

"Oh, sorry! I almost forgot. You may now kiss your bride," the man says.

And I run.

Away from the beach where they're holding the simple sunset ceremony. Away from the sight of Hunter and Cassidy together.

Married.

Having a baby.

I barely make it to Gran's back porch before throwing up in the hydrangeas next to the path. She finds me there, on my knees, panting and crying so hard I can't see.

When she finally gets me up and in the house, my knees are bleeding—cut open from the oyster shells in the path.

I still have the scars.

"I'll tell Dante to put the tile on my account," Hunter says, taking a step back from the counter.

I hop off the stool without thinking. He's leaving, but I don't really want him to leave. We're talking, and something about that feels good. We need more of it—I sense this—but I don't know how to ask him for it.

Also, I can't walk—stupid, stupid ankle—and as soon as my weight lands fully on my feet, I wince and wobble.

Hunter lunges toward me, his hand darting out to grab my elbow. "You okay?"

I close my eyes, hating that I need his help while simultaneously loving the heat of his fingers against my skin. I lean in the slightest bit, momentarily surrendering to the weird gravitational pull that wills my body to curve into his.

What would happen if I let my hands slip up to his chest? If I apologized for all those things I said about Oakley, about him, right here, with my touch, my lips, my—

Hunter's grip on my elbow tightens, and I lift my eyes to his face.

His jaw is clenched, his lips pressed together. He looks like a statue of a man ready to pounce. Or run. Or both. He does *not* look like a man who wants anything to do with my lips.

I take a shuddery breath and nod my head. "I'm okay."

Hunter lets me go, shoving both hands into his pockets, and steps away. "What does Simon think about you coming down here and hurting yourself right off?" he asks.

It's a stupid question, but the question isn't the point. *Simon* is the point, and I understand immediately what Hunter is doing. He still thinks I have a boyfriend, and he's putting that boyfriend directly between us. He's telling me I can't look at him like I want to turn him into a snack when there is another man in the picture.

I swallow. "Simon? Oh. Um, I haven't told him." I wave a hand dismissively, like it's no big deal. "But I'll be fine. I *am* fine."

I should tell him the truth. And I want to, but I also recognize that Simon as a buffer between us might make this whole renovation project a lot easier. If I'm not staying on Oakley, wanting Hunter won't do either of us any good. Besides, there are other things I need to say first. More important things that don't have anything to do with whether I'm available for a relationship *right now*.

Regardless of whether I let Hunter believe Simon is or isn't in the picture, he deserves to know why I said such awful things to him when I left.

It's time for me to apologize. I just have to figure out how.

SEVEN

Hunter

DANTE GRINS as he punches my order into the computer. It's the kind of grin that inspires violent thoughts. Like punching the smile right off his face.

"Want to tell me what you did to make *the* Merritt want to prank you? She said something about you suggesting Saltillo tile as backsplash. You didn't think she'd do her research?"

I should never have spilled my guts to Dante after a night drinking Jägermeister. Unfortunately, he knows everything there is to know about *the* Merritt. Nothing—and I mean NOTHING—good comes from drinking Jäger. Licorice is bad enough in candy form. As alcohol, it's even worse.

"What's the total?" I ask, drumming my fingers on the counter and pointedly ignoring his question.

"I'm working on it."

"Come on, man. I know you just punch in the code. It doesn't take a genius."

Dante's eyes widen, and he puts a hand to his chest. "Are you questioning my vast knowledge? I am a veritable fount of—"

"Do I need to climb over the counter and ring myself up?"

"Testy, testy," he says, and his grin widens. "My fingers are just a little stiff this morning."

I groan. "Don't pull the arthritis card, man."

"But that's the only thing it's useful for—making sure I get the last word."

Dante used to work with me on the island. For a brief time, he was also my roommate, after Cassidy, and saw me through some dark times. Hence the Jäger-fueled confession. But when he was diagnosed with early onset arthritis, he shifted away from manual labor to running the family business when his dad retired. Though he never complains, I know he misses doing the hands-on work. I would too.

"Are you going to be installing this tile yourself?" Dante asks as he slips the printed purchase order across the counter. "Sounds like a big project from what Merritt said."

Why do I hate hearing him say her name?

"This time. It's an old house. Not sure I could trust anyone else to do it right."

While most contractors typically hire out a lot of the tedious jobs, I like to do them myself. Working with my hands makes me happier than overseeing people. And other than Dante, I'd rather work alone. More and more lately, that's what I've been doing. Especially with the Markham property.

"Mmmhmm," Dante says. "Pete was in here the other day, and he said he hasn't heard from you in weeks."

I shrug. "I haven't needed any trim work done."

"You use Pete for a lot more than trim work." Dante

levels me with a glare that might look intimidating if I didn't know him so well. "It's all right if you just admit you're hanging around Genevieve Markham's house on purpose."

"Don't start with that, man. Merritt wasn't even back in town until this week."

"But you've been thinking about her a lot longer than that, haven't you? Hoping she'd come back. Knowing that *eventually*, she'd have to see the house you poured your heart and soul into fixing up. You sure *that* isn't the reason you don't want anyone else installing the tile?"

I cross my arms. "Maybe I just like being alone."

"Maybe you're a control freak."

"Maybe I am."

Dante shakes his head, smiling. "You'd never agree with me if you weren't trying to pretend Merritt isn't the real reason. Or, at least, a big part of the reason. You are also a control freak, by the way."

"Don't expect me to send more business your way anytime soon," I mutter.

He cackles. "I'm not looking. But for real, man. Whatever feelings you're feeling, I don't think they're a one-way street."

I ignore the way my heart lifts at this statement and the springing up where none has any business growing. Like a ruthless gardener, I yank it right out by the roots. Hope is a weed.

"She doesn't want to live on a small island," I say pointedly. "She doesn't want this life."

Dante shrugs away my words with an easy roll of his eyes. "You gonna hold her accountable for something she said ten years ago?"

"Yep," I say simply. It's the best way to protect myself

from moments like the one earlier when I almost kissed her in the kitchen. "Also, she has a boyfriend back in New York."

Dante frowns. "Really? That is not the vibe I got when she was drinking you in like a tall glass of water."

"Such a cliché, man. And she was not drinking—"

Dante's raised eyebrow silences my rebuttal.

"Was she?" I can't help asking, but I feel stupid the second I do.

Dante doesn't tease me this time. "Just telling you what it looked like to me. Maybe the two of you should talk."

Maybe we should.

Or, maybe I should go on trying to keep my distance. Maybe I should remember how much it hurt to lose Merritt the first time. How much I let her words set me on a path to the small life I live.

What sucks is not knowing whether I'd be living this same small life if Merritt hadn't said what she did. Is this the life I really want? Or did her words stick like some kind of label, making me think this is the only life I can have?

I drive home in silence until the silence starts to feel too loud. I switch on the Bluetooth connection in my truck, hoping whatever I last listened to on my phone will start up and distract me from my own thoughts.

Except the last person listening to anything on my phone was Isabelle, so what starts playing is some kid-friendly version of Justin Bieber.

This is *definitely* worse than silence.

I pause at a red light and shuffle through my Taylor albums. My current mood is *Folklore*. But what I *need* is *1989*, so I go with that.

If "Shake It Off" is a little too on the nose, no one but me needs to know what I'm humming along to.

I cross the bridge onto Oakley in a new, Taylor-mellowed state of mind and debate driving straight home and not going back to Genevieve's place at all. But I left tools in the front yard, and I don't trust island weather enough to leave them out overnight. What's more, I picked up the shiplap to trim out the fireplace in the front room before stopping in at Dante's. Bare minimum, I need to drop that off.

But I won't stay.

I won't look for Merritt.

I won't consider Dante's suggestion to have a conversation that's a decade or more in the making. Even if I probably should.

All those well-intentioned resolutions—and my mellow mood—go out the window when I pull up to the front of the house.

Merritt is sitting on the front porch steps. She's surrounded by sawdust and construction debris—she probably ought to be wearing a hardhat—and for just a moment, she looks like the Merritt from before. Her hair is loose, blowing in the late afternoon breeze. Her blue eyes pop against the dusty blue of her shirt. Her feet are bare.

She should really be wearing shoes with so much debris, even out here. But what is it about a woman being barefoot?

NOT in the kitchen. I'm not a total jerk. Or some kind of foot fetishist. Some men might like a woman in heels. I just like seeing Merritt barefoot. Bare feet lead to bare legs. It's the stripped-down version of her without all the polish and pretense.

I climb out of the truck slowly, and Merritt stands up, still favoring her ankle. She laces her fingers together in front of her stomach like she's worried about something.

I move to the back of my truck and open the tailgate,

partially to buy myself a little time, and partially to keep from looking like I think she's there for me. It's her house. Well—her and her sisters'. There are any number of reasons Merritt might be standing there. Except she's staring at me like she's got something to say.

I slide the panels of shiplap out of the truck and hoist them onto my shoulder.

"Can I help you?" I ask as I approach the porch, immediately regretting how cold I sound.

I can't figure out how to *be* with this woman. How to balance how I *want* to be—holding her, kissing her, caring for her—with how I'm *supposed* to be. Her contractor. A professional. NOT her boyfriend.

"Can we talk?" Merritt says gently, her voice small. "Not about the house."

I stop at the base of the stairs. "Not about tile?"

She shakes her head, her expression unchanging. No sarcasm. No judgment. She really wants to do this. Right now.

I sigh. "Okay. Just let me put this inside."

She's sitting again when I make it back to the porch, and I drop down beside her. She turns sideways, extending her injured ankle across the top of the step. I barely resist the urge to reach out and wrap my fingers loosely around her foot. To be near her and not touching her is its own form of torture.

"You should get a brace for that. It's not gonna heal if you're gallivanting all over the island and over to Savannah."

"Gallivanting?"

"Traipsing?"

Her lips quirk. "My, what a big vocabulary you have."

It's so easy to slip into this back and forth. It's like the true north to our shared compass.

But we shouldn't be sharing it. Not anymore.

She seems to be having a similar realization because her smile fades away. "I'm just going to talk for a minute, okay? And I don't want you to say anything. Or stop me. Or maybe even look at me? At least, don't make eye contact."

"Do I need to wear a blindfold? Or turn my back?"

See? There the needle goes, pointing back to our north. I never much felt the need to talk much to other people. Not until Merritt started coming around. Something about her makes it so I can't shut up. Even now.

"Hunter," she says, half laughing and half exasperated. "Seriously."

I hold up both hands. "Fine. No eye contact."

She takes a slow deep breath. "I'm sorry for what I said about you back then. About your life being too small. I didn't mean it, Hunter. Not any of it. But I was hurting. Angry at my parents for getting a divorce and determined to turn myself into someone who would never need a man as much as my mom did."

She pauses, like she knows I need a moment to digest her words. I do need a moment. Actually, these words are too much for digesting, but the pause at least helps them line up in my head. Already, I feel the sickly twist of guilt in my gut. Because when I was busy being angry and hurt and angry again, I never once considered the way Merritt might have been reacting to the news of her parents' divorce.

Merritt goes on, "Mom fell apart when my dad left. In the worst possible way. She stopped caring about things. Stopped *mothering*." Her voice catches, and she pauses, taking another breath. This clearly isn't easy for her to talk about.

"I hated her for needing him so much. It was like she didn't know how to be a person without him. I got so scared that I might turn out just like her. Needing a man. Needing *you.*"

Needing me. The words hurt to hear. They're also really great fertilizer for the hope weeds that keep trying to nudge through the surface.

This was the past, I remind myself. *And it isn't all about* you.

Still, my mind fills with things I want to say. I met Merritt's mother a few times, and Merritt isn't anything like her. Merritt is vibrant and bold and brave and determined, a *force.* But I swallow the words and hold still. I can tell by the set of Merritt's shoulders, she isn't finished. I do my best to stick to my no-eye contact promise, but it takes great effort.

"I was afraid I needed you too much. Plus, Mom made it clear we weren't coming back to Oakley. She wanted to cut Dad off completely, which meant cutting Gran off. No more summers. No more *you.* Pushing you away felt like the best protection. But I swear, I didn't really mean it. I need you to understand that. Hunter …"

She touches my arm, giving me permission to make eye contact.

I wish I hadn't.

"I especially didn't mean that you were too small-town for me. If anything, you were too big. Too much. You were the world to me. And … well. I was too immature to know how to process all that." Her smile is small. Rueful. Painful. "Took me years to realize all this."

We look away at the same time. My gaze falls to her bare feet, then I look out at the biggest palmetto in Genevieve's yard, swaying a little with the breeze.

For a few minutes, we sit in silence. I let her words settle over me like a fine dust that clouds the air before it drifts down to rest.

It wasn't the explanation I expected. The thing is, the

reason Merritt's rejection stung so badly all those years ago was because she only said things I already believed were true.

I *already* thought Merritt was too good for me. Destined for something bigger than what Oakley Island could offer. Bigger than what I could offer.

All she did was confirm what I already believed was true. And the fact is, she *did* make something of herself. Something amazing. Something that never would have happened had she wound up with me.

But it does help to hear her take on things. To have the edges softened. As much as I believed her, even then, I never quite reconciled how she used her words as weapons. Why she fought me at all.

Her explanation has the ring of truth. It fits, solving the puzzle I never understood.

It's not all that different from what her Gran tried to tell me the one and only time she brought it up. I can't even remember how our paths crossed. Maybe the grocery store? Anyway, Genevieve stopped me, met my eyes, and said, "She's hurting, Hunter. But she'll be back for you."

I guess both parts of that statement turned out to be true. Even if she came back too late.

And not for me.

"We were young," I say, because it's the only truth safe to tell.

"I'm sorry I hurt you." Merritt huffs out a breath like she's finally gotten to the end of a prepared speech. "I've always been sorry," she says. "And, um, you can make eye contact now. Not that you have to."

I lift my eyes. She's already looking my way, her face expectant. Hopeful. Vulnerable. *Beautiful*.

In this moment, I want to give her anything she asks for

—forgiveness, a hefty discount on my work, a new car. Myself—if I'm even something she'd want.

Thing is, I'm not sure I can afford to give her anything.

The cost to me might be too high.

"I'd like for us to try and be friends," she says, holding my gaze but looking suddenly vulnerable. "If you want to be."

Friends. *Only friends*. Because she has *Simon*. And regardless of what she did or didn't mean back in the day, she has a life in New York City.

I swallow. "Friends," I repeat, like I'm trying to pronounce some word in another language. Halting. Hesitant. Foreign.

She smiles, but it's the kind that says the opposite. "Don't sound so excited. We can also just work on the house and keep things totally professional and impersonal. If that's what you want."

"Yeah, because we're so good at being professional." I laugh, and she does the same.

"I'm terrible at this, aren't I?"

I'm not sure what *this* she's referencing—apologizing, dealing with the past, having a serious talk—but I know how much Merritt hates being bad at anything at all.

I once watched her wear her hands down to blisters trying to hit a baseball because some snot-nosed punk boy told her she swung like a girl. When she finally let go of the bat after nailing a ball over the fence, her hands left bloody smudges on the wood.

But she only cared about her hit. The kid wasn't even there to see it. But I was. Because she made me pitch. My shoulder was sore for days.

"You're doing fine," I say. "Except, your speech *was* a little long-winded. I'll deduct a few points for bloat."

"Bloat? That was the trimmed-down version. You should have heard the original. At least half an hour."

"Well, let's hear it while the other one is fresh in my mind. I'll compare the two and type up a critique."

Merritt shakes her head, her hair falling over her cheek as she dips her chin, hiding her smile. "You're the worst. I rescind my offer. We're definitely gonna keep things impersonal."

"I don't think I'm capable of impersonal when it comes to you, Mer." I meant this to be teasing too, but somehow it comes out as solid and weighty as the truth it holds.

A blush sweeps up her cheeks, and she bites her lip. "Friends, then?"

It's not what I want, I know that much. But I can't have what I want. Merritt has Simon. A life outside of Oakley. A life outside of me. If *friends* is all she can give me, I'll take it.

I'll hate it. But I'll take it.

"Mm," I say, which sounds like an agreement, but I have a feeling Jake would tell me it wouldn't hold up in court.

Merritt smiles and extends her hands. "Shake on it?"

Touching? If talking to her makes keeping this very request difficult, physical contact is even worse. My body has its own sort of muscle memory when it comes to her. It remembers, and it wants to go right back to the summer months when things were easy between us.

We were both pretty young and inexperienced back then. Kissing, holding hands, holding each other—that's as far as we got, even if the connection feels so much deeper than what I *ever* had with Cassidy. My body never longed for Cass the way it did for Merritt. Not before we were married. Not after.

But all this *wanting*, this desire to go back to what Merritt and I had—not just the physical but ALL of it—it's the thirst of a man lost at sea. Surrounded by water, the one thing he needs, but a kind that will kill him if he drinks.

In the interest of not revealing any of this to Merritt, I have to shake her hand.

I wrap her smooth palm in my rough and calloused one, wondering what on earth I've just agreed to and how I'm ever going to survive her *friendship*.

EIGHT

MERRITT

I SHOULD FEEL BETTER after talking to Hunter. Isn't that how apologies work? You screw up. You say sorry. You make peace and move on.

But after our conversation, I sleep more restlessly each passing night. I find myself actively avoiding Gran's house. And Hunter. Either hiding in the carriage house trying to decide how to spend days that seem interminably long without a job, or reacquainting myself with Oakley Island and its residents—most of whom seem more than happy to stop me and share a favorite story of Gran.

There's the one Frank the barber told me about Gran bringing in a man she found hanging out on the beach. She paid for him to get a haircut and a shave before she bought him lunch, then sent him off in an Uber with a thick wad of cash. No one but Gran ever knew the man's story, which I totally believe. The woman could keep a secret.

Then there was the story Harriett told me when I stopped by Sweet Tea and Toast for an early lunch. She slipped into the booth across from me, her arms resting on the smooth Formica tabletop, and told me about the famous cherry pies Gran sold in the elementary school's dessert auction every Spring. Gran kept the recipe a secret until the year before she died when she brought a faded recipe card to Harriett, handed it over, and insisted the pie be added to the restaurant's menu.

After I finished my sandwich, Harriett brought me a slice of that pie on the house, making me cry.

But aside from these totally welcome distractions, I'm feeling ... restless. *Anxious.*

My ankle is mostly better, but my head is worse. Can you sprain your brain? Certainly has a nice ring to it. I still haven't seen Hunter, and at this point, I'm not sure who is avoiding whom. But every time I see his truck at Gran's, I have a Pavlovian urge to run over there. And ... what? That's the thing—where do we go from here?

We made peace with our past (mostly) and then ... I friend zoned myself. *Really* friend zoned myself since Hunter still thinks Simon is in the picture, and I didn't tell him any different.

Because it's better this way.

Because even if I can't trust my own ability to stay away from Hunter, I can trust his ability to stay away from me. At least in all the ways he should, since he believes I'm an attached woman. Off-limits. Only available for friendship.

Not coming clean about Simon seemed like the right choice at the time. I also didn't see a way to bring it up. Like, *oh, and not that you care, but ... I'm actually single!* Or, *by the way, about that boyfriend I had ... he cheated and got her pregnant and now they're getting married!* I just couldn't work out a non-freakish way to announce this. Even if some part of me hoped Hunter would push a little, to imply that he wanted something more.

In any case, I can't remember the last time I was that vulnerable or honest with anyone at all. Maybe that's why I'm avoiding Hunter. I'm not actually sure I can look him in the face.

I've heard nothing from Eloise. Which is shocking, since she poured so much of herself into the renovation. I don't know if she's just busy with grad school or if her radio silence is her avoiding reminders of Jake like I'm avoiding Hunter.

But at least I'm communicating with Sadie more frequently. She texts at least once a day, which is so unlike her, I'm starting to wonder if she senses something is up. That I might have a secret or two. Or twelve.

On day three of my island-wandering Hunter avoidance, Sadie texts me just before midnight. I'm awake, staring at the ceiling, trying not to remember how good Hunter looked yesterday as he replaced the gutters on the east side of Gran's house.

I found a dozen different reasons to sit in my front room right next to the window just so I could watch him. I may be committed to this whole friend zone thing (loosely committed?) but I can't NOT notice the man. Honestly, it's almost laughable to me now, thinking about Simon with his starched shirts and neatly tailored suits. I'm not sure I ever saw the guy with a single hair out of place. Hunter is so much ... I don't know what he is. Just different. Messier? Manlier? Sweaty and dirty, yes, but somehow so much sexier.

I force the image out of my mind—impossible since it

literally feels like it's burned on my retinas—and focus on Sadie's text.

Sadie: I've got a surprise for you tomorrow
Sadie: (please read that text in a singsongy voice)
Merritt: No. Too loud. Too late.
Sadie: Boo
Merritt: What's the surprise?
Sadie: You'll see
Merritt: You're the worst.
Sadie: Incorrect
Sadie: I am the BEST
Sadie: Just wait
Merritt: For what?
Sadie: The SURPRISE
Merritt: When did you stop using punctuation in your texts?
Sadie: I use some
Sadie: Just not always periods
Merritt: Why not?
Sadie: They're rude
Sadie: Please note my use of a very polite and not at all rude apostrophe

I'm about to ask her why periods are rude, but I honestly do NOT have the energy for Sadie right now. Punctuation or not, she's too much at this precise moment.

Merritt: When will I know what the surprise is?
Sadie: You'll KNOW

Yep. She's the worst. And now I can't sleep thinking about Hunter *and* whatever surprise Sadie has for me.

Sometime after two a.m., I must fall asleep, because when I wake up, it's impossibly bright and a body has just landed on top of me.

"Surprise!"

My New York instincts kick in. I flail violently as my brain tries to piece together where I am and who's holding me down.

Where is my pepper spray?

My leg makes contact with something—no, someone—and there's a thud and a groan.

"Merritt! Ow!"

"Sadie?"

I lean over the edge of the bed, then lose my balance and tumble down on top of my sister, taking the comforter with me.

"Oof! Are your bones made of adamantium?" Sadie groans again and shifts under me.

"Adam—*what?!*"

"It's from X-Men," she says, as though I'm the only idiot in the world who doesn't follow Marvel. Or DC? Whatever comic book world she's obsessed with. I never remember. She continues, "Wolverine has—"

"You know what? Don't worry about it. Don't care. Why are you here?"

Sadie snakes her arms around me until she's hugging me from behind, the big spoon to my little spoon. (Despite the fact that I've got four inches of height on her.) She smells like cotton candy and coffee. Right now, only one of those two things sounds good.

"Some welcoming committee you are. Remember the surprise I texted you about?"

"Yeah?"

"Surprise! It's me. I'm the surprise."

"Oh," I say, still processing. It's early. I was asleep dreaming about … something that just slipped out of my head. Sadie is here? *Sadie is here!* "I mean, oh! Yay!"

"I will choose not to be offended by your disturbing lack of enthusiasm."

"I'm just tired."

"It's two o'clock!"

"*What?!*"

The latest I ever slept in New York was seven-thirty. Even on weekends. I guess all the restless sleeping finally caught up with me. But sleeping until two in the afternoon?! It's … appalling.

And kind of amazing.

Sadie squeezes me tighter, holding me in place for another few seconds. Then without warning, she shoves me off and hops to her feet. Her physical affection is like a fickle wind, blowing in hard and then disappearing altogether. Come to think of it—that description works very well for Sadie as a whole.

Sadie holds out one hand. "Come with me if you want to live."

"Isn't that a line from *Terminator*?"

Rolling her eyes, Sadie waves her hand in front of my face. "Yes. Now come on. Time to get you out of this funk. And you definitely are funky." She makes a show of sniffing me as I let her pull me to my feet. "Take a shower. Thirty minutes, and we're going out."

"Out where?"

"I'll make the coffee. You need it."

Sadie smacks me on the butt as I walk into the bathroom, and I throw a roll of toilet paper at her head. But as I close the door and turn on the shower, I find myself smiling for the first time in days.

———

I'M SHOWERED. Dressed for a night out per Sadie's specifications. But the very last thing I want to do is go anywhere. What if I run into Hunter? What if I don't? Despite the sleep, my eyes are puffy, and a crease on my cheek from the pillowcase hasn't disappeared even after my shower.

But when Sadie says GO, you either go or get out of the way. I might be the most dominant out of the three sisters, but even I will buckle under the sheer force of a determined Sadie.

Which is how I end up at The Round Up, shoving greasy bar food into my face so I don't drink on an empty stomach. (One wine-addled phone call with Hunter is enough for my lifetime, thank you very much.) This place wasn't around back when we spent summers here. The beachy restaurant-bar combo is a hallmark of the new, more touristy shift Oakley has gone through. Or—is going through, I guess. It's not bad though. The scarred wood floors have a light dusting of sand and open patio doors give a view of the beach just outside. "Toes" by Zac Brown Band is playing overhead.

It could be worse. Much worse.

"How's your sandwich?" Sadie asks, dipping a French fry into her milkshake.

My lip curls as I watch her eat the chocolate-dipped fry. *Disgusting.* How are we related?

"It's fine." I glance down at my plate, which is empty. "It *was* fine."

I honestly don't even remember what I just ate. Which is probably because I don't remember when I *last* ate. I'm not very good at taking care of myself even when I'm at my peak. Taking care of my clients? Absolutely. My own nutritional needs? Not so much. Unless you consider coffee and a protein bar a well-balanced meal. (There's probably vegetable powder inside those things, so it could be worse.) But I haven't been eating even *that* much since arriving in Oakley. One meal a day, maybe. And only if I eat out. I'm definitely not cooking anything at home.

Especially not after talking with Hunter. The conversation lingers like a fog in my mind. Why don't I feel peaceful about it? Why can't I stop thinking about it? About *him*?

"It must have been. You pretty much inhaled it." Sadie eats another gross shake-fry, then wipes her hands on her skinny jeans. "We should dance."

"Dance?"

"Yes, my sweet, stifled sister. You're twenty-six, not eighty-six. Now get your pert little butt off that stool and shake your groove thing with me."

"I don't have a groove thing," I protest, gripping the sides of my stool, like that will do any good against my sister.

"I've seen it. It's very neglected, but that's okay. Dust it off and let's go."

"I hurt my ankle the other day running."

"Nice try but you haven't even been limping. Time to pop and lock, Mer-Mer."

Sadie stopped using that nickname for me when she was maybe five. It startles me, but she doesn't seem to notice. She's too busy dragging me out onto an area where a handful of people are dancing. Not enough of a crowd to really hide behind, which makes me hyperaware of my stiff movements.

When was the last time I danced? Muscle memory is definitely not helping me right now. "Um, I'm not really a pop and locker, Sadie."

"Just let go," she says.

Is it really so easy for other people? To just ... let go?

Sadie, who isn't the best dancer but possesses more self-confidence than the entire room put together, has her hands up in the air, eyes closed, a smile on her face. That is, until she glances my way. Her happy expression disappears, and she wrinkles her nose.

"You look like you need a chiropractic adjustment!" she says, leaning in so I can hear her over the music, which has switched from Zac Brown to R&B. "Let loose. I know you can. I've seen it. You're a grown woman, fully capable of not caring what any of the people in this bar think of you."

With that, Sadie bumps my hip like that will somehow kickstart my sense of rhythm. It doesn't.

But as I glance around the bar, which has a decent crowd without being packed, I realize that Sadie is right. Not a single person is looking my way. I'm as invisible here as I am on any New York sidewalk. And even if they were all watching—I AM a fully grown woman. I can do what I want. And right now, what I want is to enjoy dancing (badly) with my sister.

She takes my hands, and I let her, hoping for an osmosis-style transmission of rhythm as well as attitude. I close my eyes and finally lose myself in the music, my limbs slowly cooperating as my hips sway to the thumping bass. Sadie lifts our hands up, then lets go, and I'm on my own. But it's good. I feel good.

"There she is," Sadie says, smiling as she tosses her hair over her shoulders. "Merritt's wild side, coming out to play."

She grabs my hands again, and now we're spinning. I laugh, tilting my face up to the lights. I'm not sure if someone turned up the music or if I just feel it more now. It pounds through my torso, thudding through the soles of my feet.

I'm weightless, easy, free. New York slides away like a distant bad dream—Simon beating me out for the promotion, Simon confessing he was cheating, Simon telling me she was pregnant and they were getting married.

So much of my New York life was tied up with Simon, and as I shake him off, I realize I can't go back.

I don't WANT to go back.

"I'm never going back." I say it out loud, needing the words to be real and out in the world, not just in my head.

"What?"

Sadie has to lean closer and yell because they've definitely turned up the music. The dance floor is more crowded too. How long have we been out here?

I smile. "I need a drink!"

We can talk later. A loud bar isn't the place to tell Sadie all the things I've been hiding.

Looping her arm through mine, Sadie skips toward the bar, half-dragging me. With a laugh, I skip with her. We reach the bar, collapsing against it, laughing. Clutching each other.

"What will you ladies have tonight?" The bartender is a little older than we are, with an unfortunate mustache—the kind that looks like it requires at least four expensive products to curl up at the ends.

"Vodka tonics," Sadie says. "Extra lime."

"Put it on my tab," a voice says, and Sadie's laughter evaporates.

She straightens, crossing her arms. "Cumberbatch," Sadie hisses, and I wonder how she knows this guy, and how likely it is he's related to the actor who starred in BBC's *Sherlock*.

The man in question looks nothing like his namesake.

Blond, with that whole rich guy at the beach look. Collared shirt with khaki shorts and a belt. Leather boat shoes that look weather-beaten but probably cost five hundred dollars.

"Hi," I say, reaching out my hand between him and my sister. They for sure need a barrier. He shakes my hand but only has eyes for Sadie.

"I'm Merritt," I say. "And you are?"

"Benedict."

My eyes widen. "Wait—your name is actually Benedict Cumberbatch? Like the actor? What are the odds!"

Beside me, Sadie is laughing uncontrollably, somewhere between a cackle and a guffaw. The man groans and raises his eyes to the ceiling like he's searching for patience.

"Benedict *King*. Nice to meet you, Merritt Markham."

It clicks into place exactly who this man—who obviously is a few steps ahead of me—actually is. The Kings, if I remember correctly, own this whole island. Now that I'm thinking back, Benedict might have been around the summers we were here. Hanging out with Jake, maybe? I don't think we ever hung out together, but there's something about him that seems familiar.

Still, that vague connection isn't enough for Sadie to talk like she knows the guy. And she definitely knows the guy.

"I see you seem to have some … history with my sister?"

Benedict's eyes flick to Sadie, who is still doubled over with laughter. When he looks back at me, his expression has shifted to something like wicked amusement.

"Our history is just beginning." His grin is smug.

Sadie pops up, all traces of laughter gone. She pokes Benedict in the chest. "It most certainly is not!"

Benedict grabs Sadie's finger, which is still jabbing at his sternum. "It's true. You just don't know it yet."

When he presses a quick kiss to her fingertips, Sadie gasps. "You did *not!*"

"Like I said. Just the beginning."

He must be at least a *slightly* smart man because Benedict disappears through the crowd with a cocky wave. I decide not to interfere as Sadie follows him out to the patio, a murderous look on her face. Whatever is going on there—I don't want to be in the middle. Forget being a barrier. Sadie's on her own.

I'm sipping a vodka tonic (which is a little *too* heavy on the limes) when my eyes snag on a familiar, bearded face angled my way. *Hunter.*

This bar is one of the last places I'd expect to see a man who would rather socialize with ceramic garden gnomes than most people. But there he is: at the end of the bar, facing out toward the room. But only watching *me.* His jeans are darker than the ones he wears to work. Tighter too. His black t-shirt fits just snugly enough that it doesn't look painted on, but it highlights all those muscles earned by his work.

His eyes, though—they're what pull me in. I shouldn't want to get closer. Not if we're only friends. Not if I'm leaving Oakley.

The thought that overwhelmed me on the dance floor pops back into my brain.

I'm never going back.

Not going back to New York could look like a lot of things. There are other cities. Other advertising firms. Other jobs. But all of those options feel too similar to a life I'm beginning to realize never actually made me happy.

What if *not going back to New York* looked like *staying* on Oakley?

The voice in my head takes on a Sadie-like quality as it fires off question after doubt-filled question.

What would I do for work?

Would I live in the carriage house forever?

Would my sisters care if we didn't sell the beach house?

Would Hunter feel differently about being friends if he knew I wasn't leaving and Simon was already out of the picture?

This last question gives me pause. Do I want Hunter to feel differently?

I've been flirting around my *attraction* to him since I first arrived on Oakley. But that's different than allowing that attraction to turn into something more. Is that what I want?

Something sparks low in my gut. *Oh yes, I absolutely do.*

Another sip of the vodka tonic gives me a smidge of what I know Gran would call *moxie*. Maybe it's time for me to tell Hunter another truth. I could tell him about Simon. Or about my thoughts on not returning to New York.

I take a deep breath, leave my glass on the bar, and head his way.

He watches me the whole time, and I wish I could read his expression.

I take the stool next to him, facing outward, completely aware of him but with my eyes trained on the pool tables and dance floor.

"I'm surprised to see you," I say, going for light and funny. It comes out flirty instead. "This doesn't seem like your scene."

"It's not so bad."

He's drinking coffee, because of course he is. It's about the most contrary drink you could order in a bar.

I tip my chin toward his mug. "Do they have your fancy creamer here?"

Hunter glances down, like he forgot about his coffee altogether. "No. But they do have heavy cream."

"You put heavy cream in your coffee?"

"Don't knock it if you haven't tried it."

Boldly, I reach for his mug and take a slow sip, my eyes locked on Hunter's the whole time. The drink is lukewarm—a stark contrast to the fire racing through my veins.

Hunter's gaze narrows, like he can't quite figure me out.

"Not bad," I say as I lick my lips. "Very rich."

A tense silence stretches between us as the song shifts to something slow, the couples in front of us pressing closer to each other. I'm struck with a longing so intense, my chest feels tight.

Because I only spent time here in summer, Hunter and I never went to a school dance together the way we might have if we grew up in the same town. I never got to know how it would feel to watch him open a door for me, to slide a corsage on my wrist, to put his hands on my waist as we danced.

I feel a sudden tug of nostalgia--a longing for things past that also somehow links to a very real desire for things now. Like, *right* now.

"I saw you dancing earlier," Hunter says. "I was surprised."

I elbow him lightly, careful not to spill his coffee. "Thanks a lot."

He leans closer, his breath the faintest tickle on my cheek. "Not surprised you were good at it. I was worried about your ankle."

Way to suck all the romance out of the moment, Hunter.

Now that he mentions it, I'm suddenly aware of a dull throb I've been ignoring. But my mind wants to focus on other things. Like his concern and his compliment about my dancing. Well—his *sort of* compliment.

"Right. My ankle. It's better."

"Good."

"Hunter, I need to tell you something."

His eyebrows go up. "Okay."

I take a breath to spill whichever truth comes out of my mouth first, but Sadie appears beside me, looking both irritated and energized. "That man needs a swift kick somewhere the sun don't shine. Oh, hey, Hunter."

He smiles and lifts his mug in a silent hello.

"Long time, no see. Nice beard. You didn't have that back when I used to follow you and Merritt around, watching you make out." Sadie grins.

"Sadie!" I hiss.

I want to throttle my sister, but inexplicably, Hunter laughs. "You were always sneaking around."

"*Harriet the Spy* was a very influential read for my childhood." Sadie doesn't ask if Hunter knows the book.

"Did you start a tab?" I ask. "I sort of forgot." When Sadie shakes her head, I gesture to my purse, which I've unwisely left at the other end of the bar, something I'd never do in New York. "I'll pay. Just grab my card."

"Which one?"

I shrug. "Doesn't matter."

It really doesn't. I saved for a long time for things that have since gone up in smoke—a better apartment for when Simon and I moved in together, a wedding. I need to set some new goals and figure out where those finances can go now.

"Thanks, sis. I knew you were good for something." Sadie bounces off.

"I saw her chasing Benedict King," Hunter says. "She looked angry. Usually, women are chasing him for *different* reasons."

I laugh. "Actually, I think that might have been Sadie's version of foreplay. She tends to be a little …"

I'm still searching for a word when Sadie reappears, shoving a paper in my face. "Explain," she demands.

I grab the paper. But it's not just paper. It's a very familiar wedding invitation printed on linen, the words engraved. Flowers and flourishes and gold foil everywhere. If I had to choose the tackiest wedding invitation ever, one that perfectly suited the couple, it would be this one.

I should have thrown it away weeks ago. Instead, I've been carrying it around in my purse.

I hop off my stool, shoving the invitation behind my back. "Did you pay? We should go."

Sadie steps in front of me, so close I'm trapped between her and Hunter. "Not until you tell me why you have a wedding invitation for *Simon*—your *boyfriend*, or so I thought—in your purse."

And my tower of lies has officially come falling down.

I can't look at Hunter. I don't want to look at Sadie. I'd like to go back in time and tell everyone the whole truth about everything from the start. Why didn't I? Why did I feel like holding it close was somehow protecting me?

"Let's talk back at the house," I say.

"Nope. The time for that is over. Let's talk *now*," Sadie says.

Hunter hasn't moved a muscle since Sadie practically assaulted me with Simon's invitation. I may not be looking right at him, but he's locked in my periphery.

I lower my voice. "I'd really rather not—"

"Now, Merritt."

I close my eyes. Here goes the humiliation.

"Simon was cheating on me, and he got her pregnant. We broke up, and they're getting married. Now you know everything. Oh—and he also got the promotion I wanted because I'd been helping him do his job, so I quit. Not necessarily all in that order or that fast, but there it is. My life imploded, and now I'm here. The end."

Sadie's eyes go wide, and her mouth falls open. Despite my deep feeling of shame—even though exactly none of this is *my* fault—there is some small satisfaction in shocking her. It's pretty hard to do. Most of the time, she prides herself on knowing everything. At times, I've wondered if her spying on people as a kid has just gotten more sophisticated with her use of tech. But obviously, she hasn't been tracking me.

"I always hated Simon. He's a giant jerk," she finally says, regaining her composure.

"The biggest," I agree.

"A total *Simon*."

I smile, feeling the sting of humiliation ease a little. "Such a *Simon*."

And then she's hugging me so hard one of my ribs might crack. I didn't realize how much I needed this kind of hug. A hug from someone who knows the truth, is on my side, and would probably castrate Simon if given a chance.

"You deserve so much better," she says.

"You can say 'I told you so.' It's fine."

"I would *never*." She pauses. "But is it okay if I get revenge?"

"Legally or illegally?"

"Never you mind."

"Okay—revenge is fine so long as you don't end up in jail. But I think you're breaking me. Can we conclude the hug and go home?"

"Of course. I still have to pay for our drinks. I got distracted by sniveling Simon's wedding invitation."

Sadie pats my cheek once, then darts back to the

bartender. I turn back to Hunter, afraid of what look I might see on his face. It better not be pity. I can handle just about any emotion except that one.

But Hunter's stool is empty, save for the coffee mug he left behind, a pink smudge of lipstick staining the side I drank from just a few minutes before.

NINE

Hunter

I DON'T MEAN to slam my hands on the countertop where Dante is updating what looks to be an inventory spreadsheet. But when I'm standing there for a whole minute and he doesn't look up, slam them I do. I waited as long as I could after the bar Thursday night to talk to someone—all weekend, to be exact—and now, my ability to wait is worn thin. Or nonexistent.

He finishes whatever he's writing, then methodically tucks his pencil behind his ear before grinning at me. "Hello to you too. Back for more tile? Or for the thin-set you left here the other day?"

I blink at him. "Right. Yeah."

He reaches behind the counter and grabs the bags, setting them on the counter between us. "Here you go. Anything else you need?"

In truth, I'm not here for the thin-set. I'm here to talk. A thing that now seems ridiculously hard to do. Especially with how weird Dante is being. Almost like …

"You already know." It's a statement, not a question, but there's still surprise in my tone.

"Know what?" His tone is infuriatingly cheerful. Ridiculously smug.

"Who told you?"

"No one needed to." He pulls his phone out of his back pocket, turns it on, then slides it across the counter facing me.

TikTok. Frank's TikTok. Oakley Island's only barber—a man in his sixties—has recently turned TikTok into his favorite hobby. With a specific focus on local gossip. I don't need to watch the man who's been cutting my hair since I was a kid breaking down what went down at the bar Thursday night with Merritt and Sadie.

I push the phone back to Dante without watching. "The man just can't stick to passing gossip while he's cutting hair, can he?"

"No, he cannot." Dante returns his phone to his back pocket. "So, Merritt Markham is single. And now you aren't sure what excuse to use for why you shouldn't go after her."

Dante knows me too well. At times, like right now, for example, it's a little scary.

I didn't sleep much after I bolted from the bar. I couldn't stop thinking about Simon fizzling away into a nonissue, leaving me feeling so … so … I don't even know. Whatever it is, I'm still feeling it. Merritt is single. This fact shouldn't have such a strong impact on my ability to function in daily tasks. But clearly, it does.

I only made it through the weekend because Isabelle was with me, and she's the best kind of distraction. But now that Izzy is back with her mom, the emotions I ignored while we played on the beach and ate mac and cheese and watched *Moana* five hundred times are finally coalescing into more tangible feelings.

For a long time after Cassidy and I first got together, a part of me felt like I was cheating on Merritt. What even is that? You can't cheat on someone you're not in a relationship with. And there were a good few years between Merritt breaking my heart and me trying to move on. Not that Cassidy was *just* an attempt to move on. She and I were friends. She made me laugh—a rare feat in those days. Eventually, I convinced myself the deep care I felt—and still feel—for her was love. Even if it was nothing like what had existed between Merritt and me.

But were it not for Isabelle, I wouldn't have married Cassidy. We both felt like it was the right thing to do, but her feelings were always stronger than mine. In the end, even she acknowledged we were better off as friends, co-parenting in separate households. I was less sad by the breakup of my marriage and more relieved.

I think a part of me knew my heart still belonged to Merritt.

"What are you going to do?" Dante asks.

"She said she wanted to be friends."

"Is that what you think she really wants? Is that what *you* want—friendship?"

I cross my arms. "I don't *not* want to be friends with her."

Dante regards me like I'm some new species of human he's never seen. A new, *inferior* species of human. "Are you serious right now?"

"What—you think I should just ask her out?"

These may be the most terrifying words I've ever said in my whole life. I'm sweating. My breathing is shallow. I can't look at Dante's eyes so I stare at a spot on his forehead instead.

His eyebrows lift. "Do you *want* to ask her out?"

It's not even a question. But maybe it should be. Because it's only been a few days since we dealt with the biggest issue in our past. I don't know how long ago she and Simon broke up, but it can't have been that long if her sister didn't even know. And even if she apologized for what she said back then, isn't there some truth to it? Merritt may not have her job in New York right now, but it's not like she's going to find anything comparable on Oakley Island.

"Don't tell me you're scared," Dante says.

I glare. "It's not that I'm scared."

"So, ask her out."

"I'm not going to ask her out just because you dare me to do it."

"Good. Ask her out because you want to. Because she's the only one you want to date. Because it's about time to break your years-long single streak."

"Years? Really?"

"When was the last time you took a woman on a date? And your dates with Isabelle don't count."

I smile at the mention of my daughter. Dante may be right about my lack of romantic relationships, but dinner dates with Izzy have been more than enough for me. We go out every Friday night to kick off the weekend, which she always spends at my house.

A sudden thought jolts through me. How will Merritt be around Isabelle? I can't believe it's taken me this long to consider that.

I can't believe I'm considering this at *all*.

"I don't want to be a rebound," I say.

Dante scoffs. "You, my friend, are not rebound material. If

Merritt's ready to date, she's ready to date. Let her make that choice."

I rub a hand across my jaw. "She won't be on Oakley long."

"Have you asked?"

"Don't need to." I shrug. "She's here because of her grandma's will. But Merritt has to work again eventually. And it's not like Oakley is a hotbed of job opportunities for people with an MBA."

"But Savannah has jobs. It's close."

I shake my head, immune to his reason. Or maybe just afraid of it. "It feels a little premature to think that far ahead."

Dante blows out a breath. "Then quit thinking so far ahead and just *act*. Make a move. See what happens without worrying about what *might* happen in the future."

"Not exactly my strong suit, is it?"

"It's never too late to shake things up, man. Especially when it matters. And from what I know—this one matters to you. Don't let the chance pass you by." He grins. "But a word of advice? Maybe get a couple of dates behind you before you take her home to meet the herd."

I roll my eyes. "Three dogs don't make a herd."

"What about three dogs, a raccoon, and half a dozen rabbits?" Dante asks without missing a beat.

"I don't have the rabbits anymore. I just fostered them. The raccoon, too. Banjo won't be with me forever."

"Oh, right. Totally. That makes all the difference," Dante says dryly. "But I haven't mentioned the squirrels, possums, and the deer. If anything would be a dealbreaker, it's a possum. They're like giant rats, man."

"Shut up." It's not like I have all these animals at one

time. I work too much to foster more than one or two wild animals at a time. And I'm all set on dogs. Probably.

"I'm just saying," Dante says. "You best find out how she feels about animals."

"She likes them," I say with too much confidence.

The Merritt I *used* to know liked animals. I'm not actually sure about the all-grown-up version. I've caught glimpses of the Merritt I recognize—watching her dance at the bar, and when she apologized earlier this week on the porch. But most of the time, it's like I don't know her at all, and we're starting out brand new.

"How do I ..." I don't know how to formulate the question. Or maybe I'm too embarrassed to tell Dante I have no idea how to be an adult man asking an adult woman out on a date. Because I've never done it.

But Dante has always had a way of reading between the lines, and he seems to know what I'm asking anyway. "Just start small," he says. "If you know she wants friendship, then be her friend. Take her coffee. Buy her lunch. Be thoughtful. Attentive. Make her want more."

That ... feels less intimidating. At least up to the "make her want more" part.

There were a lot of ways Merritt and I felt *right*. But Dante's suggestions sound like they're tailored for someone else. Not that I'm not a nice, thoughtful guy. More like ... Merritt and I always had fun. Joked around, teased each other, laughed until we both cried.

What I really need is to show Merritt that we can have that again. That we're good together—always were.

A memory pops into my head, the sound of Merritt's laughter echoing in my ears.

"What did you do?" *I ask, eyeing her suspiciously.*

Merritt licks her ice cream cone, her expression innocent enough to trick a stranger, but I recognize the teasing glint in her eye. "I have no idea what you're talking about."

Her eyes dart to the massive bulletin board that hangs in the entry of the ice cream parlor, full of lost dog posters, business cards, and announcements for BINGO night at the Oakley senior center.

And that's when I see it.

I stand up, abandoning my hot fudge sundae, and stomp over to the board. Right square in the middle, there's a half sheet of paper sporting a cheesy picture of me, a wide grin, two thumbs raised in a "good job" gesture, with a caption that reads, "Will mow lawns for hugs." The number under the photo is NOT my number, but one of those made up five-five-five numbers, which makes it easier to laugh. Merritt knows better than to give out my phone number. I hate talking on the phone.

"The grass is getting pretty long at Gran's," Merritt says from just behind me, her voice close to my ear. "I volunteer for the hugging part if you want to bring your lawn mower over tomorrow."

I turn to face her, shaking my head at her cheeky expression. "When did you even take this picture?"

She shrugs and takes a bite of ice cream.

"Wait, Is that my sundae?"

"Mmhmm," she says as she licks the chocolate off the back of the spoon.

I try not to be obvious about the way my eyes track the movement. The soft curve of her lips, the tip of her tongue sliding over the spoon. It reminds me of the end of last summer when she asked me to be her first kiss. She left the next day, and so far, we haven't talked about it … but kissing her seems to be all I can think about this summer. Does she think about it too?

I swallow.

"You just left it sitting there, so I figured you were done," she says, coy, but somehow still confident.

Honestly, if anyone else had taken my sundae, I might be annoyed, but not Merritt. I'd give her anything. I wonder if she knows. If that's why she took it—she knows how gone for her I am.

She holds out the spoon, offering me a bite of the sundae, and tilts her head toward the picture on the bulletin board. "There are seventy-five more of these around town. Want to go look for them?"

I chuckle as I close my lips around the spoon. I should have known ONE photo would be way below Merritt's skill level. "I'm guessing you aren't going to tell me where they are?"

"Oh, absolutely not," she says through her grin. "But I will definitely come along while you search."

I pull the picture off the bulletin board, then loop a finger around Merritt's belt loop, tugging her toward me. "You're impossible, Merritt Markham."

"Or I'm a genius," she says easily, smiling up at me. "Because now we have an excuse to spend the rest of the day together."

We ended up finding most of what Merritt put up that first afternoon, but for weeks after, I occasionally came across one on a shop window or stuck to the inside of a bathroom stall at the movie theater.

The way we would randomly come across a picture, sometimes in places Merritt didn't even remember putting one up, was the funniest and the funnest part of our summer.

Until it wasn't anymore. I found the last one two weeks after she left Oakley for the last time, and that one hit me like a sucker punch to the gut.

I clear my throat and push the thought away, choosing to focus on the brighter parts of our history. Those are the memories I need to channel if I want to make progress now.

"You've already got an idea," Dante says. "I can tell."

I have a million ideas. And a million hopes and wishes centering around Merritt. Now I just have to decide if I'm brave—or stupid—enough to try and make them happen. One thing is for sure—I'm not going to start by being thoughtful. At least, not in the way Dante meant. In fact, I'm pretty sure he'd advise me against my next plan of action, but I'm going to go with my gut.

If the goal is light and fun, then my gut says it's time to mess with Merritt. Again.

TEN

MERRITT

I WALK across the lawn to the beach house dressed in my oldest, most threadbare leggings and a shirt worn to epic levels of softness. When Hunter stopped by this morning with coffee for Sadie and me, he said I should come over later dressed to work. This is the best I can do. I hope it's suitable because it's the *only* thing I can do. Dress to work in a boardroom? I've got a million different options. Dress to remodel a house? Not so much.

After I dropped Sadie off at the airport, I contemplated driving to the nearest Target in Savannah to buy something to work in, but that felt ridiculous. And would probably be obvious to Hunter. Who buys new clothes only to do work that might ruin them?

Also, how many people know just how I like my coffee? Because Hunter does—unfussy, with no sugar and just a splash of cream. For Sadie, he brought a million sugars and creamers, just in case. I didn't miss the look she gave me when he handed them over.

I also didn't miss the way Hunter's eyes stayed trained on me. Or the smile playing on Hunter's lips when he told me he had some work for me to do at the beach house this afternoon.

Unfortunately, Sadie didn't miss any of this either, and she spent the entire drive to the airport singing about Hunter and Merritt sitting in a tree, K-I-S-S-I-N-G.

Not that I would necessarily be opposed to the activity. But after the way Hunter fled the bar last week, I don't know what to expect. All the confidence and moxie (and possibly alcohol?) that pushed me to *almost* telling him about Simon or about staying has faded. Especially now that the whole Simon thing came out the way it did.

Was he mad that I lied to—or misled—him about Simon? Does he care? Was he glad? Will he want to talk about it?

I push through the back door and into the kitchen where Hunter is leaning over the counter, installing the backsplash. The tiles look even better than I thought they would, and a surge of pride flits through me. I chose them! And they look good! It's a very small victory, but considering how few of those I've had lately, I'm happy to take the win.

"Reporting for duty, boss," I say, and Hunter looks over his shoulder, his lips lifting into a grin.

"Pretty sure you're the one in charge around here."

"True. Does that mean I should fire you for insubordination? Because it sounded like you were bossing me around this morning when you said you had work for me to do."

"Not bossing. Just asking. And you're here, so you must be willing."

Willing for more than just work. But in Gran's half-finished kitchen with the light of day streaming through the windows, my bravery is whittled down to a tiny nub.

"I'm only willing because Sadie left this morning, and I'm bored." This is not entirely untrue. I AM bored. I'm also very excited about the prospect of spending time around Hunter.

The smooth marble of the kitchen island separates us. But as we stand here with our eyes locked, it feels like less. I swear the air between us shimmers with heat like it does over an asphalt road in summer. I'm hit with an intense urge to climb right over the counter, grab his face in my hands, and see how that beard feels against my cheeks as I kiss him.

I feel the blush rising like mercury in an old thermometer —moving slowly and steadily from my chest to my neck to my cheeks. It's too much to hope Hunter doesn't see it. His eyes dip just slightly. Yep—he sees it. His tiny smirk tells me he also might have guesses as to why I'm now furiously blushing.

It only intensifies my urge to kiss him. Which makes me blush *more*. I resist the urge to fan my cheeks.

"How's your ankle?" Hunter asks.

"Fine."

"Really fine, or stubborn Merritt fine?"

"Oh, you want to talk about being stubborn?"

"No need to talk," he says. "It's a fact. You're stubborn."

"It takes a kettle to know a pot."

He chuckles. "Not how the phrase goes, but okay."

"My ankle is fine, Hunter. I wouldn't be here if it wasn't."

"Okay, then," he says. Then he turns and walks toward the back door without a word.

"Am I supposed to follow you?" I call after him.

I barely hear his grunt.

Where is he even going? I don't catch up until he's halfway across the expanse of wide lawn behind the house.

"Hey, aren't we going the wrong way? The house is back there," I say, a little out of breath as I match his pace.

This earns me some side-eye, which I had no idea could be flirty. But the look in his eyes makes my stomach flip.

We reach a large shed I've never really noticed. Hunter walks into the dark building, and I follow right on his heels, bumping into him when he stops suddenly. Now I've got a mouthful of flannel. Seriously—it's autumn but not even remotely cool. What's with the man's love of flannel?

"Oof," I say, taking a little step back.

"Sorry," he says. "Forgot where the switch is."

Hunter must locate it because the room illuminates with the kind of buzzing fluorescent light that gives me headaches. I blink and rub my eyes as he walks further inside, stopping just before an ancient lawn mower.

He points. "Here's your job."

I stare, my gaze bouncing between Hunter and the hunk of junk. He can't be serious. "I thought I was going to help with renovations. Like Eloise did."

"Lo mostly picked things out, took photos for Instagram, and talked my ear off."

"But she—"

"And when I *did* give her a job to do," he continues, "she didn't question me. She did what I asked. No arguments."

I hate being compared to my sisters. Especially if, in the comparison, I come up lacking. My competitive drive kicks in.

I walk over—maybe *stomp* is a more apt term—and take Hunter's place by the handlebar or whatever it's called. He steps back.

"I'll do it," I say.

Hunter raises a brow. "You know how to mow a lawn?"

"I know enough to figure it out." I stop just short of telling him I have an MBA—I can figure out a piece of lawn equipment. "Does this thing still work? It looks old."

And the lawn is *huge*. I'm shocked Gran never had a riding mower. Or a lawn service. Back in the day, I think she used to pay some high school boys to do it.

"It works. Are you sure you can manage?"

"Yes, I can manage."

With another grunt, one that sounds like a challenge, Hunter swings open the main double doors to the shed so I can wheel the mower out. "I'll be in the house if you need me."

"I won't," I call, and I swear, I hear him chuckle.

Only, I *do* need him. Or someone. Maybe I just need stronger arms because once I get the mower out of the shed, I can't even get the stupid thing started. There's a cord to start it—that much I know—but I'm either not pulling it hard enough, or it's out of gas, or something else is wrong.

"Need a hand?"

I glance up to see Jake walking along the path in a suit, briefcase in hand. I'm about to tell him no when I think of the alternative—telling Hunter I need help.

"Actually, could you just help me start this thing?"

"Sure."

With two good yanks from Jake on the same cord I spent ten minutes pulling, the mower roars to life. *Sexist machine*, I think.

"There you go," he says over the roar of the motor.

Jake tries to say something else as he steps back, but it's impossible to hear. And I suddenly see a bearded face watching from a window in the house. A smiling bearded face. I hope against vain hope Hunter didn't just see me accepting Jake's help.

"Thank you!" I call as Jake heads back to the path.

I try to move the mower forward and holy mackerel—does this thing put the *push* in push mower. Even holding down the self-propel lever, I feel like I'm trying to force an armored tank across rocky ground. I don't look at the house again to see if Hunter is still at the window when he *should be* finishing the backsplash. Sweat trickles down my back as I dig in and heave my weight behind this thing. I *will* do this.

Not gonna lie—my MBA is proving totally useless in this particular activity. The lawn is like some optical illusion that gets larger and larger as I mow. How big is this property? I try to remember the specs Jake went over when he was going over Gran's will. A full acre? Whatever the official measurements, it's never-gonna-finish large.

I'm definitely hiring a lawn service after today. There's money in the accounts marked for renovation, but I feel like I remember Jake mentioning funds for maintenance and upkeep as well.

Almost as though they've been conjured by wishful thinking, a pickup truck towing a trailer with a riding mower pulls up to the curb near Gran's. It must be here for the neighbors, but I really wish it was here for *me*.

Maybe it *can* be …

With a quick glance at the house to make sure Hunter isn't watching, I dart over to the truck. I leave the mower running because I don't trust myself to get it started again without help from a man. Since the mower is sexist. Not because I apparently need to work on my upper body strength.

"Hey," I call, waving to the man with sun-worn skin and bleached blond hair.

He pauses at the back of the trailer, eyes moving from me to the still-running mower, which smells very strongly of gasoline and exhaust. Which likely means I smell like gasoline and exhaust. And sweat. So much sweat.

I stop out of smelling range. (I hope.) "I don't know if you'd be interested in picking up another job, but I've got one for you."

"Sure," he says easily. "What kind of job?"

I sweep a hand behind me, indicating the half-mown lawn. "This. Not today, obviously. But maybe we could get on your schedule?"

"Right. Um." He scratches his cheek, glancing again at the lawn like he's confused. Or thinking really hard about my offer.

"I could pay you extra," I say quickly. "Whatever you normally make, plus … twenty-five percent." My legs begin to shake, and I realize exactly how exhausted I am from mowing just this tiny fraction of the yard. "More if you start today. If you aren't too busy."

He grins. "I can't say I'd mind the extra money, but I have to decline."

I slump. I already got my hopes up. "Thirty percent? Fifty?"

With a laugh, he drops the ramp of the trailer and climbs up. "Again, as much as I'd like to accept, I really can't."

"Do you know anyone who could?"

"No—you don't understand. I already take care of the yard. Twice a month during the winter, once a week in summer. You're welcome to give me a raise though, if you're offering."

It takes a moment to sink in. When it does, my glaring eyes move right to the house, where I swear I see Hunter ducking away from the window.

"You're here now to do *this* lawn?"

"I am. Want me to take care of the mower for you? That thing is ancient. I forgot your grandmother had asked me to haul it to the dump. But if you want to keep it for sentimental reasons or something, I'll put it back in the shed."

Hunter is a dead man.

I FIND Hunter in the kitchen, spreading grout between the backsplash tiles like he wasn't just spying on me. He doesn't move or turn though I know he heard me slam the door and stomp in here.

I open my mouth to say whatever irritated words tumble out of my head when Hunter says, still with his back to me, "Versailles tile."

I pause, wishing my eyes had laser beam properties so I could glare holes through the back of Hunter's flannel shirt. In case I had any question about Hunter messing with me, I have zero now.

"You knew there's a lawn care service."

"I did."

"And that it was coming today."

"Yep."

Oh, I want to kill him.

Why do I also want to kiss him just as much?

I weigh my options: Escalate the prank war. Tell Hunter off with a string of angry verbiage. Order him—as his boss—to do some other form of labor as punishment.

Or ... I could play dirty.

This last option sounds like the most fun. And I know just how to hit Hunter where it hurts.

"Well that's good." I sink onto one of the stools at the island. "I really wanted to push through and finish but ..." With a heavy sigh, I lift my foot, propping it on the rung of another stool. "My ankle is really bothering me."

Hunter drops the tool in his hand and spins to face me. I make sure I'm wincing as he does. I almost feel guilty because of the concern on his face. *Almost.*

"Stay there. I'll get you some ice," he says.

The new fridge hasn't arrived yet, so this means a trip to the carriage house.

"There's an ice pack in my freezer," I call after him. He's already halfway out the door. "And will you bring me a Diet Dr Pepper?"

He grunts a response, and the door slams behind him. When he returns a few minutes later, he's breathless and there's a fine sheen of sweat on his forehead. Like he ran to the carriage house and ran back. Again, I have to squash the guilt trying to make its presence known.

The sound of the riding mower out back is a good reminder of why I don't need to spend even a second feeling bad.

Hunter comes to a quick stop in the doorway, staring. I hold up his phone, which he had the misfortune of leaving unlocked. I've already changed my contact name to The Best Woman in the World and added a silly photo of me making a duck face—for the first and last time ever. I'm not sure who thinks that look is attractive, but it's perfect for Hunter's phone.

He still hasn't moved. I'm not sure if he's stunned into just staring because I've got his work playlist blasting through the Bluetooth speaker or because he's realizing I had to walk across the kitchen on my supposed bad ankle to retrieve his phone.

"Nice playlist! I didn't know you were a Swiftie." The man's entire musical library consists of Taylor Swift. Well—Taylor and a handful of Otis Redding songs, which makes for an interesting combination.

Hunter gives me a wary look and then sets a bag of ice on the counter along with a can of Diet Dr Pepper. "I have ice. And your drink."

"Thank you," I say sweetly. "So, what's your favorite album? Personally, I like *1989*. It's just so … catchy."

With a grunt, Hunter carefully lifts my ankle and sits on the stool next to me, settling my foot in his lap. Unlike the other day, he doesn't take off my shoe and sock. Instead, he grabs the bag of ice and gently places it over my ankle. I try not to suck in a breath when his other hand brushes over the bare skin just below my leggings.

"This okay?" he asks, not meeting my gaze. One of his fingers traces a tiny circle on my skin.

I bite my lip. "Mm-hm."

"I'm sorry," he says, still not looking at me. "I wouldn't have had you do that job if I knew it would hurt you."

His kind words make something squeeze tight in my chest. "Hunter—"

"It's my fault. I'm sorry, Mer. It was supposed to be a joke—I knew Mitch was coming to mow today and figured it would just be a few minutes. He was running late, and now you're hurt as a result of my actions. I'm sorry," he says again.

His fingers continue running over the tiny slice of skin between my sock and my leggings, making tiny circles and likewise making my breath catch. It's just part of my leg. Not a particularly sensitive area. Or, it shouldn't be. Maybe it's just the fact that it's *Hunter* touching me. And being so sweet and thoughtful …

Leaning forward, I grab his hand and squeeze. "Hey. Please don't feel bad. I'm really okay."

"No—I shouldn't have let you. I knew it, and I still had you do something that could have hurt you."

I give his hand another squeeze, wishing I could lace our fingers together or take his hand and press it to my cheek. There's no way to shove down the guilt now. I feel awful. I'd forgotten how tender Hunter's heart really is.

"Shake it off," Hunter says, squeezing back.

"What?"

When he looks up, the spark of mischief in his eyes makes my heart go haywire. I am totally thrown. So when he says, "My favorite Taylor Swift song," it takes me a minute to realize he's answering my earlier question.

It takes me another minute to realize that he's been messing with me. Again.

"At least, that's my pick from the *1989* album. My favorite album altogether is probably *Lover*, but I have a lot of respect for *Reputation*," Hunter says, with the same easy confidence with which he talked about tile choices.

A real Renaissance man, this guy. Can tile a backsplash, carry an injured woman off the beach in his arms, and has Serious Opinions on Taylor Swift albums.

"You know I wasn't hurt."

"I figured it out."

"What gave me away? Was it the fact I got up to get your phone?"

"That—and I was watching you outside. You seemed fine. I mean, other than the fact that you can't mow a lawn to save your life."

"Hey!" I protest, but I really can't argue. The man is tenderhearted. It's true. He's also some kind of evil genius. I lean a little farther forward and poke him in the ribs. He used to have a ticklish spot right around ... *there*.

He giggles. A very manly giggle, but definitely a giggle and not a chuckle or laugh. He grabs my hand and holds it tight as I try to pull free. Not like I could.

Not like I *want* to.

"Versailles tile," he says.

"Versailles tile," I agree, loving that we have new code words, just like we used to back then. "Truce?"

He raises a brow. "Is that what you want? A truce?"

I shrug because I honestly don't know. I mean, does a truce mean we have to stop playing? Because this is fun. I also don't think I can beat Hunter at this game.

"What *do* you want, Mer?" This question feels loaded. And it doesn't at all feel like he's asking about the pranks.

Friends, I told him the other day. And being friends is fine. I want to be Hunter's friend.

I also want him to pick me up and pull me into his lap. I want to feel his strong arms banded around me. I want to know what kind of beard burn kissing him might give me. I want to drink in the scent of him, feel his warmth surrounding me.

"I'm sorry I didn't tell you about Simon," I say, which is not any kind of answer to the question he asked.

He studies me. "You don't owe me an explanation."

"I kind of feel like I do. At the least, I want to give you one."

"You went through something," he says gently. "I don't blame you for not wanting to talk about it."

"I appreciate that. But I don't want to have any secrets, Hunter. At least, not from you."

Fire sparks in his eyes, and his grip tightens around my ankle. He moves the ice pack to the counter and shifts my foot off his lap.

For a moment, I'm sad about the loss of contact, but then he scoots his barstool forward so we're sitting closer, his knees bracketing mine.

"Okay," he says softly, leaning forward. "How long ago did it happen?"

A valid question, but he's close enough for me to catch a faint whiff of sandalwood—I *love* the smell of sandalwood—and I'm not sure I can put words together to answer him.

Focus, Merritt. FOCUS.

"Um, a few months, I guess? Well. A few months since I found out about the cheating and called things off. Learning about the baby and the wedding, that was a little more recent."

He nods. "Must have been tough."

"Honestly? The worst was watching Simon get the promotion I wanted. I know that sounds awful. But I wasn't heartbroken about the end of us, you know? Not really. I don't think I ever loved him." I lift my shoulders in a tiny shrug. "Actually, I'm not sure I've ever loved anyone." I pause and swallow. "Except you."

Hunter jumps off the barstool so fast, he nearly knocks it over. He paces to the window, one hand clasping the back of his neck, and I suddenly wish I could reel all my words right back into my mouth.

What was I thinking, admitting THAT to him?

"Hey. I'm sorry. I just meant *back then*. I loved you back then, and I'm sure you knew that. I didn't mean now. Obviously, I don't mean now. I mean, we hardly know each other now." I'm babbling, but I'm not sure I can stop. The silence feels almost as threatening as whatever nonsense I might spill out of my mouth. "And I'm only here for a little while, so that would be weird, right? If I were to—I mean, if we were—not that I wouldn't want—"

My words end abruptly, because am I ready to end that sentence? Not that I wouldn't want *what?* To date him? To try to love him again? Love this grown-up, wiser, sexier version of Hunter?

"I, um, I should let you get back to work." I reach for my Diet Dr Pepper. "Maybe I'll just go drink this on the beach."

Hunter moves around the island and back to where he was working, like he's going right back to putting in the grout. As a boy, he was terrible at talking about his feelings. But that's the thing—I didn't mean to start talking about feelings at all. I hover by the back door, practically choking on my disappointment. Is he seriously going to say *nothing*?

Apparently, that's exactly what he's going to do.

Ugh—you're an idiot, Merritt.

"Okay, well. See you around?" I nudge open the door, but before I can walk through, Hunter's voice calls me back.

"Mer, wait."

I turn slowly, not wanting to get *more* disappointed or feel *more* stupid. But is that possible?

"Thanks for telling me." He holds my gaze for a long moment before he adds, "I loved you back then too."

The air whooshes out of my lungs, and my hand holding the drink trembles. The past is the past—I know this—but my body is reacting like the past is *right now*. Like I'm hearing *today* Hunter say the words to *today* Merritt. Which is silly. Completely unrealistic.

And also totally something I want. Badly.

I'm only going to need a little nudge to fall *back* in love with him. If I even fell out of love to begin with. Meeting his deep brown eyes from across the room, I'm not so sure I ever did.

Because I'm too flustered to be rational, I lift my Diet Dr Pepper like I'm making a toast and say, "Cool. Good luck with the backsplash," before walking out the door like the idiot (or coward) I am.

ELEVEN

Hunter

I SPEND the rest of my afternoon finishing the grout and mulling over my conversation with Merritt. Admittedly, I would have planned better if I'd known where the conversation was going to go. I wouldn't have just confessed that I loved her like that.

But she did it first! And I'm still reeling from that revelation.

She loved me.

I loved her.

And now ... is it too much to hope maybe we could try again?

I don't know how to do this. *Obviously*. How to keep my cool when my feelings are flaming hot. How to ask her out like it's a first date when she's already imprinted on my heart, stamped into my memories.

I also can't ignore the worry pulsing on the periphery, like those flashing caution signs you see when you're driving through heavy fog. *She might leave. She might leave. She might leave.*

I won't ignore the warning. But I also won't let it stop me. If I do, I might not ever get this chance again. Which is why, after work yesterday, I drove to an art supply store in Savannah, where I took entirely too long and spent entirely too much on art supplies Merritt may or may not want.

Now, the next morning, in the bright light of day, I'm sitting in my truck rethinking or overthinking this gift. *Start small*, Dante said. And like an idiot, I basically came back with, *I'll see your "small", and I'll raise you a love confession and a few hundred dollars on art supplies.*

I guess "small" isn't really my thing.

Second-guessing, however, most certainly is.

"Get on with it, Hunter," I tell myself before picking up the box of supplies and climbing out of the truck. It's early yet, but Merritt is usually up and sitting on her front porch, coffee mug in her hands, when I show up to work. Not like I make a habit of watching her from the windows of the big house or anything.

It took me hours to pick out the right paints and brushes. Does Merritt still like acrylic? Would she prefer oil now?

Not knowing means I bought some of everything. *Too much* of everything. This is about as obvious as an adult version of a note reading *I like you. Do you like me? Check yes or no!*

I leave the canvases in the truck for now, because I bought too many of those as well, and they're bulky. Heading straight for the carriage house, I tell myself this is the kind of thing old friends do for each other—drop a cool few hundred on possibly unwanted art supplies. No biggie.

Jake appears around a curve in the path, his eyes stormy

and his face set in the frown he's been wearing since the day Lo left.

"Hey man, you okay?" I ask his retreating back.

"Peachy. I'm just going for a run. This is my running face."

He takes off as if to prove the point. Whether to me or himself, I'm not sure. But *running face?* I bet he's regretting that ridiculous statement already.

Speaking of ridiculous, when I reach the porch of the carriage house and see Merritt standing in her doorway, my mouth goes dry. I clutch the box, wishing I could hide it behind my back or toss it in the bushes.

Box? What box? I don't have a box!

"What happened to him?" I say as I climb the steps. I already know the answer but need to talk about anything but why I'm here.

"Um, pretty sure he's in love with my little sister, and I just called him out on giving up."

"He's *definitely* in love with your little sister. You should have seen them before she left. I'm not sure there's a person in Oakley who didn't see the two of them kissing."

Her mouth drops open. "And you didn't think to tell me?"

I shrug. "I guess I thought you knew."

She shakes her head. "Eloise didn't tell me much. I mean, I assumed, but I didn't know it had actually turned into a kissing-all-over-the-island thing."

I chuckle. "Definitely that." I wrinkle my nose. "And all over your Gran's house."

Merritt covers her eyes. "I don't need details!"

Me neither, but I got them anyway when I walked in on them more than a few times. "Honestly, I'm surprised she left."

Merritt nods slowly. "I have a feeling something happened

with Jake that made the *leaving* part easy. But that doesn't necessarily mean she's happy to be gone."

"I hope they work it out. They seemed good together."

Her gaze lifts to mine, and our eyes lock. Like always, I nearly lose myself in the intense blue of her irises, in the way they seem to reach in and hold me. I couldn't look away if I tried.

"I, um, I brought you something," I finally say, holding out the box.

She leaves the doorway and takes a small step forward.

"I don't know if you're still painting," I say quickly. "Or if you even want to. But since you've got some time on your hands, I just figured ... maybe?"

I shove the box forward, and she pauses, glancing back at my face. Am I sweating? I feel like I'm sweating. This close to fall, it oughta be cooler, but the temperature and humidity don't take much of a break on the island. Not for a few months yet.

Yeah, I'm just hot because of the temperature. Not because I'm panicking about the gift I'm holding.

My mouth keeps going, like it's on a mission to fill the silence. "You don't have to take it. I can return all this if you aren't interested. Or you can donate everything. Or throw it all out. I don't care."

I *very much* care. I'm sure it's obvious, given the way I'm babbling like this.

When Merritt doesn't move, I pull it toward me and take a step backward. This was a bad idea. A horrible idea.

I'll take everything back to the store myself. No. I don't care how much it cost—I'll throw it all away. Or dramatically hurl it into the sea.

"Hunter?"

I jerk when Merritt's fingertips graze my arm. "Yeah?"

"I'm interested," she says, holding my gaze.

I wish we weren't just talking about paint. Wait—*are* we talking about paint? Every conversation we have seems six layers deep.

"Sorry," she continues. "I was just surprised. This is ... you are ..." Laughing a little, she shakes her head. "You actually shocked me speechless."

"Wow. Didn't know that was possible."

She swats my arm. "Hey! I don't talk *that* much. Just maybe compared to you, and that isn't a very high bar."

I grunt in response, and the air between us shifts. Her smile is fast and unguarded. The kind that feels like both risk and reward.

Merritt bites her lip, and I can't help but track the movement. "Can I look?"

I hold out the box. But not too far because I want her to come closer. It's the same technique I use when I'm trying to get some new animal to trust me.

Merritt is not *some injured raccoon or stray dog, dummy. Terrible comparison.*

It is. Probably highly insulting.

Definitely highly insulting.

And yet ... as Merritt cautiously steps closer, I realize, whether the comparison is rude or not, her trust has been broken. If I want her to trust me, I have to earn it.

Not just with art supplies. Or with food, like I would with one of the animals I'm fostering.

Merritt grasps the other side of the box, but I don't let go. I don't step back. She's near enough that I can smell the floral scent of her hair. She frowns as she looks at everything. "Hunter, this is hundreds of dollars of supplies."

"It's—" I can't finish my sentence. Because it *is* hundreds of dollars of supplies. I won't lie to her. "They gave me a discount."

"You didn't need to do this. I can buy my own supplies."

I do my level best not to read into that, not to see this as a remark about my financial situation. I do just fine for a life on Oakley. But I wouldn't be able to afford a month in New York. Not even in some terrible apartment.

But Merritt never played that kind of game, the one where every sentence can be heard two ways, where each word is a pointed barb. When Merritt meant to wound me, her words were clear and direct. No need for subtext.

"Yeah, well. Maybe you can. But I bought these for you. Whether you keep them or not or use them or not—that's up to you."

"Let me pay you. Do you use Venmo? The cash app?"

"No." I don't clarify that I have both apps on my phone but won't accept either from her. Even if she never uses them. "Take it or don't. But don't try to pay me."

Merritt hesitates, and the air between us feels thin and stretched. Finally, she smiles, and I can breathe again.

"Thank you."

She goes back to pawing through the box, taking in the tubes of paint, the packs of brushes, the turpentine and linseed oil the guy said she'd need if she wanted to do oils.

"*Are* you still painting?" I ask.

Her hand stills, and it takes her a long moment to respond. "Not much since I left the island. I ... I'm not sure I remember how."

I don't even attempt to stop myself from brushing a lock of hair behind her ear, and I don't miss the small sound she makes when I do. Once again, the atmosphere around us shifts. Now a different kind of tension hangs heavy in the air.

"I think you'll remember," I say, unsure what, specifically,

I mean or what I hope she *thinks* I mean. Could be anything or everything.

Definitely not *nothing*.

"I think it'll come right back to you." *As though you never stopped. As though you never left.*

I want so badly to touch her again. To brush my knuckles over her cheek. To take her hand or, better yet, take her in my arms. But I remind myself that she just got out of a relationship—one where she was badly hurt.

"Muscle memory," she whispers.

All I can think about is how the heart is a muscle too.

"Merritt, have dinner with me."

Again, I'm failing with Dante's suggestions to start small, to start as friends. But suddenly, I don't want to wait anymore. And Dante also said to let Merritt choose when she's ready.

"Okay," she says easily. But then her expression shifts, taking on a teasing glint. "But I thought we agreed to be friends."

"Friends have dinner."

"This is a *friendly* dinner, then."

"If that's what you want it to be." I'm standing on the edge of some great height, trying to decide if I'll die if I jump or just break *most* of my bones. "Or it could be something else. A *more than* friendly dinner."

My heart is thudding in my ears and practically beating out of my chest. But Merritt smiles, a teasing smile. Playful. The kind of smile that tells me exactly how much trouble I'm in.

"When do I have to decide what kind of dinner it is—friendly or more than friendly?"

"I'm not looking for an official RSVP, Mer. Just come and see. No need to make any declarations. Yet."

Making sure she's got a firm hold on the box, I finally let go and step back. "I've got canvases in my truck. And an easel."

Her eyes soften. "Hunter, it's too much."

It's not nearly enough, but I won't risk scaring her by saying so. Instead, I give her a playful grin before I start down the steps. "What are friends—or *more than friends* —for?"

Merritt calls after me before I can get too far. "When are we having this yet-to-be-determined level of friendship dinner?"

I turn but continue to walk backward. "When are you free?"

She rolls her eyes. "I have no job. I'm free all the time."

"Then, why wait? Let's go tonight." My heartbeat is like a battering ram against my ribs while I wait for Merritt's response. When she finally grins, instead of calming down, my stupid heart redoubles its efforts.

"Then I'll see you tonight," she says.

I nod before turning around and letting a full grin loose on my face. *Tonight*, I think, barely keeping a skip out of my step. *Tonight.*

TWELVE

Merritt

WHAT DO you wear to a friendly (or more-than-friendly?) dinner with a man you fell in love with when you were both just kids? A man who still doesn't know how spectacularly he broke your heart after you first broke his? A man who you might be falling for again—that is, if you ever fell *out* of love with him in the first place?

These are non-rhetorical questions for which I have no answers.

Strangely enough, googling variations of my question does NOT produce any solid outfit suggestions. And New York Merritt's style does not translate well to Oakley Island. The business suits hanging in the carriage house closet in black, gray, and navy? Not a chance. Other than that, I've got my running clothes, pajamas, and a few casual outfits, none of which feel right.

When there's a knock on the cottage door, my heart leaps.

Hunter. Excitement and desire and nervousness form a tight braid in my chest as I close the bedroom door. Must hide the clothes covering every surface showing a woman freaking out before a date.

I am more disappointed than I should be to see a woman I don't recognize standing outside the screen door. She waves as I push open the door.

"Hello," I say cautiously. Not because she doesn't look friendly. Her smile is warm and open. But I find after years in the city, the friendliness of other places still unsettles me a little.

"Hey. I'm Naomi, Jake's sister." She hooks a thumb toward the other side of the carriage house. "You must be Merritt. I figured I should come over and say hello. Be neighborly and all that. Jake watches Liam a lot. Liam's my son. I'm a single mom. Wow—I'm kind of botching this whole introduction thing. Did you ask for my life story or what?" She laughs, running a hand through her brown hair, a few shades darker than mine.

"No worries. I think it might be an island thing. At least, I've found myself doing a lot more talking myself."

Probably more than I should. Like saying yes to dinner with Hunter, who left it up to me whether this is a friendly or more-than-friendly dinner.

Hunter, who carried me off the beach with anger and hurt brewing like a storm in his eyes. Hunter, who listened as only he can and forgave me for what I said and did years ago. Hunter, who bought me hundreds of dollars of art supplies I can't bring myself to take out of the box. I'm not sure if I'm more afraid of trying to paint and realizing I can't, or trying to paint and thinking about *him* the whole time.

Would that be so bad?
I don't know!

I realize I'm staring, but my gaze snagged on Naomi's outfit, which is a romper—I think that's what the one-piece shorts and top combo is called—in a soft navy material. Strappy sandals wrap around her calves and big gold earrings brush her shoulders. It's the kind of thing I could see Eloise wearing.

Except the romper would be covered in anchors or parrots or something like that.

"You're cute," I say, then realize how weird that sounds. "Sorry. I mean, I like what you're wearing. The whole … everything." I gesture toward her whole body, like this will convey what I'm stumbling to say. "I'm sorry. See? The talking thing. Bad."

She laughs, but it feels like laughing *with* me, not *at* me. It puts me at ease.

"It makes me feel better about awkwardly dumping so much information on you," she says. "Don't worry about it. And thanks. I've got a date."

Some kind of eager longing must show on my face because Naomi tilts her head. "What?"

"I just …" My eyes dart back toward my room and the rejected outfits. "I actually have a date, too. I think? *Maybe* a date. A dinner. I don't know what it is exactly. Which means I don't know what to wear. Do you … do you think you could help me?"

Naomi's eyes light up. "Yes! I have a little time before I need to go. I love clothes."

Well—that was before she saw what she had to work with. I want to laugh at her expression when she sees the bedroom littered with dark, corporate clothing and workout pants.

"New York, huh?" she asks, picking up a navy blazer and

dropping it over the back of a chair like it's disease-ridden. It makes me want to laugh.

"Yep. It's bad, huh?"

Naomi grins. "It's not bad. It's a challenge. You and Lo really are different." When she sees my expression, she holds up a hand. "I do not mean that as an insult. Not good or bad different—just different. Lo and I became friends. And I get the sense maybe you and I could be friends too?"

Friends. A prickle of warmth threads its way through me. I think of Jana in New York. We worked together. Got drinks together after work. Complained about work. And ... after I left, she texted once to say she was there if I needed anything. That's it.

What's more—I've barely thought about her. Not once have I gotten the urge to check in or text. So, yeah—I could use a friend.

"Friends sounds really great, actually." I drop onto the bed. "I probably need to do a whole wardrobe revamping, huh?"

Naomi inspects a pair of leggings and folds them, adding them to a pile on the corner of the desk. "I mean, not if you're planning to go back to the corporate world."

Am I? Definitely not if I'm staying on Oakley.

"You know what? Don't worry about it. I think this might actually be impossible."

Naomi grins. "Oh, I love a challenge. I'll make magic from this."

And she does. Twenty minutes later, Naomi has not only found an outfit but helped make a pile of clothes to put in storage until—or if?—I go back to office life. *Or donate them because you don't want to go back to that life,* a small voice says. But it's a reasonable voice. Kind of an alluring one.

From my various unsuitable outfits, Naomi picked out a

pair of black pants and paired them with a short-sleeved white blouse, which she tells me to leave mostly unbuttoned to reveal a turquoise tank top. The tank top came from Naomi's purse.

Yes—she really did pull clothing out of her purse like some sort of Mary Poppins. And now I am a woman who wears clothes pulled from the purses of near-strangers.

"Look at you!" Naomi says. "Casual, but also hot. Perfect for a maybe date."

It is. And I'm not sure why I couldn't have paired this together, but I never would have.

"Do you feel good? Comfortable?"

"I feel like … me."

The old me, I don't add. Because the longer I'm here and away from New York, the more I feel like I'm excavating myself. Slowly, because it's terrifying, so I'm using one of those tiny brushes scientists use on fossils to sweep away the dirt.

"Good. The best outfit is when you look hot but also feel like yourself." She hands me a pair of black flip-flops.

"These?"

"Trust me."

Oddly, I do. The flip-flops that I would never have paired with these pants (except maybe on my morning commute, to be replaced with heels at the office) complete the whole casual but pretty vibe I wanted.

"Hair up or down?"

"Down." Naomi does not hesitate to plunge her hands into my hair near the roots and do some kind of tousling. The end result is the same natural waves but with a little more body. "Yeah?"

"Yeah. I'm shocked and impressed. Thank you."

"Anytime! This was fun. So—who's the lucky guy?"

"You might know him since this island is tiny. His name is Hunter."

Naomi grabs my arm, her eyes wide. "Hunter Williams?"

When I nod, she groans, then smiles. "Oh man, you definitely need to lock that down. The island vultures have been circling for years. When they see he's finally dating, it won't take seconds for one of them to try and sink her talons right into him."

"Island vultures?"

"Bunch of single or divorced ladies. Desperate. Hungry. Not in a good way. Hunter is one of the good ones. He's the white whale of Oakley Island."

I choke out a laugh, completely unsure how to respond. My pink cheeks probably say it all. "The white whale, huh?"

"*Moby Dick* references feel more relevant on an island, you know? I guess maybe some people might consider Benedict King the true white whale. But he's more of a unicorn. Island owner, charming, billions in the bank—unicorn. Oh!" Naomi laughs. "Ben could be the narwhal—a white whale with a unicorn horn. It's perfect."

I bet Sadie would love that description. I make a mental note to text her about it later. By the time she left, we were fine and she'd forgiven me for not telling her about everything. But I'd like to check in to be sure. If I'm turning over a new leaf though, communicating with my sisters more, I probably need to tell her about this maybe date with Hunter. And also check in with Eloise.

"You weren't, um, interested in Hunter, were you?" I ask Naomi.

"Oh, I never would have turned down a date with him. But no—we've been around each other enough for me to know there is zero interest. And it's not like I was *into* him, specifically. He's just a good guy. Speaking of ..." Naomi glances at her phone. "I need to boogie. I like to be late for first dates. It's a good test to see how guys react. But I'll be super late if I don't go now. Anyway—good to meet you! Bye!"

And then Naomi is gone, leaving me staring at my reflection. This outfit should look like it's straddling worlds—mostly my old clothes just styled a different way. But I see nothing of New York Merritt in the mirror. I just see ... me.

―――

I DO my best not to overthink the date. My *best*, as it happens, is not very good. My brain is like an overcooked noodle at this point. Rubbery and sticky and best thrown out.

I consider Naomi's test of being late on purpose. But I can't bring myself to do so—a compulsion to be on time is one thing about me that has not changed. I step outside with a good ten minutes to make the five-minute walk to the restaurant Hunter mentioned via text. It was me who suggested we should just meet at the restaurant. I'm not even sure why I insisted.

But it doesn't matter, because Hunter is cresting the top of the porch steps as I open the door. When I swallow, my throat seems to get stuck. The man couldn't look bad if he tried. But dressed in dark jeans and a faded blue button-down open over a tight white t-shirt, he is perfection. His hair looks shower-damp, and his beard looks freshly trimmed. The scent of him, woodsy and spicy and strong, reaches me, and I try not to take a visibly deep inhale.

Just a subtle deep inhale.

"Hey." Hunter's smile is adorably shy. "Is this okay? I took a chance coming here rather than meeting you. I was too early and figured it was a nice night for a walk."

Is it a nice night? I did NOT notice the night. But he's right—it's a little less humid but still warm enough I don't worry about finding a jacket or sweater. I do worry about the end of the night. Because if Hunter walked me here, Hunter will walk me home. And if Hunter walks me home, what will happen when we get to the door? An awkward goodbye? A handshake? A hug?

A kiss?

My brain goes into meltdown mode immediately, and I realize I'm standing here NOT answering Hunter's simple question.

"Sounds good," I manage.

"Are you sure? You don't sound sure."

Laughing a little, I shake my head. "I am sure about very little these days. But walking with you sounds great."

"Great," he echoes.

His smile has my heart testing the limits of my cardiovascular system. All the systems, really. They're all still in meltdown mode after the mere thought of a kiss at the end of the night.

"Oh, and I brought you this." Hunter pulls something from his back pocket and then opens his palm.

I stare down at it, confused. "A penny?"

"Flowers felt like too much, and I didn't want you to feel pressured. Do you remember this?"

Suddenly, I do.

"Are we watching a comedy, action-adventure, or drama tonight?" Hunter asks. I don't miss the way his lip curls slightly when he says *drama*.

"Definitely a drama," I tease, and he groans.

"Please just not another historical one. I can't handle all the buggies and corsets."

I laugh. "I was kidding. I'm more in the mood for ..." I pause, and our eyes lock.

"Comedy," I say just as he says, "Action."

We both laugh now. And honestly, I don't care what kind of movie we choose. I'm way more interested in Hunter. He got taller this year. Filled out a bit. Most guys our age still have that scrawny, boyish look to them. Hunter looks older. His voice is deeper, and it makes my stomach feel all fluttery, especially when he teases me. Which he's been doing a lot more this summer than before.

Could it be that he likes me too? Ugh—*likes* isn't the right word. Somehow, over the years, my summers here with Hunter have become the best part of my life.

"Guess it's time to invoke the penny," Hunter says, pulling a coin from his pocket. "Heads or tails?"

"Like you even have to ask. Heads."

Hunter nods seriously and flips the coin in the air. But I'm not watching the penny. I'm watching his face.

Reaching out, I take the penny. I can't meet his eyes. "Is this *the* penny?"

His smile is soft. "No. I lost that one years ago. Probably left it in my pocket and threw it in the wash."

"Oh."

He must read my disappointment (which is so, so stupid) because he gently closes my fingers around the penny. He holds my hand in his for a few seconds before letting go.

"This is a *new* penny, Mer."

I can hear what he's not saying. New penny, new us. New start. Hunter always had more to say to me than anyone else. But even with me, he's always been a man who spoke volumes in silence. I love that about him.

When I look up, Hunter's hands are jammed in his pockets. I can tell they're in fists. I'm not the only one nervous about tonight.

"Thank you," I tell him, wanting to say more but unsure exactly what. These pants don't have pockets, so I tuck the penny into a zippered part of my purse where it won't fall out or get lost.

Hunter holds out an arm. I hook mine through his, letting my hand rest on his elbow. Even this contact sends a thrill through me.

"How very gentlemanly of you—giving me your arm," I say as we start down the porch steps.

"If it worked back in the old days, I figured it couldn't hurt," he says, and I get the sense he's trying not to scare me off.

Not a chance.

Okay. Maybe a chance.

It's fifty-fifty.

Because surely, I can't get used to this. Can I? Walking down Oakley's quaint streets on Hunter's arm feels like a waking dream. We pass the brightly painted doors and shutters, palmettos waving and seagulls laughing overhead as a soft dusk falls around us.

The island was always a vacation for me, an escape—never *real* life with its day-to-day monotony. I try to picture this place being something more. Something permanent.

Could this be my real life? What would my day-to-day look like here? Where would I work? What would I do? The questions start to ping through my brain like a string of unanswered texts.

And Hunter—I may have apologized, and he may have asked me to dinner, but can we wade through all the baggage? Do the people we are now fit together as well as we used to?

Hunter stops, just in front of a darkened window. "What?"

I try to manage my expression, to keep the inner turmoil *inner*. "What?"

He studies me, and my face heats under his gaze. "You tensed up as we walked. And I could practically hear your thoughts banging away in there."

He lifts his hand and uses the calloused pad of a fingertip to smooth away the line I imagine is between my brows.

"Don't overthink it," he says in a low voice. "Just dinner. Okay?"

"Yeah. I know."

"Do you?"

I laugh. "No. I can't stop my brain from spiraling into worry."

"Worry about what?"

"Everything?" I say with a shrug. "What does this mean? What happens next? Will there be a second date? A third?"

"So you decided this is a first date?" he says, a smile playing on his lips. "A more-than-friends date?"

Yes. Absolutely yes. I nod. "Yeah. I did."

He studies me, one hand running across his beard. "Good. That's what I want too. But we have to do something about all this overthinking."

"I'm open to ideas if you have one," I say, half-joking.

He tilts his head and waits for a minute like he often does before speaking. "I do, actually, but it's a risky one."

"I don't mind risky."

This earns me a small smile. "It might sound a little out there," he cautions. "I'm not sure if—"

"Hunter. My heart is racing. The backs of my knees are sweating. I can hardly breathe. Yes to the idea. Just ... yes."

His brows pop up. "Are you sure? You don't know what the idea is."

"I trust you."

The words settle over him or maybe settle into him slowly, resulting in a wide smile. One I haven't seen in years.

I wave my hands over my hot cheeks. "Please. Whatever your idea is, just—"

Hunter steps forward, cups my face in his hands, and kisses me.

It is the very last thing I would have ever expected from Hunter. Yet my body reacts as though it has been waiting years for exactly this moment. *Finally.* I melt into him, grateful when his hands move from my face to my back, pulling me closer, holding me up as my legs tremble.

Hunter may have been my very first kiss, but I still remember everything about that moment. And though this kiss holds something familiar—his scent, his hands, just *him*—it's completely NOT the same kind of kiss.

No hesitation.

No awkwardness or questioning.

No giggling and trying to find the right angle.

Hunter *owns* my mouth. But only in the sense that he's taken the control I've willingly given. Nothing feels forced or coercive. He's playful and yet sensual. I want to laugh. I want to slide my hands under his shirt and lay my palms flat over his heart.

Check, please!

As though sensing the way I'm ramping up, Hunter slows down. He presses a few more quick kisses to my lips as he slowly releases me and steps back.

I am wobbling. Totally a good thing I didn't wear heels. My breath comes in shallow pants, and I feel like I need to make a run for the ocean and hurl myself in to cool off.

"What was *that*?" I demand, practically gasping for air.

"My risky idea." He looks suddenly unsure, the smile sliding right off his face. "I'm sorry. I thought—"

"Don't be sorry. I just … need a minute. But also—you thought that would *calm me down?*"

There is no chance of calm. Zero chill. I am *wrecked*.

"You said you were worried about what happens next. I mean, I can't guarantee tomorrow or next week, but I figured if I kissed you now, you at least wouldn't spend the whole night wondering if we would kiss at the end."

I gape at him.

He shrugs. "Made sense at the time."

It honestly *does* make sense. In a way. Because yeah—I was already thinking too much about the possibility of a goodnight kiss. I'd pictured the awkwardness at the end of the night, the struggle of trying to read what he wants while deciding what I want.

"Also," he says, a little hesitant now. "I didn't want to wait."

He didn't want to wait to kiss me. A thrill zips through me at the thought.

"Now, you don't have to worry about deciding if it's something you want to do," he adds. "You get to decide if it's something you want to do *again.*"

Hunter's smile turns a little wicked then, like he can already tell that I one hundred percent want to do it again. Now, preferably. And then again in ten minutes. An hour. Basically, all the time. If our date consists of parking like two teenagers and making out in his truck, I'll be fine with that. It would be only fitting since, when we kissed as teenagers, we weren't old enough to drive.

I take his elbow, needing to touch him, needing the live wire of my body to be grounded by him.

As we start to walk away, I don't miss movement behind the glass window of the store. Not a store—the barbershop. Neither does Hunter. He groans as an older Black man pulls the blinds shut. I don't miss his broad smile before he's gone.

"That was very poor planning on my part," Hunter says. "Hope you're okay being Oakley Island famous."

"Why?"

"Because that was Frank. He runs the most gossipy island TikTok account you can imagine. And I'm guessing that kiss is now on his profile for the whole island to see."

I should care. Maybe be embarrassed or even upset that my privacy was violated. You can't just film people without permission and put it on social media!

But instead, I'm only thinking of what Naomi said about the island vultures—the women who have been after Hunter.

I hope they *all* see the video of us kissing.

I've never really felt possessive like this, especially not when there are still so many unanswered questions about what happens next, what this is even going to look like. But I'm filled with smug satisfaction at the idea of people knowing. People seeing.

Hunter leans close to me, swinging open the door of the restaurant and holding it for me. "Here's a secret," he whispers, his breath tickling my neck. "I was planning to kiss you at the end of the night anyway."

THIRTEEN

Merritt

DID I expect Hunter to turn our walk to the restaurant into a scene right out of a romance novel? No, no I did not.

Did I mind? Not even a little.

And weirdly, sharing a kiss really did break up the tension between us. I'm breathing normally, at least, even if my cheeks still feel a little warm and my brain is repeating over and over the phrase: I can't believe this is happening.

Because honestly. *I can't believe this is happening.*

We walk inside, and multiple sets of eyes turn our way as we wait by the hostess stand. Like, an *unusual* number of eyes. A man at the table closest to us grins.

"Way to go, Hunter," he says under his breath.

Behind me, Hunter sighs. "Frank works fast."

"Seriously?" I whisper to him as the hostess leads us to our table. Even *she* smiles like she knows about the kiss. She also looks at Hunter in a way I don't like. "That guy was at least seventy years old. You're telling me *he* is on TikTok? I'm not even on TikTok."

"You are now," Hunter says with a wry grin. "It's a small town, Mer. And everyone knows Frank. They're on TikTok because *he* is on TikTok. Or, *The* Tiktok, as the older set of Oakley residents like to call it."

"Honestly, it sounds like a subplot of a Hallmark movie, not real life."

"Hallmark has filmed movies here before," Hunter says easily, opening his menu. "One summer just after Isabelle was born. They hired me to build sets."

Building sets for a Hallmark movie—that's really cool. But I'm more distracted by the mention of Hunter's daughter. It's still hard to hear my middle name fall so easily from his lips. His daughter's name. Hunter has a daughter. Hunter is a *dad*.

I don't want to make a big deal about it, but I do want to talk about it. About her.

But maybe not quite yet.

"The island doesn't seem all that changed," I say, wanting to kick myself for making stupid small talk.

"It's more touristy than it used to be. But we're not Myrtle Beach yet."

"And hopefully never will be." I'm not sure where this sudden bout of protectiveness for Oakley comes from. Then again, this place always had open arms for me. Even now. I can't help but wonder what might have changed if my parents hadn't gotten divorced. If I'd kept coming here, summer after summer. Would my whole life's path have been different?

Hunter looks like he's going to ask me something, but the waitress appears, so we busy ourselves for a few minutes, asking questions about the menu, placing our orders. When she's finally gone, Hunter extends a hand across the table, palm up, and I slip my hand into his.

Easily. Like breathing. His palm is warm and a little rough—a working hand. It feels strong. The kind of hand I'd like to feel cupping my face again. On the back of my neck, pulling me toward him. On my lower back or maybe my hip …

I clear my throat—and my head. "I didn't notice the name of the restaurant until I looked at the menu. This place is really called The Big Tuna?"

"The owner is a fan of Jim Halpert from *The Office*." He smiles. "And, you know—it's seafood, so it makes sense."

I laugh. "That's fun." I pause, suddenly running into the big gap of things I don't know about Hunter. That he doesn't know about me. Namely … everything in the last ten years. *The Office* was on back when I still came to Oakley, but streaming wasn't what it is now. I watched the whole show long after it went off the air. "Did you like *The Office*?"

"Yes, but not the British version, even if it was the original. I tried and just couldn't."

"Same. Do you have a favorite show?"

"*Longmire*," he says.

"I haven't watched that one. What's it about?"

Hunter and I fall into what could be considered normal first-date conversation, but it feels like catching up, the way we did every summer when I first arrived back on Oakley. It's easy. Comfortable. And yet … there's still so much *past* hanging between us, like I'm watching Hunter through some thin curtain as we continue talking.

I learn that he got a license to rescue and rehab wild animals like possums and raccoons--one of which he currently has at home. He also adopted a collection of rescue dogs as well, most with some kind of disability. There is something so very … *Hunter* about this, and it makes my chest ache. At heart, he's a caretaker.

I tell him some of the things I love about my job—consulting on print and digital advertising campaigns. Which isn't all that interesting to anyone outside the field, but his attention from me never wavers.

Even if *my* attention keeps snagging on his mouth as he eats his coconut shrimp. *That mouth kissed me an hour ago. I want it to kiss me again now.* When not caught up in memories of kisses, my thoughts keep circling back to the things we *aren't* talking about. Finally, there's a brief pause after the waitress stops by to refill our drinks.

I swallow, my eyes dropping to my almost empty plate of blackened mahi-mahi. "Hunter, will you tell me about Cassidy?"

And Isabelle. But for some reason, that feels like a harder question. Because I don't know how to NOT connect the name to our life *before*. To the conversations we had. The *plans* we made. Not to mention the way I'm still trying to get my head around the idea of Hunter being a father in the first place. I mean, I saw Isabelle, but not with him.

He takes a moment to gather his thoughts, wiping his mouth before he pushes his plate back and clasps his hands on the table. "What do you want to know?"

"You guys got together after . . ." I don't know how to end the sentence. *After me.* But just because my life is divided into two distinct parts—before Hunter and after Hunter—that doesn't mean his is, too. For all I know, his life is marked by before his marriage to Cassidy and after.

"You remember her right?" Hunter asks gently, and I nod. "We went to school together. But we were just friends."

He may think so, but she didn't want to just be friends

with him. In the brief interactions I had with her around Hunter, I saw it. Even if he didn't.

It shouldn't sting that she got him all year long when I only got summers. But somehow, it does. Unfair though it may be, I want all of Hunter. His friendship, his happy memories, just … *him*. I don't want to share, even his past that I wasn't a part of.

There's that possessiveness again, the same one I felt when Naomi said other women were interested in Hunter. It's starting to feel like a too-familiar burn right behind my sternum, rising in my throat.

"After that last summer you were here, I was—" He pauses and runs a hand through his hair. "I was kind of a mess, Mer. I don't mean to make you feel bad," he says. "It's forgiven."

"Okay." My eyes are starting to sting, the familiar swell of tears nearing the surface, and it takes all the control I possess to force them back.

"Cassidy made me laugh," he continues. "It was easy between us. We started spending time together and …"

I can fill in the rest of the blanks, though I'd rather not. Thinking about Hunter with her or anyone else is just—no. No. No. NO.

He reaches across the table again, offering his hand like he did before. Not pressuring. Letting me decide. I slide my hand into his. I don't realize how hard I'm squeezing his fingers until he squeezes mine back and clears his throat.

"Sorry," I say, starting to ease my fingers away.

He grips me tighter, keeping my hand right where it is. "I don't mind."

I exhale, letting out a slow, intentional breath. "Okay. Continue."

Hunter hesitates, and I get the sense that this is hard for

him too. Not because he's still hung up on her or because it hurts him to remember, but because he's thinking about *me*. That's the kind of man he is. Hunter is (correctly) worried I might not want to *hear* about him and Cassidy.

Which is good. I don't want my sudden bout of possessiveness to make me want to fight a pregnant woman. I asked him to tell me after all. I just didn't realize how this conversation would make me feel.

Remember the kiss. He kissed you on the sidewalk today. YOU.

It helps a little. Until he says her name again with such familiarity.

"Cass was seven months pregnant when we graduated from high school. We got married right after, and then came Isabelle."

This is the perfect time for me to tell him that I know because I was there that day. I may not have had all these details then, but I got the gist. Hunter in a suit. A pregnant Cassidy looking beautiful and perfect in a wedding dress. Oh, how it *burns* to remember.

He's making the marriage part sound very practical. Gran did tell me that's all it was when she helped me into her house and bandaged my knees from where the oyster shell path had cut them. She said it was a decision they made more because of the baby than because they were truly in love. But I didn't believe her. Or maybe it didn't matter? Because either way, he married *her*.

I came all the way to Oakley without even telling my mom for one reason. I came to tell Hunter I loved him, that I never got over him, that I was so sorry I hurt him.

And he married *her*.

"Did you love her?" I ask simply.

He rubs one hand across his jaw. The other still rests in mine. "Of course I did. I still do. She's the mother of my daughter. And a good friend." Something flashes in his eyes. "But I never *love* loved her. We had good intentions, but eventually, Cassidy and I both realized there was a reason we didn't work together. We never felt *right* together."

There is so much warmth in Hunter's expression. And a spark, too. I can't decide if I want to cry about the past or just crawl across the table and settle into his lap so we can pick up the kissing where we left off outside of Frank's barber shop.

Instead of doing either one, I pull my hand away and lean back, needing a second to catch my breath and think clearly. Which I absolutely cannot do as long as Hunter's skin is on mine.

"Hunter! There you are!" a voice calls.

"Oh no," Hunter mumbles.

An older couple quickly bustles their way toward us, the woman waving like we're long-lost friends she hasn't seen in years. The woman looks vaguely familiar but—

"It's my parents." He shoots me a weary look. "I'm sorry in advance for … *everything*."

Now I remember Hunter's mom—her wide smile, the deep brown eyes that match his. Her hair is now pure white, a neat bob ending just below her chin. I only met her a couple of times. I never met his dad, but there's no mistaking who he is. He reminds me so much of Hunter, I want to laugh. His beard is a little shorter and neater than Hunter's, and his hair is darker. But it's his reserved countenance that really clinches it.

"You might not remember me, dear," his mom says. "I'm Carol, Hunter's mama." She pulls two more chairs over from a nearby table. "And this is Grant, Hunter's daddy."

Before she sits down like it is no big deal to jump right into her son's date, she pats Hunter on the shoulder and kisses his bearded cheek, then turns right back to me. "What are the odds that we would just run into the two of you like this?"

Hunter's dad snorts and gives his wife a look as he takes his seat.

Carol's eyes gleam mischievously. "Well, it *was* a coincidence that we just happened to be right down the street when I saw the TikTok. Bob Harley commented and said he saw the two of you come in here."

I swear, I haven't given TikTok as much thought *ever* as I have in the past hour. Am I the only one on this island *not* using the app?

"Oh. Perfect," Hunter says, giving me a look saying he's so sorry. "And crashing our date felt like the best course of action?"

"I told you it wasn't a good idea," Hunter's dad says, his tone even. The cadence of his words is so similar to the way Hunter speaks, I practically do a double-take.

But then Hunter's mother squeals and starts dabbing her eyes with a tissue. "So, it *is* a date! Oh, Hunter." She sets down the tissue and takes my hand. "Merritt, you have grown into such a beautiful woman. I'm so happy to see you back. And here. With our Hunter."

"I—thank you." I'm slightly embarrassed—I mean, this is a LOT to handle—but Hunter looks ready to blow a fuse.

Kicking off my flip-flop, I extend my foot under the table and hook it around his calf. When he looks up to meet my eye, I shrug and smile, hoping he understands at least a little of my meaning. *They're here. We might as well make the most of it.*

Hunter pulls out his phone while his parents are busy grabbing a waitress and placing orders. He taps something out, then nods in my direction. I slip my phone out of my bag to find a message he apparently just sent.

Hunter: I cannot apologize enough.

Merritt: Your parents are adorable. So are you when you're embarrassed. Your ears turn red.

As he reads this message, they turn even redder. So do his cheeks. And I wasn't lying; it *is* adorable.

Hunter: Stop it.

Merritt: I'd like to see you make me in front of your mom.

Hunter: We aren't finished with our date.

Merritt: Fine by me. As long as we also aren't finished kissing.

I rub my foot up his calf to his knee while he's reading my message. Not too far. Just far enough. Hunter clears his throat and puts his phone face down on the table and shoots me a look that says I better behave, even if he doesn't truly want me to.

I slide my foot back down to his ankle, realizing how deliciously *fun* this feels.

I can't remember the last time my life felt *fun*. Or when *I* felt fun. Sadie is fun. Eloise is fun. Somehow, I've turned into the serious one. The responsible one. The least likely to play footsie with a man on a first date.

I could get drunk off this feeling, this buzzing, almost reckless excitement.

Suddenly, I become aware that Hunter's parents have finished ordering and are both watching us. Hunter's dad looks embarrassed, as though he walked in on us kissing or something. His mom, however, has her elbows on the table and her chin in her hands, smiling as her eyes bounce between Hunter and me.

"Are you texting each other while you're at the same table? That is *so* adorable."

Hunter groans. "Mom, you need to stop."

"I can't."

"Then take it down a notch," Hunter says.

"She is physically incapable," his dad says. "This is her lowest setting."

I laugh, partly because it is funny and partly because I see exactly where Hunter's understated humor comes from.

"It's fine," I say. "It's really good to meet you both."

Hunter glares. He stops glaring when I slowly move my toes a few inches up his calf.

"Merritt," Hunter's mother says, turning my attention away from Hunter's leg. "We sure were sad to hear about your grandmother's passing. She was a wonderful woman."

My breath catches at the mention of Gran. I know I'm living on her property, but the reality of her being gone only hits me sometimes. When it does, it usually hits hard.

Carol must see that I'm struggling because she flits right on to asking me about my sisters and the renovations and if I still paint and how I liked living in New York. I'm not sure I've met a more talkative woman, which is so funny given the way the two men at the table are silent through most of our exchange. Except when either Hunter or his father feels the need to jump in and correct something or drop an unexpected one-liner. I get a very clear sense of what dinners might have been like at their house.

Hunter's phone vibrates against the tabletop just after his parents finish eating, right as a debate starts about whether or not we're going to order dessert. I'm silently voting no, agreeing with Hunter's dad, but probably for very different reasons. Namely: I am really looking forward to walking back to the carriage house with Hunter. I meant what I said in my text about the kissing.

Hunter's expression shifts the second he puts the phone

to his ear. "Hey, hey, slow down," he says. "I can't understand you."

The argument stops, and we all fall silent as we watch Hunter and wait.

"I'll keep trying to call him," Hunter says. "You don't worry about that. No—it's fine. And I'll come to the hospital right now."

Hospital? Carol gasps and reaches out and grabs her husband's hand. Cold dread pools in my stomach, and I reach up to rub my arms.

"I'm on my way, okay?" Hunter is already pushing back from the table. "You're going to be fine, Cass."

I knew it was probably Cassidy on the phone. But hearing Hunter call her *Cass* hits me all wrong. All the camaraderie from moments ago has vanished. I suddenly feel like the third wheel.

No—like a spare tire jammed into the trunk.

Hunter hangs up his phone and drags a hand through his hair. His eyes land briefly on me, then slide away. "Cassidy is in labor," he says to his parents.

"But she's still six weeks out," Carol says. "It's too early for her to be in labor."

"They're trying to stop labor, I think, but Adam is in surgery, and Izzy's with her. I'm going to pick her up."

"Will you bring her back to your place?" Carol's shrewd gaze finds me, and she pats my hand. "We could take Isabelle if you want to finish your date?"

Hunter shifts his weight, obviously eager to leave. "That's okay. Cass asked me to stay until Adam can be there."

Is this ... normal?

I mean, don't get me wrong, I love how thoughtful Hunter is. But when it comes to his ex-wife? My parents' divorce was so ugly, they haven't seen each other since. They talk through lawyers and through lawyers *alone*. For Hunter to be with Cassidy at the hospital while she's in labor feels weirdly intimate.

"You're on a date," his mother says sharply.

I wasn't embarrassed by anything she said tonight, even though she clearly doesn't know the meaning of the phrase *personal boundaries*. But now—I feel tiny and humiliated.

You know it's a great date when your date's mom has to remind him he's on a date at all.

"Carol," Hunter's dad says.

Hunter walks to me and presses a quick kiss to my temple. "I'm so sorry to leave."

I shake my head quickly. "It's family. Of course you have to go."

"Yes, but you don't have to stay," his mother insists again. This sounds like an old argument, one that's been had again and again.

"I'll call you," Hunter says to me.

I nod. Try to smile. Fail.

But he's already gone, leaving me with his parents, a VERY awkward silence, and the check.

FOURTEEN

Hunter

"LET'S SEE," the woman behind the desk in the ER says. "If she's in labor, she should be in labor and delivery."

"But she's early. They're trying to stop labor. Would that make a difference?"

I'm doing my level best not to snap at the young receptionist who can't seem to find any trace of Cassidy at the hospital. It likely isn't her fault. It's definitely not her fault my date with Merritt got cut short.

"Ah! Here we are. Room 417."

Finally. I charge through the doors once she opens them, doing my level best not to hyperventilate. I hate hospitals. I'd trade most things I own if it meant never setting foot in one again. I don't even like it when medical shows come on TV. It's not that I'm afraid of doctors or needles or blood. I've done my fair share of helping wounded animals, and I'm not squeamish.

But doctors rushing by in scrubs and that antiseptic smell—it all brings me back to the night Isabelle was born.

After she was here, a red-faced, impossibly small and perfect baby with a powerful set of lungs, things were completely different. I got hit with the kinds of feelings I didn't know existed until I held my daughter in my arms. There aren't words for that warmth, for the way my heart seemed to grow another chamber just to contain all the things I felt.

But it's not those sweet memories that come rushing back to me as I make my way to the elevator. No. No elevator. *Too closed off.* I turn down the hall and take the stairs two at a time. Isabelle might have been perfect, but getting her here was traumatic for almost everyone involved.

Cass's labor was long. Rough. She was scared. I was scared. And I felt powerless to help. Guilty because I couldn't. Guilty because it felt like my fault she was in pain. Guilty because, despite my vows, I didn't really want to do this. Hours and hours of two teenage kids stumbling toward something bigger than either of us could understand.

Cass had a whole birth plan written out and printed up on cardstock. Laminated. She had a labor playlist, a special lamp with a soft light she made me carry, and an exercise ball. Her hospital bag was packed a month in advance with everything she needed and then some. We went through not one birth class, but two.

That's Cassidy—organized and overprepared.

Then the contractions jumped from every five minutes to every two minutes, and all that went out the window. Cass panicked. "It wasn't supposed to be like this," she kept saying. When she *could* talk, that is. Sometimes the contractions came in double waves with no break between.

The nurses talked about back labor and posterior position. They kept pressuring her to get an epidural. Cassidy yelled at them to get out. She yelled at the doctor when he said she was only dilated to four centimeters. She yelled at me for reasons I'm still not sure about and threw the exercise ball, which broke the lamp with the soft light.

My worst fear is having the people I care about hurting when I'm unable to help—and that's exactly what Cassidy's labor became.

I said all the wrong words. Whatever training we had in the birth classes flew right out of my head. When I tried to touch her, she screamed. When I didn't touch her, she cried. All while contractions rocked her body.

Cass called me useless, and that's exactly how I felt. It's how I still feel now, pausing outside of room 417, trying to steady my breathing. It's quiet inside, the lights dim.

This won't be like before, I tell myself. But I am counting down the minutes until Adam gets here, so I can get out of the hospital.

And back to Merritt.

I force myself not to think about dinner, about leaving her there alone, about our kiss. *Later.*

"Cass?" I call, pushing open the door but hesitating in the doorway. "It's Hunter."

"Duh. I know your voice. And I called you." She laughs. "Come on in; I'm decent."

She's smiling, sitting up in a hospital bed and wearing a gown she clearly brought from home. It's pink and purple with flowers and a little lace around the collar—definitely not a cheap hospital-issue gown. Wires from some kind of monitoring thing extend from under the gown to a machine next to her. The television in front of her is silent, playing a *New Girl* rerun.

Isabelle is glued to a tablet, earphones in her ears. She doesn't even notice me come in.

Despite the peacefulness in the room, sweat starts prickling on my lower back. "Hey. How are you?"

"Better. Can you hand me a ponytail holder? They're on the table," Cassidy says.

I pass her a rubber band, watching as she ties her hair up, looking just as calm as can be.

"You're okay?" I ask. "When you called, you were ..."

"Freaking out?" She smiles, then yawns. "I might have panicked a little more than necessary. Isabelle calmed me down."

I'm not surprised by this. A flare of warm pride expands in my chest as I look at Izzy's face, washed blue in the screen's glow. "Did she, now?"

"Yeah. She and I took a mommy and daughter birth class. Not that I want her to be around for the birth." She laughs. "I can't be the only one who has flashbacks to the last time."

I glance down at my feet. "Yeah."

Cassidy points, smiling. "You're terrified to even be here. I can see it in your eyes."

"Maybe."

I'd rather not relive everything from before. Not only because the memories are traumatic, but also because we're not those kids now. We're not together anymore. I'm her ex, not the man here to support her through labor. I'm not wholly sure I should be here now.

I've always tried to do my best by Cassidy. Even after the divorce. Maybe especially after the divorce. My parents—fine, specifically my mom—have made comments about this not being the healthiest of situations. That I'm doing too much, that Cassidy relies on me when Adam is busy being a surgeon or whatever.

Not until tonight, when I had to leave Merritt at dinner, when I saw her face before I left, did I really *get* what Mom meant.

But what am I supposed to do? I had to come. At least for Izzy.

But where I want to be at this exact moment is wherever Merritt Markham is. And since Cass seems just fine, I'm itching to go *now*.

"Have you heard from Adam?"

Cassidy's mouth tightens, but she forces it into a smile. "No. The hospital said surgery should be done in an hour. Maybe two."

"You're okay, though?"

She glances toward the machine. Maybe I should remember what kinds of things it's tracking, but I don't.

"I think so. They gave me some drugs to slow the labor down, and now it's a waiting game to see if that works. You and Izzy can go. I'll be fine until Adam gets here."

"You sure?"

Cassidy nods, but then her expression shifts. "But even if the labor does fully stop now, it looks like I might be here for a while."

"I can take Izzy for a couple of nights. No problem."

This was always the plan once Cass went into labor. We're just doing a little trial run.

I'm already thinking of Isabelle's schedule and what I'll need from the store. Last I looked, my fridge had some medications for the dogs, expired milk, and not much else. I always keep clean—or, pretty clean—sheets on the twin bed in her room. The dogs will be excited to see her. Banjo will be thrilled. Izzy gave him his name and bottle-fed him when I first brought him home. We're all always happy to have her around.

Except, maybe not this exact moment. Because one thing Merritt and I didn't get to talk about was the fact that I'm a dad now. And I have a daughter who shares Merritt's middle name. The name we once dreamed about using for our own child. Definitely a conversation about *that* is coming.

"No, Hunter," Cassidy says, shaking her head. "What I mean to say is they're putting me on bed rest and want to monitor me until delivery. You'll need to take Isabelle for the next few *weeks*."

At that moment, Isabelle looks up from her screen. "Daddy!" she cries, launching herself across the room and into my arms. "You're here!"

I crouch down to catch her, then stand up, taking her with me in a giant hug. "Hey, ladybug."

"I calmed Mommy down," she says, leaning back so she can look into my eyes. "Did she tell you?"

"She did. I'm glad you were here, Izz."

"Me too. The nurses said they should offer me a job. Oh!" Her eyes dart nervously to her mom before she leans in again. "One of the nurses was really pretty," Izzy whispers in my ear. "I might have given her your number."

MOM MEETS me as soon as I cross the bridge onto Oakley, and I transfer a sleeping Isabelle into her car. "M&Ms," she mumbles as I buckle her in.

"Got it, ladybug," I tell her, closing the car door as softly as I can. "You'll be okay getting her in the house?"

Mom scoffs. "I can't carry her, if that's what you're asking. But I have a feeling she'll hit her second wind. We'll be fine." She pauses, and I don't miss the smirk on her face. "You have fun *getting groceries*. Take your time."

The way she says getting groceries sounds like a euphemism, and I really don't want to think about what, exactly, my mom means.

"I've got all night," she adds with a wink, and now I know *exactly* what she means.

"Mom. Please. No."

Sobering a bit, she asks, "And you'll have Izzy for a while?"

"A few weeks. Until the baby is born, however long that takes."

"The timing," she mutters. "Well, your father and I are around. We'll help any time. Especially if you need to *get groceries*."

"Mother!"

Cackling, she gives me a wink before climbing into the car.

Obviously, she knows I plan to stop by Merritt's. But I also actually need to get groceries.

The literal kind. I have zero plans tonight to consider the figurative kind.

Unfortunately for me—and, apparently, my mom—all the lights in the carriage house are off. Merritt used to be one of those ridiculous people who went to bed by nine o'clock every night. Guess she still is.

On the quick drive to Gator's Groceries, I consider the ramifications of my new short-term reality. Adam is very hands-on with Isabelle, but he's a surgeon. He's barely around. Which means I'll be a full-time single dad until Cassidy gives birth. Maybe a little longer, depending on recovery and all that.

Normally, I would hardly blink at this. But given the fact that I just convinced myself to take tiny steps with Merritt—

tiny other than the kiss, which was more like an Olympic broad jump—the timing here is tricky.

How does Merritt feel about kids—her own *and* ones belonging to someone else? I know when we were younger, we talked about it, but we were fifteen. Dreamily optimistic and naive. Now Merritt is a career woman, even if she is between jobs. She could want a totally different future now.

Part of the reason I haven't dated since Cass is because I haven't met anyone worth pursuing. Or maybe it's just that no one else was Merritt.

Whatever my reasons, this means I've given little thought to how to navigate dating as a dad.

The challenges are obvious, though. Dating when you have a kid is weightier. Less casual. I'm only twenty-six years old. Most women my age are just starting to think about kids, if they're even thinking about them at all. Expecting someone to become an instant mom is a lot.

I can't know how Merritt feels about Isabelle. But I'm going to have to ask. Talk about being thrown straight into the fire. We've barely had one date, and now I'll have Isabelle with me at all times.

I ease into a parking space at the grocery store, my thoughts still swirling. Gator's is closing in half an hour, but I should be able to get in and out quickly.

"Well, if it isn't Hunter Williams! I heard Oakley's most eligible bachelor list just got a little shorter."

Maybe NOT so quickly.

"Hello, Mrs. Hopkins."

I try to politely steer my cart right past the older woman with pale skin and bright purple hair. But she turns her cart full of bagged and purchased groceries right around and matches my brisk pace to the produce section.

"How was your date tonight? I'm surprised to see you here. Thought you and Merritt might be—"

Do NOT want to hear the end of that sentence.

"Cassidy went to the hospital. She's fine," I add quickly when Mrs. Hopkins gasps. "She and the baby are both fine. But she'll be on bed rest for a while."

"Oh, my!"

This is way more information than I'd normally give a woman I know to be as notorious a gossip as Frank. Unlike Frank though, Virginia Hopkins gossips the old-fashioned way, right over the landline, something I know after replacing her backsplash last year.

She spent most of the time I was working sitting at the kitchen table in a short nightdress and heels, fanning herself with a copy of AARP magazine. I've never done a quicker tile install.

Cassidy may kill me for telling Mrs. Hopkins, though right now, I'm more concerned with not having to talk about Merritt. I'm practically throwing produce into bags, grabbing bananas, apples, and oranges, knowing full well most of it will rot while Isabelle begs me for Frosted Flakes and peanut butter sandwiches.

"How many babies do you and Merritt think you'll have? She's certainly got a big house to fill."

The entire bag of oranges slips out of my hand. And wouldn't you know it—one of the contrary fruits rolls right under Mrs. Hopkins's foot.

"Oh!" Her arms flail like propellers and I barely manage to catch her—realizing as I see her sly smile that her fall was entirely orchestrated.

Still. I make sure she's set back on her feet before I let go of her shoulders. I'm not going to the hospital a second time tonight, especially not for a broken hip.

"Aren't you a gentleman," she purrs. "That Merritt Markham sure is lucky. I thought she was a city girl, though."

Woman, I correct silently. I don't know what kind of woman Merritt is now, not yet, but I don't plan to discuss this with a woman who might broadcast her version of whatever I say to half the island.

I hate that Mrs. Hopkins is bringing up the very thing causing me the most concern when it comes to Merritt. Because it means I *have* cause for concern.

I put the last of the oranges in the bag and tie it tight. "I really do need to head on before the store closes, if you don't mind."

"I don't mind at all," Mrs. Hopkins says, picking up her pace as I practically sprint back to the frozen food aisle. "I skipped my yoga today, so this will be my workout. You know how it is—we women need to keep up our flexibility and stamina."

I do NOT know how it is, and I'm very positive I don't ever want to.

But I'm not able to shake Mrs. Hopkins, who's the human version of super glue. Not even when I stop at the men's room. I don't need to go, but I take a long time splashing my face with water, then check my phone for any notifications. I even lean against the counter and play a round of Angry Birds, confident I've wasted enough time that Mrs. Hopkins waiting for me would both be awkward *and* socially inappropriate.

Socially inappropriate must be Mrs. Hopkins's middle name because when I finally emerge, she's still there.

"I hope you don't have anything frozen in your bags," I tell her as I look through the bread for the brand Isabelle likes.

"Don't you worry about me. Though I appreciate the

concern. My, my," she tsks. "My book club will be mighty sad to hear you're off the market. A man like you. Sexiest Single Man on Oakley has been neck and neck between you and Benedict for years."

I could have lived my entire life without knowing about this.

"Book club?" As far as I know, that's usually code for wine and talking. Then again, I can't remember the last book I read. Maybe book clubs actually read nowadays.

"I'm sure you know about it. Your mother attends most months. It's called Panty Melters."

She chuckles while I'm busy trying not to think about my mother being involved in anything called by such a name.

"We like to keep those fires lit, if you know what I mean. Extend an invitation to Merritt! We'd love to have her. And I bet we could impart some real pearls of wisdom."

I don't bother with the peanut butter but break into the fastest walk of my life to the front registers. Mrs. Hopkins finally takes the hint and heads outside, waving as she goes.

"Don't forget to tell Merritt about the Panty Melters," she calls, cementing my mortification. "You'll be glad you did. *Trust me.*"

The teenager ringing me up looks as horrified as I feel. The tips of his ears are flaming red, and he looks at me like I had an actual choice in the subject matter of that conversation.

"Sorry," I tell him, though none of this is my fault.

Before I forget, I grab two bags of M&Ms for Izzy.

Sexiest Single Man on Oakley Island is a title I'll happily cede to Benedict. I'm fine just being a dad. A contractor. A woodworker. A wild animal rescuer.

But there is one more title I'm suddenly wishing for, one

that would knock me off whatever real or imagined list Mrs. Hopkins was talking about. *Husband.*

It hasn't mattered for years, but since Merritt came back, it's suddenly all I can think about.

I can only hope it's what she's thinking about too.

FIFTEEN

Merritt

"ARE you sure I can't bring you anything else?"

Harriett, the owner of Sweet Tea and Toast, slides a full mug of coffee onto the Formica table in front of me. Her long white braid is draped over her shoulder, giving her the air of a woman much younger than she probably is. The deli is mostly empty. It's too late for the breakfast rush and too early for lunch. But that suits me just fine. Everyone I run into—Harriett included—looks at me with a sly smile, like they know all my secrets. Which they do. Frank's TikTok has a lot of followers.

"No, this is good," I say, wrapping my hands around the mug. "Thank you."

She hesitates for a moment, her eyes narrowed. "I've got just the thing," she says. "Be right back."

Just the thing for *what*, I'm not sure. But I nod and check my phone again. Still no messages from Hunter.

Did Cassidy have her baby? Is she okay? Does he have Isabelle? The questions are like persistent mosquitos buzzing in my ears.

He didn't show up at Gran's house bright and early like he usually does. He could be working at another location. I have no idea if he's the kind of contractor who has multiple projects going at once. It feels like a strange thing not to know. We leap-frogged right over several important topics last night—this being one.

Another being ... Isabelle.

For so many years, I've been telling myself and anyone who asked that I didn't want to have kids. Childless by choice. But it's not lost on me that I didn't come to this decision until after seeing Cassidy pregnant.

With Isabelle.

Hunter and I might have cleared up some of the past hurts, but that doesn't mean it's *all* clear. Or that there's some easy path forward. If I really want something with Hunter, that means accepting Isabelle. His daughter with my middle name.

Harriett slides into the booth across from me with two plates. Each holds what looks like the most perfect double chocolate muffin I've ever seen. I half expected another piece of Gran's pie, but this is fantastic.

"You look like your morning needed a little sweetening up."

"Do I?"

"Yes."

"And how about *your* morning?"

"I'm just here for the gossip," she says, winking as she takes a big bite.

I have to appreciate the honesty. I also appreciate the

muffin, which is good enough to make me moan. "This is amazing. Did you bake these?"

"I wish." She dabs at her mouth with a napkin. "I order them from a bakery in Savannah. Best I've ever had."

"So?" she says.

"It's delicious," I say, taking another bite.

Laughing, she shakes her head. "No, child. I don't mean the muffin. I mean, what's got you looking all mopey after your date with Hunter last night? I'd have thought you'd be all smiles."

I probably would be—if our date hadn't ended the way it did. Even when his parents crashed our dinner, I still enjoyed every minute.

Before answering, I take another sip of coffee, weighing how much to share with a virtual stranger ... who happens to already know almost everything. She probably even knows Cassidy's in the hospital.

"We had a great date," I say, watching her smile grow brighter. "But he had to leave early because Cassidy went into labor. I'm still waiting to hear from him."

Harriett sits back, clucking her tongue. "He didn't call to tell you?"

I shake my head. "Not even a text."

"That boy. Cassidy's fine. They stopped labor, but she'll be in the hospital for a bit now. Hunter's got Isabelle for a while."

I blow out a breath. "Do I have to start using TikTok to know what's going on?"

Harriett laughs. "I don't have time for those things. I get my gossip the old-fashioned way—on the phone. Virginia Hopkins ran into Hunter at Gator's last night and got the scoop."

"I wish I had the scoop," I mutter, dragging my finger across my plate to get the last few crumbs.

"Want me to add you to the list for fresh gossip?" Her dark eyes twinkle.

"That's okay. But thanks."

"How about a little bit of advice, then?"

Advice doesn't sound half-bad at this point. I'm not going to ask for it, but I won't turn it away either. "Sure."

"Hunter Williams is as loyal as they come. A little serious sometimes, but I think that's a good thing. He doesn't play around."

"No—he doesn't, does he?" This knowledge thrills and terrifies me in equal measure.

She eyes me knowingly. "He also hasn't dated since Cassidy, and believe you me—every woman on this island, young and old, has tried. His daughter even set him up on a few dating apps."

Jealousy is a flash flood, intense and immediate in its force as it tears through me. "Dating apps?"

Harriett laughs again, reaching across the table to pat my hand with her weathered one. "Don't you worry, child. That boy has only *ever* had eyes for you."

It's a strange thing knowing that some of the people on this island like Harriett knew me as a girl when I don't remember them. As a kid and especially as a teenager, I wasn't paying much attention to adults. How much did Harriett see? How much does she remember?

And is she right about Hunter only having eyes for me?

The front door chimes, and a handful of people wander in. "It's going to be okay," Harriett says as she shifts out of the booth. "Give that man a minute to figure himself out. I promise he will."

I offer her a warm smile I mostly mean. "Thanks, Harriett."

I finish the last of my coffee and look at my watch. Still no texts. No missed calls.

This is not good. What else am I supposed to do with all this time on my hands? Hunter said something about stripping the wallpaper out of Gran's downstairs bathroom—it's the only room with wallpaper left—but I don't feel up to tackling a job like that without him to guide me through it.

I suppose I could always paint something.

A pulse of uneasiness runs through me. Do I *want* to paint something? I can't quite explain why I feel scared to paint. But I do.

When my phone buzzes from the table beside me, I jump, startled, and almost knock over my empty coffee mug. *Finally.*

I look up to see Harriett smiling at me from across the deli. "Told you," she says breezily as she leads the newcomers to a booth in the opposite corner.

Hunter: Cassidy and baby are both fine. They stopped the labor, but Cassidy is on bedrest until baby is born, so Isabelle is with me full-time until then.

The text brings both a sense of relief and a sense of anxiety. Knowing Isabelle was with Cassidy most of the time made Hunter feel a little more … accessible. Like maybe I could ease myself into seeing him as a dad, into knowing Isabelle and figuring out what my role is there. But now, if she's with him all the time, I'm not easing into anything. I'm in it. Full stop.

It feels selfish to think about how this will impact things with Hunter and me. But it does. It *will*.

I tap my phone against my palm as I try to figure out how to respond. I finally settle on something benign and hopefully supportive.

Merritt: Do you need to bring her to work with you? I don't mind if you do.

If he brings her, will I get to meet her? Will he want her to? Will she like me? Will I like her?

Hunter: Not today. She's got a fever, so she's home from school. That's why I'm not there. Most days, I'll just need to cut out early in the afternoons to pick her up. Or else go grab her and bring her back for a couple of hours.
Hunter: Sorry I didn't text sooner.
Hunter: Also, I miss you.
Hunter: Drove by last night after the hospital but it looked like you were asleep.

The worries I've been beating back all morning finally subside.
Hunter misses me. He even came by last night. A thrill shoots through me, and I catch myself smiling at my phone like a dummy.

Merritt: So sorry Isabelle is sick! Do you need anything?
Merritt: Also, I miss you too.
Hunter: We're okay. She's resting. What are you up to today?
Merritt: Thinking about painting, maybe? Some guy I know gave me all these supplies...
Hunter: Must be an amazing guy...
Merritt: He's all right.
Hunter: Tell me about him.
Merritt: Hmmm. Nice eyes. Decent personality. Really great butt. Exceptional taste in art supplies.

Hunter: Sounds like a winner. You should hang onto that guy.
Merritt: Word on the street is he's a pretty hot commodity. Think I stand a chance?
Hunter: Honestly, Mer, you're the only one who ever really has.

I press the phone up against my chest. My smile is so wide it hurts my cheeks.

What is happening right now? HOW is this happening?

Me and Hunter. Texting like this. Talking like we did last night. *Kissing* like we did last night. Of all the things I anticipated when moving down here to take over for Eloise, I never imagined this.

I respond to Hunter's last message with three red hearts, then flag down Harriett and ask her for a to-go container of the chicken noodle soup her menu claims is the best in all of Georgia and a pimento cheese sandwich after she assures me it's Hunter's favorite. That makes me want to laugh. Hunter may look like a lumberjack, but he drinks his coffee with fancy creamer and eats pimento cheese sandwiches. Why do I find this so adorable?

Once Harriett has disappeared back into the kitchen, I pull up Naomi's number, which I got while she was helping me pick out my date outfit. We talked about the possibility of shopping this weekend in order to expand my wardrobe. I'm definitely down for shopping, but right now, I'm hoping she can help me with something else.

Merritt: Hi. Would you happen to know where Hunter lives? I've heard it's almost off the grid. Can you tell me how to find it?

Right as Harriett returns with my food, Naomi texts back an address and a string of flame and eggplant emojis, which makes me laugh.

Naomi: The island vultures are still circling. Stake your claim, woman.

The mention of vultures has that jealous wave surging again. Clearly, I want this man for my own. But before I can do any kind of claiming, I need to meet Isabelle.

―――

WHEN IT COMES to Hunter's house, *off the grid* feels like an understatement. The man lives in the literal middle of nowhere. Or maybe more like the edge of nowhere? Apparently, the southernmost point of Oakley Island is a protected wetland. Marshland? A combination of both? I'm not sure I know the difference.

All I know is, no one lives there. Except Hunter, apparently. After driving down a narrow, gravel road for what felt like an eternity but was probably only three or four minutes, I stop my car in a sandy parking area just behind Hunter's truck.

The main house is to my left—a rustic cabin I immediately wonder if Hunter built himself. It looks cozy and comfortable and like it belongs exactly where it is. Almost like it sprouted from the surrounding landscape. I can't see the ocean from here, but I sense where it is, just beyond a thin line of scrubby plants, palmettos, and live oak trees draped with Spanish moss. Opposite the truck, there's another building almost as big as the house, which seems like some sort of garage or workshop. The sides are corrugated metal—worn, but painted a light blue.

I climb out of my car, suddenly nervous to be here as I approach the house. Will Hunter be mad that I just showed up? Will he be happy to see me? Will Isabelle think it's weird I'm here? Will Hunter even want me to meet her?

And maybe the most pressing question—are the dogs barreling toward me friendly?

Hunter talked to me about his rescue animals and didn't mention that they're aggressive, but multiple dogs barking and running right at me doesn't inspire confidence. Recognizing the inevitability of my possible demise, I back up against my car and close my eyes, my arms lifted to shield my face.

A sharp whistle cuts through the air, and I open my eyes to see two dogs sitting at my feet, tails wagging. They're much less intimidating now, even though one of them is the size of a small pony.

"Sorry if they scared you," Hunter calls, quickly descending the porch steps. For once, he's sans-flannel, wearing jeans and a plain white t-shirt, his feet bare. I am suddenly entranced by how sexy I find this. He's so casual. So comfortable. So *delicious*.

"That's Sunbeam, and she's Lilith," he says, pointing to what looks like some kind of shepherd, and then a Great Dane. "They are both very enthusiastic about people."

"I'll say." I offer my hand for sniffing as Hunter steps around the dogs and wraps an arm around my waist. When he presses a kiss to my temple, I nestle into him. It is the tenderest welcome, and I want to rewind and do it all over again. Minus the almost-dog mauling, maybe. Now that they're wagging their tails and licking my hand, it's all good.

Any doubts about showing up uninvited vanish as Hunter squeezes me tighter.

"What are you doing here? And that is not a complaint. I'm very glad you are."

"Um, I brought Isabelle some soup." I bite my lip. "I hope that's okay."

Hunter pulls back, just enough for me to see his smile. "That was thoughtful."

"It's from Harriett's."

"*Very* thoughtful. Anything for me?" He raises an eyebrow.

"I might have brought you something. Like a mint."

Hunter's hands wander up my ribs, finding a ticklish spot. "Is that all?"

I try to twist away, and he tightens his grip. "Maybe a pimento cheese sandwich. But only if you're good."

His mouth finds my ear, his breath hot and his beard prickly as he whispers, "I thought you knew, Mer. I'm definitely *not* good."

I shiver. From the feel of his lips grazing across my eyelids. From his words. From his strong hand circling my waist.

And then I feel a tug on my leggings, glance down, and shriek. "There's a raccoon!"

Hunter laughs, the sound deep and rich. "It's just Banjo. I told you about him, right?"

"Oh. Right—your rescue raccoon," I say, remembering this from our conversation last night. The raccoon, who darted behind the dogs when I screamed, pokes his masked face around, peering at me with bright eyes. "Sorry, Banjo. You startled me."

Crouching, I hold out my hand. He waddles over, sniffing

my fingers before climbing on to my legs and sticking his cold, wet nose right in my ear. "Ah!"

Hunter plucks the raccoon from my lap, holding him with one hand as he uses his other to pull me back up. "Sorry about that. Banjo has no manners. And he really likes ears and shoving his nose where it doesn't belong." He sets the wiggling raccoon back on the ground before lacing his fingers through mine. "About that pimento cheese sandwich ..."

I laugh, tugging Hunter toward the passenger side of the car where I've got the takeout bag. "Right. We need to discuss your taste in sandwiches."

"I have excellent taste in sandwiches."

"I agree. It's just that I don't know many men who like pimento cheese."

"How very sexist of you." Hunter takes the bag from me, still keeping our hands linked. "Why don't we ..."

He trails off, glancing back at the house like he's nervous about something, which reminds *me* I'm nervous about *everything*.

"If you're busy, I can totally just leave it and go."

"No, that's not—I'm not busy."

Hunter gives my hand a gentle tug, and we head toward the porch, trailed by the horde of animals. He hesitates again, the same expression taking over his face. "Let's sit out here," he suggests.

"Don't you want to give Isabelle the soup?"

"Yesssss," he says, drawing the word out. "But she's ... sleeping! Fast asleep. And she's a light sleeper, really, so I don't want to risk waking her up."

Okay. I don't know if he's lying about Isabelle being asleep or if he has some other weird reason for wanting to keep me outside, but Hunter is definitely hiding *something*.

My insecurities start whispering. "Hunter, you can just tell me if you want me to go. I'll leave the food. It's fine if this is a bad time. Or … if you don't want me to meet Isabelle yet."

"I don't want you to go," he says a little more calmly. "That's not it. And I'm fine with you meeting Izzy. When she finds out about you, she'll stop trying to set me up with strangers and creating profiles for me on dating apps."

I bite my lip, happy, at least, that the jealousy eating me at the deli isn't overwhelming me here. Hunter's hand still holding onto mine might be helping in that regard. "Harriett mentioned the dating apps."

Hunter gives me a charming grin. "Izzy is too smart for her own good. She wrote profiles for me, listed preferences, she even included a picture."

"Sounds like a girl I need to meet."

"You do. I know she'll love you."

"Good." I pause. "But you don't want me to come inside your house," I say, because I can still tell there's something he's not saying.

He glances toward the door, then quickly back to me. "I live like a bachelor. So messy. Stuff just … everywhere."

Lies. Hunter was never messy. I have trouble thinking that, as a grown man, he's gotten more slovenly, not less. I tell myself not to take it personally. If he doesn't want me to come inside, he's got a reason. He'll tell me when he's ready.

"Tell you what," he says. "Let me take the food inside and check on Isabelle, and then I'll show you my woodshop."

"Is that a pickup line? Do you show all the ladies your woodshop?"

He chuckles and nods his head toward the building on the other side of his truck. "No pickup lines here. I have an actual woodshop. Do I need a pickup line?"

"Not with me you don't." I smile.

There's definitely something he isn't telling me, some reason he doesn't want me to come inside his house, but the warmth and sincerity in his eyes are compelling enough to ease my worries.

"Should I just wait here?"

He nods, hesitating only a moment before leaning forward and brushing a quick kiss against my lips. "I'll be right back."

I lower myself onto the top step next to Sunbeam, who immediately lifts his head and drops it into my lap, scooting closer and rolling over. "Aww, you like your belly scratched, huh? That's a good boy."

Soon, Lilith drops down on my other side, the look in her eyes saying she'd love some scratches if I'm giving them out.

"You're going to be a lady about it though, aren't you, Lilith?" I say, lifting my free hand to scratch behind her ears. "No begging from you." She closes her eyes and nudges the palm of my hand with her nose, and I immediately love her. "What's your daddy hiding inside that house of his? Does he live like a pig? I'm not buying it."

Banjo climbs the steps but gives me a wide berth, like he's taken personal offense because I didn't want his nose in my ear. He climbs on top of Sunbeam and the two start gently wrestling.

"Okay, buddy, there you go," Hunter says from behind me. "This is Vroom."

I turn to see him coming through the door, a tiny dachshund at his feet, who is, quite literally, vrooming his way around the porch. His front paws touch the floor, but where his back legs should be, there is a two-wheeled cart.

"Oh my word. He is *adorable*."

"Oh, hey, careful, buddy. Be chill." Hunter sits beside me, positioning himself so his body is blocking the steps from

Vroom. "He's got a ramp but likes to forget he's not like the others sometimes."

I didn't even notice the ramp, which is clearly a newer addition based on the lighter color of the wood. "You built that for him?"

Hunter looks slightly embarrassed. "I mean, it's good to have the house be accessible. Just generally speaking."

"Mm-hm. That is good. But you did it for the dog."

"Yeah. I did it for the dog."

Vroom leans in, wedging between me and Sunbeam, who's still wrestling with Banjo. I scratch Vroom's ears, which are velvety and soft. His tiny butt cart—because what else do I call it?—wiggles back and forth as he wags his tail.

"Hunter, this dog is perfect," I say, leaning down so Vroom can lick my cheek. "He's absolutely perfect." Lilith snuffles and nudges my shoulder with her oversized head. "Sorry girl. I promise I won't play favorites. You're pretty perfect too."

"They like you," Hunter says in a way that makes me feel like this is important to him.

"I like them too." I look around, my eyes drifting across the yard. "And this. Out here. This place is beautiful, Hunter."

The tips of his ears turn pink. "It's a work in progress. There's still so much to do to make it … I don't know. To make it everything I want."

"It feels like you. Like what I would have imagined for you." *For us.*

"It's getting there," he says slowly, holding my gaze with those dark eyes. "Still a few things missing."

Could he mean me? I really, really want him to mean me.

"Come on," he says. "Let me give you the tour."

Instead of taking the stairs, which would make sense

because we're sitting on them, Hunter laces his fingers through mine and leads us down the ramp, Vroom following right behind.

He's taking the ramp for the sake of his dog.

Forget our history. Even if I'd only met Hunter ten minutes ago, my heart would already be in a melted puddle at my feet.

"How's Isabelle?" I ask. The dogs race ahead, then turn and head down a path toward the marshy side. Hunter doesn't call them back, so this must be okay, even for Vroom.

"Still sleeping. I gave her medicine a while ago, so her fever broke. She'll probably be ready to eat when she wakes up, and the soup will be perfect. Thanks again for that."

Hunter's face changes when he talks about his daughter, and that does weird things to my heart. Weird, nervous things. But also ... seeing him talk about Isabelle with such affection fills *me* with affection for *him*. He swings open the creaky door to the metal shed. With a light tug on my hand, he stops me, and his face looks so vulnerable, it makes something pinch tightly in my chest.

"No judgment, okay?"

Did my words from long ago embed in his brain? Does he think I would judge him? Based on the question, he must. I'll be honest—the realization hurts.

My relationships with my sisters are complicated. We love each other. We bicker. We have layers of history, shared memories that hit us all differently. What Hunter and I have is sort of like that in terms of all the layers. But it's so much more complex because of the deep wounds.

Ones I inflicted on purpose. Others he still doesn't even know he inflicted on me and never intended to cause.

Which you should tell him about, I remind myself. *It's not a huge thing—just tell him. You were here on his wedding day. You came back for him.*

But ... I don't. Instead, I choose my words with care, choosing to stick with the present rather than bringing in the words I said in the past. "I promise not to judge."

When he still looks unsure, I take a breath and lean forward, pressing a soft kiss to his lips. I mean it as a comfort, maybe even as a sort of promise, but to me, it's more like an engine revving.

"I will love whatever is inside because you made it," I whisper against his mouth, loving the softness of his lips and the light scratch of his whiskers.

Then, before I slam my lead foot against the gas pedal, I pull away and offer a reassuring smile. Hunter's eyes are hooded, and when he licks his lips, I shiver.

Maybe I should rethink hitting the brakes ...

But I don't get to consider it too deeply before Hunter pulls me inside and flicks on a light switch. I clutch his hand, taking in the room with wide eyes.

The workshop is exactly what I would have imagined for him. The cement floor is swept clean. Every saw and tool I can't name looks like it's been recently wiped down and immaculately maintained, though none look new. It's tidy and efficient.

But his work, on the other hand ... I don't have words.

I drop Hunter's hand and step forward, drawn forward to a tabletop leaning vertically against one wall.

"This is ... breathtaking." I reach a hand out to the smooth wood surface, then pause with my fingertips inches away. "Can I touch it?"

"That one's finished curing. Go ahead."

I place both palms flat against the surface and walk, letting my hands glide over the polished wood. This is no ordinary table. It's made of two large wood slabs with natural edges—rough, irregular, and darker than the wood top. In the very center between the two wood edges, there's a burst of unexpected color. Swirls of deep blue threaded with turquoise and even a few lines of pink and purple. The finish is smooth and glossy.

"It's called a river table," Hunter says.

I understand why because that's exactly what it looks like—a table with a river running right down the middle.

"It's stunning." I turn and meet his gaze. "Absolutely *stunning*."

The walls are lined with more finished tops, large and small, and similar designs. All have the natural edges, and some of them have multiple places where the color swirls, giving the effect of something wholly natural, plucked right out of a forest.

I don't miss the way he's made this small building into a gallery of sorts. A private gallery, hidden out here on the loneliest part of the island.

I wonder if I'm the first one to see these.

"Are these commissions?" I ask, hoping my curiosity doesn't sound like the extreme nosiness that it is. "Do you sell them in any of the stores on the island or in Savannah?"

When I glance over, Hunter has one hand on a work table and the other on the back of his neck. "No."

My brow furrows. "Then where do you sell them? To your clients?"

"They're just for me. Not a job or a side hustle. It relaxes me."

I have so many questions, but Hunter's voice is tight. There are lights flashing telling me to slow down, and a sign warning me of dangerous curves ahead. Though everything in me wants to press him—because this is what I do, the firstborn urge to fix and correct and offer practical suggestions—I make a choice to let it go.

For now.

It involves biting the inside of my lip to keep my words contained.

In the center of the room, another table is in progress. The blue is lighter here, almost clear in some places. I can't tell for sure because the whole thing is sitting in a kind of oversized tray.

"That one's still curing," Hunter says.

"I won't touch," I say quickly. One more tabletop, a little smaller than the biggest two, sits in the back corner, looking completely finished.

"I'm planning to put that one in my house," he says. "I just need to buy chairs."

"I love it. I love it all. Hunter …" I get choked up for a second, and I can't pinpoint why. I swallow, then sniff, mentally ordering my emotions to get it together.

I step closer and take both of his hands in mine, letting my fingertips trace the calluses on his. "I am blown away, yet not at all surprised by the beauty these hands created," I say softly.

I haven't ever thought of hands in and of themselves as being attractive. Or sexy. I mean, sure—obviously hands are important for touching, which can be very sexy. But I've never looked at a pair of hands and thought about what they are capable of making or building and had a visceral reaction like this.

I'm not the only one having a visceral reaction. Hunter crowds me, urging me to step backward until I'm up against his table, a little breathless.

"You don't know what you do to me," Hunter says, his

eyes darkening. "Your words. Your touch. The way you look at me."

"Same."

This pulls a grin from him. *Same.* A simple word Hunter and I used all too often back then, like an echo, a refrain. His smile does nothing to slow what's building between us, and it shifts into something else altogether when he suddenly takes me by the hips and lifts me until I'm sitting on his table.

"Will this hurt the finish? I don't want to—"

He quiets me with a fingertip to my lips, tracing my mouth like he plans to memorize the shape.

"You won't hurt it, Mer."

But once upon a time, I really hurt him, I think, lifting my hands to cup his bearded jaw. Even if I apologized and he forgave me, it doesn't take away the scars left behind.

What's more, I could still hurt him. I *will* hurt him when I leave Oakley. *If* I leave?

At some point, whatever this is, I need to make some decisions. Hunter and I will have to talk.

But not now.

Maybe it's selfish or immature, but for this moment, I want only this. Only my hands on his cheeks, his hands on my hips, his eyes with their darkening desire.

When he leans into my touch, I let my hands roam over his face. Exploring, learning the curve of his cheek and the lines of his beard. I love the feel of his thick hair under my fingers. I relish in the soft groan he makes when he closes his eyes.

I never did this with him, just let myself touch his face and his hair, exploring his broad shoulders and his muscled arms. He wasn't bearded, or so broad, or this muscular back then.

Things never got super physical aside from some kisses—we were young and I think we were both afraid of screwing up the friendship we'd built over the years by giving into the teenage hormones raging through us.

But the raging I felt back then, when he kissed me or held me, doesn't even compare to the molten fire roaring through me now.

His eyes pop open suddenly, hazy at first and then practically glowing with intense clarity.

"I am going to kiss you," he says. "Unless you don't want me to, in which case, please speak now or I won't be able to—"

Stop? Hold back? Survive?

I have no idea what Hunter would have said because I tug his face to mine and answer him without words.

SIXTEEN

Hunter

I HAVEN'T EVER TESTED my tables to see if they can hold an adult human. But as my mouth moves against Merritt's and my hands sink into her hair, feeling the soft strands, I'm glad to know the table can hold her weight.

Even if it didn't—*worth it.*

If I ever do get around to selling my tables, I wonder if this could be a selling point?

Will withstand a heavy makeout session! Money-back guarantee!

Mer pulls back. Her pupils are wide and dark, but she blinks and the expression in her eyes is suddenly full of concern.

"Are you with me?" she whispers. "It feels like you're a million miles away."

I start to answer yes, then realize I've been thinking about my tables instead of the gorgeous woman I was kissing. The one I've dreamed about kissing for years, thinking it would only ever be a dream.

So, why am I not here in the moment? Why am I thinking about the features of tables I'm not even selling?

The answer is immediately obvious. And it makes me feel small.

I'm afraid.

Merritt lightly strokes my cheeks. "I can't read you like I used to. But I'm getting some mixed signals. You wanted to kiss me, but you're distracted. You didn't want me to come inside your house, and I can't for a minute believe that it's because you're messy."

I swallow, looking past her, to where a row of familiar tools hangs on the wall. I'm not ready to explain why she can't come inside. I should have known she wouldn't miss me being weird about it. And as for why I'm distracted ... do I *really* need to confess my fears?

Her hands tug a little on my jaw, drawing my gaze back to hers. "Hunter?" Merritt whispers.

I'm suddenly filled with a new fear. She's going to tell me she's leaving or that this was a mistake or—

"I'm scared too," she says.

Merritt was wrong—she can read me like I'm the book she kept on her bedside table all these years, picking it up every night to read.

Maybe it shouldn't, but her confession makes me bold.

"I don't know if I can stand losing you a second time," I confess. "I want this. I want you. But not if it's going to end."

She nods, then looks away. "I feel the same, which I know isn't fair because I was the one who hurt you. The one who left you."

"The one who's here temporarily."

I want her to argue—I *need* her to argue—but her mouth

opens, then closes. She gives a halfhearted shrug and sniffs. I'm horrified to see her eyes wet. The last thing I wanted was to kiss her and make her cry.

"I'm sorry," I say, my tone gentler. I run a hand up her back and don't miss the way she shivers under my touch.

"I can't make promises, Hunter." She swallows, my eyes tracking the slight movement in her throat. "Not yet. I'm in limbo here. No job, no home, no idea what comes next."

Though I completely understand, some caveman part of me I didn't know existed wants to *tell* her what's next. She'll move in here with me. Or if she doesn't like being all the way out here, I'll move to wherever she wants, so long as it's on the island. It'll be more complicated with Isabelle. And with the dogs, used to having free rein of acres, but it would be fine.

Only ... I can't make the choice for Merritt.

I can only hope that in the end, I'll be her choice.

"Do you want me to go?" she asks, her voice sounding watery.

I curl my hands around her waist. "You leaving is the last thing I want, Mer."

I hope she knows I don't just mean now. I mean *ever*. But I won't say more. I won't push. I won't be her anchor if she wants to leave the island again, leave *me* again.

"But you don't want to do this without a commitment." She states this like it's a fact, not a question.

I mull over the words, my mind sifting through possibilities and scenarios like I'm thumbing my way through a file cabinet, looking for just the right one. Only, here, there is no one right thing.

We both made mistakes back then. She might have pushed me away, but I think I knew, somewhere deep down, that she didn't really want to. That she couldn't mean such hurtful words. Merritt wasn't—*isn't*—a cruel person. I think she knew exactly what she needed to say in order to push me away. To protect herself but to protect me too.

Even when I considered that possibility in my teenage pea-brain, I didn't do anything about it. I didn't call her or text her or try to find her on social media. I didn't push to see if something else was going on with her.

No—I took her words, as out of character and out of nowhere as they were—at face value. I wallowed in hurt and bitterness. Then I tried to move on with someone else. Cass was more to me than a rebound or someone I used for that purpose, but I wouldn't have ever pursued her with Merritt anywhere in the picture.

Back then, it was easier to simply let Merritt's words keep us apart. To believe them. To let my fear keep me from fighting for her. Because *what if she did mean it? What if I was too small for her?*

The same fears exist now.

The only difference is that I'm a *man* making a decision, instead of a boy.

It feels like hurling myself into a stormy sea, hoping the skies will clear and I won't get dragged under. But it's worth the risk, isn't it?

She's worth the risk.

I slide my hands to the curve of her waist. Merritt is so strong, but I see who she is underneath. Not weak, never that, but *vulnerable*. Soft. As scared as I am.

But brave enough to call me on it and be the first to confess her fears.

It only makes her more beautiful to me.

"I don't want to pressure you to decide something today. I don't want to unduly influence your choices, even if I have some strong opinions about what I'd like."

She grins at this, and it's like the sun beaming through a bank of gray clouds.

I lick my lips, not missing how her eyes track the movement, and the hunger I see there matches the one building in me. With intentional softness, I trail my hands up her back again, then twine them in the hair at the back of her neck. I smile when she bites her lip.

"The question is—can we keep doing this without knowing the end yet?" I ask.

"*This* as in kissing on one of your tabletops?" she teases.

I give her hair a gentle tug, watching her eyelids flutter a little. "That. For sure *that*. But more. Are you willing to risk the hurt to see what could be between us?"

The question hangs in the air, like a held breath. But she doesn't make me wait long.

"Yes. Are you?"

Instead of answering right away, I let my hands dance down her neck, fingertips lightly dragging over the skin of her bare arms when I reach the bottoms of her sleeves. I lean forward, sliding my beard against her cheek, and the sound of my bristly hair against her softness does something to me. Flames lick through me, building, building, building.

My lips find her ear, and I keep them close enough to brush as I speak. She whimpers softly.

"I would rather risk everything for a chance than live another moment without you in my arms."

She slumps against me, as though this answer is one she's been waiting years to hear. I kiss the shell of her ear, working my way slowly from her ear down her neck, back up to her jaw and toward her mouth.

Mine, mine, mine, I think with each kiss. I figure it's okay to let that Neanderthal part of me at least have this much sway.

But there is another unspoken phrase scaffolding these

kisses. *I love you.* This one I don't say because it would be too soon, pushing too hard. But that doesn't make it any less true.

When I brush my lips over hers, barely a ghost of a touch, Merritt's whole body trembles. I pull her closer to me, aware of her warmth against my chest, her hands fisting my shirt.

"I never knew how much I needed to kiss you on a table I made," I whisper against her mouth.

"You don't bring all the women to your workshop for this purpose?"

She's teasing, but I hear the question in her words.

I pull back enough to meet her eyes. "No other woman has *ever* been in this workshop. Not even Cass. And Merritt?" I pause, unsure how this next part will go over. "There wasn't anyone else before or after. Only you, then Cass."

If she's seeking answers, looking for reassurance that this means something to me, she needs to know. I stop just short of telling her that when it comes to my feelings, it was only ever her. *Always* her. Meanwhile, I have no idea how many guys she's dated or kissed or said *I love you* to. I find that it doesn't much matter so long as she's here with me now.

Forever.

I shove THAT thought away and, as a smile breaks over Merritt's face, I return to her lips, taking her mouth with all the restraint I have.

Which, to be honest, is not very much.

We're breathing heavy if we're coming up for air at all, our mouths ravenous and greedy. Her hands trail over my arms and my chest and shoulders, like she's trying to familiarize herself with the man I am now. Her touch is like fire, or maybe it's more like an accelerant to the flames burning in me already.

And then—dogs barking. All of them at once, right at the door to the workshop.

I lean my forehead against hers, breathing heavy and ragged. "Like little chaperones," I growl.

"Or, maybe like a warning bell?" she says, and that's when I hear it—Isabelle, calling my name.

Faster than I thought I could move, I lift Merritt off the table, set her down, and meet her gaze.

"Are you ready to meet my daughter?" I ask, this question feeling so much bigger and riskier than any other thing I've said today.

I expect hesitation or maybe reserve, but Merritt only smiles, making something turn over in my heart. "You really think she'll like me?"

I chuckle and quickly kiss her soft cheek. "I think she'll latch onto you like a tick."

"Ew." Merritt makes a gagging noise.

I wince. "Bad analogy. But what I mean to say is she'll love you."

And she's not the only one.

SEVENTEEN

Merritt

HUNTER HOLDS my hand as we cross the workshop but drops it as soon as we're outside. I immediately miss the contact, but I can't really blame him. I have no idea what he's told his daughter about me. Probably nothing at all. Definitely *not* that he planned to kiss me senseless in the middle of his workshop.

Which was ... the highlight of my year.

Meeting his daughter requires a sudden switching of gears. Have she and Hunter talked about him dating again? He mentioned dating apps, so I'd assume so. But has he ever mentioned me specifically? Has Cassidy? She and I were never each other's biggest fans because we both wanted the same thing: Hunter.

What if Isabelle doesn't like me? What if I don't like her? What if I meet her and still don't want to have kids? Is this just ... the end?

"Mer." Hunter's voice, low and deep, is like an immediate off switch to my swirling thoughts.

"Yeah?"

He taps one finger on my forehead, right between my eyebrows, where I know there's a crease of worry. "I've got you."

His voice steadies me, his words the reassurance I didn't know I needed. As fiercely independent as I am, I could get used to the idea of Hunter's protection.

"Breathe," he says.

I do. "Thank you."

Isabelle stands on the porch, a blanket held snugly around her shoulders like it's the dead of winter in New York, not a humid Georgia fall. Hunter's pace quickens as he crosses the driveway and climbs the steps, but only after looking at me over his shoulder as though to tell me he's still got me.

I follow behind, taking the ramp with Vroom and stopping a little ways back. However this meeting goes, it needs to happen on Hunter's terms. On Isabelle's. Not mine.

I watch as he scoops Isabelle into his arms. She wraps around him like a baby koala, her head dropping onto his shoulder. My heart climbs out of my chest and flops around on the floor of the porch like a caught fish.

On his own, Hunter is dead sexy.

But Hunter as a *dad*?

I ... had no idea this was a thing I'd love. But I do. Heat surges through my body, fueled by some chemical reaction I cannot control. The meaning behind it feels biological. Primal.

I want to have this man's babies.

Or at least, my biology has deemed it desirable, for the continuation of the species, to procreate with his biology.

No. That's inaccurate. It is *true*—some of this has to be related to my genetic programming. But I am, immediately and consciously as a *thinking* woman (who, mind you, has said for the past eight years I didn't want children), very much *consumed* by the sudden idea of babies (and *baby-making*) with this man.

The feeling is startling and strange. Me? *Wanting babies?* What is happening to me?

Except, it shouldn't feel so foreign. There was a time I did want kids. When I played M.A.S.H. and dreamed about raising a family the way you do when you're too young to understand all the ways your dreams can go wrong.

But all that dreaming stopped when I saw a pregnant Cassidy marrying Hunter. Actually, the seeds might have been planted when my parents split. Hunter and Cassidy—and Isabelle—were just the fertilizer the seeds needed to grow into a staunch conviction that family life was not for me. Too much risk. Too much hurt.

But this feeling, this yearning—it makes the risk feel worth it.

It's a strange moment—the sharp ache of what I wanted *before* leapfrogging over all those years I wanted something else and landing here, right now, wrapping around my heart in a way that makes me wonder if I was only ever pretending I didn't want a family. It's trippy to have it all happening in the presence of the very kid who kicked me off the family path to start with.

Hunter turns toward me, a gentle smile on his face. "Izzy, this is my friend, Merritt."

Friend. Hm. Okay. The baby-making urges pump the brakes.

Logically, *friend* is a solid place to start. Though, if pressed to answer, I'd tell anyone who asks: I DO NOT KISS MY FRIENDS LIKE HUNTER AND I JUST KISSED.

Isabelle lifts her head and eyes me curiously. "Are you the artist?"

Hunter stiffens the slightest bit, and when his eyes cut my way, I see a hint of sheepishness. So he *has* talked about me. Enough that his daughter would recognize my name and think of me as a painter. Even if I'm not sure that's still how I think of myself.

I like the idea of Hunter telling her about me maybe more than I should. So much so that it makes me briefly mute.

He leans toward Isabelle and whispers something in her ear.

Isabelle's eyes go wide, then she nods, which only increases my curiosity.

"I don't know if I'm *the* painter," I say slowly, "but I used to paint a little. It's nice to meet you, Isabelle. I'm sorry you're sick."

She nods. "Me too. I'm missing game day at school. I was going to be the Monopoly man." She sniffs and looks at Hunter. "Can I pet Vroom?"

Hunter shifts and sets her down on the porch steps, dropping down beside her and motioning for me to join them.

I nudge Sunbeam out of the way and sit down next to Isabelle, more nervous than I've been in I don't know how long. The dogs were easy, but Isabelle is a *person*. One with thoughts and feelings and opinions.

And one I *really* want to like me. Which is another weird discovery. Normally, I see kids and run the other direction. They are sticky and strange, and I don't know how to talk to them.

But Isabelle is different. Isabelle is Hunter's.

"What do you do besides dressing up on game day?" I ask.

"All kinds of things," Isabelle says, her face lighting up.

"We go from classroom to classroom and then to the gym and the library and there are teachers in every room with different games. My favorite is the matching one. Because I'm the best at it. I remember better than everyone else."

"Izzy," Hunter gently chides.

"What?" she says, a little indignantly. "I didn't say I was the smartest this time. Just that I'm best at matching."

"Just so long as you're only telling *me* you're best at matching, and not telling all the other kids."

Isabelle rolls her eyes. "I don't *have* to tell them. They see me win. They all want me on their team."

I find my lips curling up in a smile. Isabelle is absolutely endearing. Precocious and vibrant. And already, I'm looking for ways she's similar to and different from her father. Hunter would have faded into the wallpaper before wanting to compete with a team on game day. I didn't need to go to school with him to know this.

And yet, I see Hunter in her intelligent eyes, and even somehow in her sass, which isn't a characteristic readily visible on the surface with Hunter. But it's there.

It's not bad if I'm just completely ignoring what parts she might have inherited from her mother, right? Because I don't want to think about Cassidy. Even if she's married to a new man and having his baby.

Great. Now I'm thinking about Cassidy.

I clear my throat. "Is the matching game like Memory? The one where you turn over the little tiles looking for a match?"

Isabelle nods. "Just like that, but the tiles are this bigger." She stretches her arms out to either side. Her blanket falls to the porch and Hunter arranges it over her shoulders again. "They spread them out on the floor, and they fill up a whole classroom with all the desks pushed to the sides. Memory is a little kid game, but it's fun like this." She perks up and looks at Hunter. "Can we play a game with Merritt?" She turns her attention fully on me. "Do you want to play?"

I look at Hunter. I have literally zero places to be, so I'd love to play a game, especially if it means catching a peek of the inside of Hunter's house.

But I don't know the rules here, about dating or whatever, with a kid. And I don't want to impose.

Especially when Hunter got a look of panic in his eyes at even the hint of me coming inside his house. I really hope this isn't some Bluebeard's secret room kind of thing.

"It's a nice day," Hunter says easily. "Why don't we play out here?"

Thwarted again. What is this man hiding? I shove the macabre thoughts of Bluebeard and a room full of skeletons right out of my head. Isabelle can go inside, so obviously, there isn't anything dangerous or weird. Except, does that mean it's just a *me* problem?

"On it!" Isabelle calls, jumping up from the porch.

"Hey, hey, slow down," Hunter says. "You're still sick, Izzy."

She stops at the door. "I don't *feel* sick."

"Because I gave you medicine. Better still take it easy, okay?"

She frowns. "So we can't play?"

"We can still play. Just slow down. No need to run like Vroom's chasing you. And one game, then it's back to bed with you."

"Okay, Daddy."

Hunter's eyes stay on his daughter until she disappears through the front door, two of the three dogs hot on her heels.

"You're good at this," I say, motioning toward the house.

"Good with *her*."

He shakes his head, laughing lightly. "Sometimes it doesn't feel like it. Parenting is a little like being thrown into a pit of vipers. Or, like a pit with one viper, whom you really love and want to take care of but ..." He stops and runs a hand over his beard.

I grin. "That analogy got away from you a little bit, didn't it?"

"It did." He chuckles. "Point is, I felt like I got tossed in and am still fumbling around trying to find my way."

"I think that sounds completely normal."

I'm basing this sudden parenting expertise on one work friend who had a baby last year. Former-work friend, I guess, since Eleanor decided not to come back after maternity leave ended.

I brought a meal to her once and found her with one breast hanging out of a nursing top, a cabbage leaf poking out of the other side, and what looked like a smear of chocolate across one cheek. She put her infant daughter in my arms, wept, and told me to ignore her tears because it was just hormones. Ten minutes later, she had showered and was nursing her daughter like everything was normal. Eleanor described it in a similar way, like being thrown into a deep end with no arms or legs and only baby books, the advice of the internet, and your own internal compass to keep you afloat.

And yet you just thought about having babies with this man, a voice from the depths of my brain scoffs.

Yeah. I did. And the idea still doesn't sound horrifying. I'll have to spend some time considering whether this is a Hunter-specific shift or if I'm rethinking my thoughts on the subject altogether.

We're both quiet for a beat before I say his daughter's name slowly, with a little more purpose this time. *"Isabelle."*

My middle name. OUR name—the one Hunter and I talked about using back when we were planning out and hoping for a future together. Banjo yawns from a sunny spot on the porch and waddles over, nosing Hunter before climbing in his lap, reaching up his tiny paws to touch Hunter's beard. Hunter redirects, picking up a dog toy shaped like a lizard and handing it to Banjo.

"I didn't choose her name to hurt you," Hunter says softly, his eyes on the door, ready to switch gears back to low whenever Isabelle returns. He strokes Banjo's back.

Even if I wanted to resist the man, the sweetness of how he is with Isabelle and the way he looks with a raccoon in his lap would make my resistance utterly futile.

"I know."

He shoots me a quick glance. "Do you? Because I know how it might seem."

I shake my head. "That's not you. You don't do spite or play games or get passive-aggressive. I may have missed some years in there, but I know this much about who you are, Hunter."

His smile is quick, then his face turns serious. "Isabelle is also Cassidy's grandmother's name. When Cass suggested it right before Izzy was born, I didn't have the heart to tell her that you and I had talked about—" He shakes his head. "I was trying so hard to make the marriage work. To be a good husband, even though I was barely out of high school. A stupid kid." He lifts his eyes to mine, fire sparking in the depths of his irises. "Mer, I'd be lying if I told you a part of me didn't want to use the name *because* of you. Because I knew that every time I looked at Isabelle, I'd think of you."

Heat courses through me, sharp and heady. It's a soul-deep fire. I want more of this. More of him.

A sharp yearning presses against my heart. Beyond my growing feelings for Hunter, being on Oakley is showing me something about myself, too. I want to be the person I *was*—the person I *am*—when I'm with Hunter on Oakley. This island—or this man—seems to bring out the best version of myself.

When I left that fateful summer, I told myself it was best to make a clean break. But the break wasn't just between me and the geographical location. It was a break between me and the people here I'd come to love. Hunter, but Gran too.

I also created a cavernous rift between who I was and who I decided to become. Because when Mom and Dad divorced and we stopped coming to Oakley and then moved across the country, I let my new circumstances dictate the new me. I became who I needed to be to get through it, to get my sisters through it. My personality was always the orderly, take-charge kind.

But I also used to cultivate space for a girl who ran around the island with no shoes and no watch. A girl who felt most like herself with a brush in her hand, letting brilliant colored strokes fill a white canvas. Who laughed while my hair whipped around my face from a strong wind, who dove off the end of docks, and maybe even sometimes snuck out after curfew to watch a meteor shower with Hunter.

I was *both*. And I cut one half of me off without fully realizing what this would mean for the person I became. I couldn't know how it would impact me to lose the part of me that was free and creative.

I think of the gorgeous tables inside Hunter's shop, artwork in functional form. He didn't cut off that part of him. But he is hiding it away.

Which is maybe not so different from what I've done, just in his own way.

"I picked Bananagrams!" Isabelle darts back out the front door, startling Banjo. The raccoon makes a chittering sound and climbs right on top of Lilith, sniffing the big dog's paws and then her ears.

Isabelle plops onto Hunter's lap like it was made for her. She is easy, comfortable in her dad's presence, which says a lot about the kind of father he is. Hunter wraps his strong arms around Isabelle, and she nestles against his chest, holding out a little yellow pouch shaped like a banana.

"Have you ever played this?" Hunter asks, and I shake my head.

"You'll catch on," Isabelle says. "It's like Scrabble, but no board. Just letter tiles. You'll see."

As Izzy explains the game, a hundred different worries flit through my brain, distracting me. Am I supposed to let Isabelle win? Is that something parents do? Or do I just play like I would play a game with any adult? I don't know how any of this is supposed to work.

Or, in a bigger sense, how *parenting* is supposed to work. My anxiety rears its head again as I start to overthink. As though completely in tune with my feelings, Hunter nudges my foot with his and nods encouragingly. *Breathe,* he mouths. I shouldn't need the reminder. But I do.

"Split!" Izzy says, and we're off, flipping over our individual tiles and racing to make words.

I catch on pretty quickly, but I'm not as quick as Hunter or Isabelle. My competitive nature flares up, and I shove away my worries to line my letters up into a scrabble-like grid. We can only get new letters or exchange letters we don't want by saying banana-themed words, which I'm mostly tracking, but I'm still slow. Hunter finishes first, winning the first round by calling out, "Bananas!"

He lifts an eyebrow at Isabelle. "Who did you say was the best at this game?"

Isabelle flashes him a smirky little smile. "Let's see who wins the next round," she says, her tone and cadence an echo of her father's.

"You're going down," Hunter says, dropping his voice into a growly grumble.

Okay, so we definitely *aren't* letting Isabelle win. In our next round, I'm on fire and am the first one to call out for more letters. It seems like she has a pretty solid vocabulary for an eight-year-old. But I also don't know exactly what's typical for this age.

"Ooh, Izzy, looks like you've got some competition." Hunter's eyes lift to mine, and a pulse of something electric sparks between us. Will that ever stop happening?

I hope it never does.

Isabelle purses her lips and looks me over, like she's sizing me up. "I can handle it," she says, sounding eighteen instead of eight.

And she totally *does* handle it. She wins the second round, even though Hunter and I were obviously trying our best.

"Good game, ladybug," Hunter says.

"I told you," Isabelle says through a yawn.

"You are good at the game," Hunter agrees, shooting me a look that seems to say he can't really argue with her now. "But let's work on mixing a little humility in with that confidence, k?"

"Remind me what humility is again?"

"When you don't talk or act or think like you're the best, even if you are. Not calling attention to your successes but letting them speak for themselves."

Does parenting also somehow turn you into an oracle or fount of wisdom? Because Hunter's response is perhaps the best definition I've ever heard for humility.

"Let's pick up," he says.

"One more game?" Isabelle pleads.

"Nope. Time for soup and a nap. Merritt brought you some from Harriett's."

"Thank you," she says, throwing me a megawatt smile. But then her expression shifts, her eyes darting from me to her father and back again. When the last tile is in the banana bag, she holds my gaze for a long moment before she asks, "Are you dating my daddy now?"

My eyes dart to Hunter's. "Um."

He lifts his shoulders in a tiny shrug.

"Yes?" I finally answer, hoping it's the one I'm supposed to give. "I think I am."

"You *think*?" For just a moment, Isabelle channels Sadie with her tone and the look she gives us both. "You should really *know*. We don't do things halfway, do we, Dad?"

Hunter shakes his head, giving me a look that's at once amused and apologetic. "No, we give things our all."

Isabelle crosses her arms. "So, maybe you should make sure Merritt knows where you stand."

I want to laugh, but Isabelle—full of mischief though she is—is also dead serious. I suspect the fastest way to lose her approval would be for her to think I'm making light of her words. So I just stare at Hunter, whose ears turn pink, then red.

"Well?" Isabelle says, looking exasperated. "I can't ask for you. I can only lead the horse to water."

Okay, this child is TOO MUCH. In the best way. And, mostly because it's fun to see Hunter squirm, I love it.

Hunter clears his throat. "I think this should maybe be a private conversation, Izzy. Between Merritt and me."

She gives her dad a serious nod. "I can give you a few minutes."

"Where you're not listening at the door?" Hunter arches an eyebrow, and she giggles, finally sounding like an eight-year-old again.

"No promises."

"Let's get you inside. Be right back," he tells me, then turns and Isabelle climbs onto his back. She yawns and her head droops onto his shoulder. "Izzy, can you say goodbye?"

She cracks open sleepy eyes. "Bye, Merritt. Thanks for playing with me. And don't go easy on my dad. But I hope you say yes."

Hunter groans as I step closer and lift the blanket, draping it over Isabelle. I smooth it out, patting her back a few times in a gesture I hope feels motherly. "No promises," I say, echoing her words from earlier while biting back a smile.

Hunter pins me with a look that does not feel like the kind he should be giving me with a kid on his back. "Don't move."

Yes, sir. Whatever you say, Bossy Hunter.

The dogs stay with me, shifting closer to take up the space Hunter left. I scratch Vroom and Sunbeam at the same time, listening to the low rumble of Hunter's voice through the screen door. Banjo wanders through the yard, digging around the dirt, sniffing everything.

Voices carry from inside, and if I were a better person, maybe I wouldn't be straining to listen.

"What did we say about meddling?" Hunter asks.

"That it's an act of love?" Izzy's voice is hopeful.

He harrumphs and says something too low for me to hear. Then: "Maybe now you can lay off the dating profiles for a while, yeah?"

I don't hear her response, only the low murmur of her voice. But then she says something a little louder. "Are you going to kiss her goodbye? You should kiss her goodbye."

I *definitely* agree about the kissing.

Vroom seems to agree as well, as he's wagging his butt cart with unbridled enthusiasm.

"Are you all in on this?" I ask him. "Playing matchmaker?"

Vroom wiggles even harder and Sunbeam thumps her tail on the porch. Yep. They're definitely in on it. Thing is—I don't even need any nudges. I'm all in all on my own.

When Hunter returns, I stand to meet him.

"I've gotten strict instructions to make sure I kiss you goodbye," he says, his brown eyes sparkling.

"I heartily approve the suggestion," I say, and he moves in, slipping a hand around my waist as he pushes me back against the porch railing.

"Is this going to hold me?" I ask.

He snorts. "I built it. Yes. It'll hold."

"Hm. I see where Isabelle gets her humility."

This earns me a kiss, one that steals my breath and my ability to stand on steady legs. But I've got Hunter's hands on my hips and the railing he built behind me.

I lift my hands to his chest, pressing my palms flat against his t-shirt, momentarily distracted by the feel of all that solid muscle. *Wait.*

"Hunter, are you flexing right now?"

"I thought maybe you wanted me too. You're rubbing my chest like I'm a magic lamp and you're hoping for a genie."

I drop my hands like he's on fire, but he catches them and lifts them back, pressing them to his chest and holding them in place with his own as he chuckles. "I didn't say I minded. But don't get too excited. I've got a dad bod now."

I roll my eyes. I don't buy that for a single second. "Right. Absolutely. This feels very Dad-bod-like. And when you picked me up on the beach the day I hurt my ankle, you *definitely* seemed like you were struggling to carry me."

"You were checking out my butt, weren't you?"

"No!" I attempt a horrified face, but he only laughs. "Fine. But it was *right there!*"

"Mm-hm. Well, as far as I'm concerned, you can check me out all you want." He flexes again, his muscles jumping underneath my palms.

"I can't seem to stop," I say as my hands slide across his chest. I mean the words to sound teasing, but instead they sound wanton and breathless.

He leans down and presses his lips against mine. "I don't ever want you to," he whispers when he finally pulls away.

We walk to my car, hand in hand.

"I know it's a Saturday, but I was thinking I'd be by the house tomorrow anyway, as long as Isabelle's up for it." He makes a face. "She'll have to come with me. My parents can help some while I've got her, but tomorrow they've got plans."

"Isabelle can hang out with me while you're working," I volunteer, immediately hoping I don't regret it. Playing Bananagrams while Hunter is present is one thing. But entertaining a kid I barely know one-on-one is another matter entirely. "I'm certainly not busy. We could go down to the beach. Or play games."

"She likes you," Hunter says. "I bet she'd love that."

"I like her, too."

Hunter kisses me again, right up against the car. The man seems to like kissing me up against things or on top of things. I will not even pretend to mind. The kiss is longer this time, but with the measured control I'm beginning to sense dictates everything Hunter does in life.

It's a selfish thought, but I find myself wanting to push against that control. What would it take to make this man let go? To kiss me like he doesn't have to stop. Like he doesn't have to worry about whether his daughter is watching. Or whether we're going to break each other's hearts again.

I can't lose you a second time, Mer.

His words echo through my mind, and I pull away. Even though I don't want to. Even though, if he asked me to stay and keep kissing him for the next twelve hours, I wouldn't be able to say no.

But he won't ask, and I have to understand why. Despite wanting to make him lose control, I need to be as careful with him as he's being with me. As careful as he's being with himself. And his daughter.

We aren't just kids now. The stakes are higher. And there's an actual kid now, one whom I imagine would suffer right alongside Hunter if he were hurting. If *I* hurt him.

Which I won't, I vow. *Not again.*

I pull back the slightest bit. "See you tomorrow?"

He nods and kisses my forehead, one hand wrapped around the back of my neck. "I can't promise I won't text you a hundred times between now and then."

"You don't like talking but you like texting?"

Laughing a little, he says, "I like everything when it comes to you, Mer."

It occurs to me, as I drive back to Gran's house, that I'm not just looking forward to seeing Hunter again. I'm looking forward to whatever comes next, too.

For once, there's nothing looming over me. No deadlines. No meetings. No stressful schedules or client quotas or emails to answer. For the first time in I don't know how long, my future is entirely unknown. New York Merritt would have been terrified of that.

But now? All I feel is *free*.

EIGHTEEN

Merritt

MY CONFIDENCE in spending time alone with Isabelle lasts until six a.m. when I wake up in a sweaty panic.

What was I thinking?!

I don't know what to do with her. Not without Hunter. What if I accidentally say the wrong thing, like bring up an inappropriate topic for an eight-year-old?

I mean, I don't even know what topics *are* appropriate for an eight-year-old.

Like, what if I accidentally drop the bomb that Santa's not real?

Why that would come up, I have no idea. Isabelle may not even believe in Santa. Do eight-year-olds still believe in Santa? Somehow I can't see Hunter keeping that particular tradition. But what if he does, and what if I tell her, and what if she cries and hates me, and Hunter tells me this will never work between us because I ruined Christmas?

I head to the kitchen to make coffee, my thoughts still spiraling. If Isabelle doesn't have a good time, I could ruin everything. And I *really* don't want to ruin everything.

Finally, I get completely desperate and call the one person in my life who just might be able to help me.

"What's wrong?" Eloise demands when she answers on the fourth ring. I definitely woke her up.

"I need help."

There's a pause. A long enough one to make me irritated because it's not like me asking for help is enough to stun my sister into silence.

"Are you there?"

Eloise sputters. "I just … I've never heard you utter those words before. I was taking a moment to process."

Okay, so maybe me asking for help IS enough to make my chattiest sister swallow her tongue. Whatever.

"I need to know what to do with a kid for a few hours." Or more. Maybe it's going to be all day. I start to sweat, pacing the tiny kitchen.

"Like … babysitting?"

"Yeah, kind of." Only with stakes that feel much higher.

"Do you know what time it is here?" Eloise asks, sounding irritated for the first time.

Outside, the light has the diffused gray, dreamlike quality of pre-dawn. Which would make it practically the middle of the night on the west coast.

"I'm sorry. I just … didn't know who else to call."

This earns me another pause, and I'm not sure if I'm more irritated with Eloise for being shocked or with myself for being so closed off that a phone call asking for help is so shocking.

"And why would you think to call *me*?" Eloise asks, then yawns loudly.

"I met Naomi, and she said Liam comes over a lot to be with Jake. I thought maybe you have some fresh experience with this kind of thing."

When she still says nothing, I pull the phone away from my ear to make sure the call didn't drop. Nope. Still going. "I guess I thought maybe with you dating Jake—"

"I'm not dating Jake," she snaps.

"Well, yeah. I figured with all his moping, y'all must have broken up before you left, but it was pretty obvious there was something going on—"

"Nothing's going on."

Where Jake turned into a veritable Eeyore after the breakup, my sister apparently turned into a hedgehog. Or maybe a porcupine. I'm not sure which is pricklier, but whichever it is, that one is Lo.

"Fine. You're not dating. But my powers of deduction lead me to believe you spent time with Liam, and I really need advice." I pause, and Eloise still doesn't say anything, so I pull out the big guns. "I'm desperate, Lo."

It's easier than I thought it would be to confess my complete ineptitude. Maybe all these years I held things together, I could have just been falling apart like everyone else and it would have been totally fine. I actually feel weirdly relieved.

"Wow. This is … a surprising turn of events."

"Yeah, yeah. Rub it in. But *later*. Now, I need you to tell me what to do."

"Merritt, I have full confidence you can handle whatever child you're watching. You're good at *everything* without even trying."

"I am not," I say quietly, but she's still going, clearly not hearing me.

"Just use common sense. You'll figure it out. This isn't so hard."

"I appreciate your vote of confidence, but you're clearly underestimating my lack of experience here. What if I break her? Or accidentally spill the beans about the birds and the bees?"

There is a snorting sound I'm pretty sure is a laugh on the other end of the line. "You aren't going to break her. And no one calls it the birds and the bees anymore. Plus, why would you be talking about sex with a kid?"

"I wouldn't!"

"Okayyyyy. Does this have anything to do with a man?" she asks.

"What man?" Now who's the queen of denial?

Me. It's me.

"Because Sadie told me about turd-face Simon. Good riddance, as far as I'm concerned. Also, I'm sorry. But he's the worst."

"Yes. He is."

"I'm trying to plan something I can mail him that's not quite anthrax but might make his hair fall out."

Wow. Heartache apparently gives Eloise an edge.

"You sound *way* too much like Sadie."

"We're planning it together."

I shouldn't feel a stab of jealousy, some remnant of years past when I had to be the mature one, the sister who acted like a mother while our actual mother fell apart. Which often resulted in Lo and Sadie ganging up against me.

But right now isn't the time to examine all of my sister issues. I have more pressing, current issues. Primarily an issue named Isabelle, who will arrive in a few hours.

"Back to how to do this kid thing."

"I'm getting the sense this is about more than babysitting."

Now, I'm the one who's silent. Maybe confessing one weakness per decade is my limit. Not that liking Hunter is a *weakness*, per se, but weakness and vulnerability feel remarkably similar.

"Just tell me how to make a kid like me, Lo. Please? While also being a responsible authority figure."

"You know what?" Eloise says, yawning again. "As much as I'm *very* intrigued by this whole conversation, I'm going back to bed."

"What am I supposed to do?"

"Google it."

And then my baby sister hangs up on me.

TURNS OUT, I didn't need to worry about what to do with Isabelle, who is feeling much better and has more energy than my sisters and me put together. She came with a bag full of board games, three books, her bathing suit ("In case we have an unseasonably warm day," she said), an array of snacks, and enough words to carry the conversation for the both of us. I swear, she's more like eight going on eighteen or maybe even twenty-eight.

"I'll be right over there," Hunter said at the start of the day, pointing before giving Isabelle a kiss on the forehead and tromping across the path to the main house in his work boots. I did my best not to stare at his butt as he walked away.

Now, we're on our third game, and I've been annihilated and humiliated by Isabelle in all of them. Which is not sitting well with me. Clearly, island living is making my brain dull.

"Are you letting me win?" she demands, after beating me for the second time in some game involving castle-building, dice rolling, and using disaster cards to wipe out the other person's resources.

"I would never," I say, even if it's tempting to let her think I'm doing just that. It's pretty embarrassing to lose a game when the suggested player age listed on the box is seven. "You just kept getting all the tornado cards."

"I did," she says, smiling sweetly. Then, as though remembering the existence of sportsmanship, she holds out her hand. "Good game. I'll clean up. Do you have any sandwiches?"

"The one thing I do have is sandwiches. I've got ham or turkey and a few kinds of cheese. Also some really juicy tomatoes."

I have a real weakness for tomatoes. And I swear, the very best ones I've had are grown on this island. Ms. Sylvia has a little produce stand I'd all but forgotten about until I passed it on the way back from Hunter's yesterday. I grabbed maybe more than I can eat. Maybe. I've been known to eat tomatoes like apples, which Sadie likes to tell me is disgusting. She doesn't know what she's missing.

"Do you have mayonnaise?" Isabelle asks, then makes a face. "The real stuff, not the fake kind. Daddy bought some weird fake kind. It was gross."

"I *only* use the real stuff." I lift an eyebrow. "Tomato sandwich?"

"*Please.*"

She grins, and I can see where one of her top teeth is growing in a little crooked, overlapping with another. It only makes her smile cuter.

I wouldn't expect a kid to like tomato sandwiches, but then, I did. I've always been a tomato girl.

I've got bread and plates on the counter when Isabelle joins me in the kitchen. "How do you feel about being a big sister?" I ask as I slice through the biggest tomato. It's juicy and crisp, and my mouth is watering as I sprinkle salt over the slices.

Isabelle doesn't answer right away. It's the first time she's really been quiet all morning.

"Okay, I guess," she says finally.

"You've been flying solo for a while. It will be an adjustment. Would Hunter—would your dad like a sandwich?"

She smiles again as she sits down at the small table, facing me. "Yes. But maybe *two* sandwiches. Do you have brothers or sisters?"

"Sisters. Two of them. I'm the oldest. But we're a little closer in age so I can't remember a time being an only child."

"Do you get along?"

It's my turn to consider how to answer, and I do so while laying out slices of white bread on the counter. I turn and pull the mayonnaise out of the fridge.

"We didn't always. I mean, we always had each other's backs when it came down to it. But we fought a lot."

"How about now? Mama says even if I don't like my baby sister, we'll be glad when we're older. But I think that's because Mama and Aunt Cici are so close even though Cici lives in Atlanta. They're always on the phone."

I try to remember Cassidy's sister. Cassidy and Cici—hearing those names together is familiar, but I can't remember details about her or even a face.

"My sister Sadie just came to visit. And I talked to my youngest sister, Eloise, this morning."

I'm not sure why I feel the need to prove my sisterly worth to Isabelle. I'd rather be honest, even if it's not the prettiest picture. Even if I'm talking to a child. I'm sort of over having the kind of life that appears picture-perfect.

"But we're not very close. I wish we were closer," I confess, not realizing how true it is until the words leave my mouth.

I wish, when I called Eloise this morning, I'd been honest about Hunter. That she'd been honest with me about Jake. My sisters and I feel a little like a string of islands whose connecting bridges have washed out. I wonder what it might take to rebuild them.

I sit down across from Isabelle and slide her plate over. Her eyes light up. "Can we eat now?"

"Yup. I didn't finish making your dad's yet. Didn't want it to get soggy while we ate. We can walk it over in a few minutes if that's okay."

Isabelle has already taken a bite, tomato juice running down her chin. She uses her tongue to get it rather than a napkin. I approve.

She sets her sandwich down suddenly. "What if I don't like her?" The words are muffled because her mouth is still full.

"Your sister?"

She nods, and I consider while licking tomato juice from my wrist. Do I go with honesty? Or a pat answer that's what I should say? I vote honesty.

"You might not like her. Especially at first. Babies cry and poop"—Isabelle giggles at this—"and they need a lot of attention. Your mom's attention, especially. It will change things," I tell her, hoping being *this* honest is okay.

"Mama says I have to be her helper."

Her nose scrunches up in an adorable way. I don't smile because I know she's being serious. I remember how I hated it when I was serious as a kid and adults laughed. Like once, in a mock trial for school we did in a real courtroom, I asked the very best question cross-examining a witness. I remember thinking that if my life were a movie, this would be that dramatic moment where the heroine solved the case.

Instead, all the adults laughed. Even the judge. I still don't know why, mostly because I forgot my questions and Mom forgot to record the mock trial. But I still remember the feeling of hot anger swirled with shame.

No way will I be the kind of adult who makes a serious kid feel stupid.

"I think you'd make a great helper. Moms do need lots of help, and I'm sure your mom would appreciate you being so responsible."

"How do *you* know I'm responsible?" This comes out like a challenge or demand, and I'm beginning to see just how sore a subject this is.

I tip my chin toward the coffee table, where the game we played is put away, the box stacked neatly on top of the others. "It's in the little things," I tell her. "I can see it. I know I'd be glad to have you as my helper."

She perks up, straightening in her chair. "Really?"

"Yup."

"Cool. So you've got two sisters. Do you want a lot of kids?"

I almost inhale a slice of tomato and definitely inhale some pepper because I have to set my sandwich down as I hack up a lung. At least it gives me time to think about my answer.

Honesty, I remind myself.

But what *is* the right answer? I wanted kids. Then I didn't. Now, I maybe do again?

"I never planned on having kids," I say, relieved when she nods like this is a perfectly acceptable answer. "I mean, when

I was little, I thought I would. Then I focused on my career and ... yeah."

"Daddy says you have a big important city job."

Did he, now? I'd love to know what other little tidbits Hunter mentioned, but it feels wrong to ask.

"I do. Or, I did. My focus was more on work, not on being a mom. Not that there's anything wrong with being a mom. It just wasn't part of my plan."

I should add something about plans changing. Maybe even tell Isabelle that spending time with her makes me think I *could* be a mom someday. But before I can say anything else, Isabelle slides her plate forward and drops her folded arms onto the table. "That was yummy."

A tiny beat of regret pulses through me, an opportunity lost.

I take the last bite of my sandwich and lick the juice from my fingers. "I want another," I confess.

"Maybe we should eat Daddy's and not tell him." Isabelle's grin has a naughty edge to it.

Remind me not to get on this child's bad side.

"How about we make more and carry them over to the house to eat with your dad this time? We don't have to tell him we're on our second sandwich. Our secret?"

"Our secret," she promises. "But you should make him two. He eats a lot."

We don't get the chance to walk over the sandwiches because Hunter knocks and then walks right in as I'm spreading the mayonnaise. The sight of him after only a few hours makes my pulse race. He gives me a grin that's fast and flirty before turning to Isabelle with an entirely different expression.

"Hey, ladybug," he says, ruffling Isabelle's hair. I don't miss the way he does so carefully, not making knots or a bird's nest. It's just a soft, playful touch.

Thoughtful man, I think. *Even in the details. Maybe especially in the details.*

"We made tomato sandwiches," she says and pats the chair next to her. "Sit."

"Yes, ma'am."

Hunter smiles at me as he sits, and I wonder if I'll ever stop feeling this fluttery sensation in my belly. As I pass out the plates, Isabelle makes a face, and I realize she's trying to wink. It's only clear when she mouths, *Our secret.*

I give her a quick nod. Hunter may not know what we're talking about, but he doesn't miss the silent exchange. I catch sight of a grin before he takes a big bite.

He closes his eyes as he chews, making a deep hum of appreciation that stirs feelings in me I don't exactly want to have with Isabelle sitting here.

"This is delicious," he says. "Haven't had a good tomato sandwich in ... I don't know how long. Perfect tomatoes."

"They're from Ms. Sylvia's," I tell him. "I couldn't help myself."

Hunter nods, and without thinking about it, I reach out and pluck a tiny tomato seed from his beard. He goes still, and I know my cheeks are starting to flush.

"Sorry. You had a seed." I hold up my fingertip because now the seed is stuck there.

"Blow it off and make a wish," he says, his dark eyes holding mine.

Isabelle giggles. "That's eyelashes, Daddy. Not tomato seeds."

"You're right. But maybe tomato seeds need their own tradition. I'll make a wish."

And then his hand grasps my wrist, holding my hand

steady as he leans forward and eats the tomato seed right off the tip of my finger.

Okay—this moment is *one hundred percent* not one we should be having with Isabelle right here watching. At least, based on how my body reacts to his lips and tongue on my fingertip, with all its millions of nerve endings firing at once and shouting *MORE! MORE! MORE!*

But he was quick and goes right back to eating. Isabelle laughs like it's the funniest thing she's ever seen, not like I'm over here completely melting down from the hot flame of desire Hunter just stoked.

"Daddy, ew!" Isabelle says. Then adds, "What did you wish for?"

Hunter's gaze meets mine, and his eyes are part amusement, part a sort of smug pride because clearly, he can see what effect he has on me.

"I can't say it out loud," Hunter says, and the look in his eyes sharpens. I can almost feel his gaze on my skin like a caress. "Or it won't come true. And I really, *really* want this one to come true."

NINETEEN

Hunter

IT TAKES no time at all for Merritt to cozy herself into every corner of my very ordinary life. Bringing lunches over to the beach house which we share right in the middle of a half-tiled bathroom or partially refinished floor while we peruse Lo's design boards for decor and paint colors. Sitting on the porch swing, waiting for me to finish work and give her an end-of-the-workday kiss. Coming out to my place where she plays with Banjo and the dogs and does her best to beat Isabelle at board games. Or my favorite—walking with me on the beach, our feet bare, our fingers laced together.

I haven't let her inside my house yet, but she's in my heart, which is far more dangerous.

As I maneuver my truck into the crowded restaurant parking lot, my phone pings with a text. "Wanna check that?"

Merritt swipes my phone from the cup holder and shoots me the kind of grin that makes me want to pause everything and kiss her right on the mouth. "Are we already at the level of trusting each other with our messages?" she asks.

Yes. At least, I am.

To be honest, I don't know what level we're at. Are there levels now or is that a joke?

The last time I dated, I was in high school—basically a child. For all I know, they've added actual dating levels to go alongside the terribly cliché baseball analogy with the physical stuff. If so, I'm at whatever level makes me a total sucker for Merritt. The kind of sucker who wants to spend every possible second in her company even while I'm simultaneously terrified I'll blink and realize it ended, she's gone, and I'm alone again.

Merritt is an overachiever. Driven. Talented. She's obviously in an in-between place right now, but I'm desperate to be a part of whatever's next for her. If she has an inkling what that is, I don't know about it.

But it can't just be talking to me while I lay tile.

"You can check my phone anytime," I say, though her face is already bent to my screen.

"Dante says he and Jasmine got us a table because it's crowded. Have you been to this restaurant?"

"Nah. I don't come out here much, aside from getting supplies."

Out here being Savannah, where we're meeting Dante and his girlfriend for dinner at some trendy place where I'll probably feel out of place in my worn jeans and flannel shirt. Not that I care what a bunch of trendy hipsters think. I care more about college basketball, and to be clear, I do not care at ALL about that.

Also, from what Isabelle told me today, flannel is what the trendy hipsters are wearing now. How *she* knows this, I don't know. But—take that, hipsters! You aligned your style to mine.

I shift my truck into park and look Merritt's way. My phone is still in her hands, but she's staring out the window, eyes locked on the restaurant.

"Hey, you okay?" I ask.

"You would tell me if my outfit looked stupid, right?" She looks down at her clothes and frowns.

I raise an eyebrow. She's wearing a dress. It's blue and … it's a dress. Her feet are in sandals. It all looks nice on her. That's about as far as my understanding of women's fashion goes.

What does she have to be worried about?

"This looks like something Eloise would wear," she says. "Doesn't it?"

Her deep blue dress *is* a little more colorful than what Merritt normally wears, but honestly, I like this better than the muted blacks and grays she brought from New York. She looks more like herself this way.

I shake my head. "Nah. It would need pelicans on it for Eloise to wear it."

This at least earns a chuckle. "Really, though—it's okay?"

I'd forgotten it's possible for Merritt to be insecure. Even when we were kids she had this solid sense of self, a confidence I envied. A few times, I saw the cracks like this, where the shell of strength broke just a little to reveal a very human sense of self-doubt.

I brush my fingertips down her arm, and she stills, looking up at me with those ocean-blue eyes. "Mer, you look perfect. The color does amazing things for your eyes. Are you sure there isn't something else going on up here?" I tap a finger to my temple.

Her shoulders drop the tiniest bit. "There's nothing going on. At least, there shouldn't be." She breathes out a little huff. "I never felt insecure in New York. I owned every room I walked into. I could intimidate people with a single word, even just a single look. So why does this feel so scary?"

I tilt my head, studying her. I have a few ideas about why, but I'm not sure how to phrase them without overstepping. Things are still so new between us, and it seems highly possible for me—a man not good with words anyway—to say the wrong thing.

"You should just say whatever it is," Merritt says softly. "Your thinking is very loud."

"I was just thinking . . . maybe you're butting up against memories, against past versions of yourself, and it's disconcerting. With all you've been through lately—it's enough to have anyone feeling a little off-kilter."

She nods slowly. "That's very insightful."

"I have my moments."

"You have a lot of them."

I can tell she has more to say, so I stay put. Making Dante wait a few minutes is the least of my concerns right now.

Merritt finally looks at me and holds my gaze. "On Oakley, it feels like there's more at stake. Which is weird, because there was always *so much* at stake in New York. It was high stakes, lots of money on the line, big deals. But it was never *personal*. Here though …" She chokes out a laugh. "Honestly, it feels like every single thing is personal. My heart is so tangled up in this place."

I sure hope it is. Specifically, I hope her heart is way too tangled up with mine to consider going back to that high stakes, New York life.

I hold out my hand, palm up, and she slips her fingers into mine. "I've got you." I give her hand a tiny squeeze, and she squeezes back—hard enough to cut off circulation in my fingertips. "And your outfit does not look stupid. In fact," I say, leaning closer, "that dress makes it very hard for me not to do things like *this*."

My mouth finds hers, and we continue the conversation—this time without words. Only, I know the things my lips are saying—*you're so beautiful, stay, I love you*—but I don't know what Merritt is saying back.

She pulls away after not nearly enough time, tugging a loose strand of hair from where it's caught on my beard. Smiling, she says, "Don't we need to go? They're waiting."

I let my lips trail over her jaw, a little ways down her neck, and back to her lips. "They're fine."

This time, when she pulls back, it's all the way to the door of the car with one firm hand on my chest. "I really want your friends to like me. Making them wait isn't the best first impression."

I give her an easy smile, then climb out, meeting her in front of the truck where we lace our fingers together and walk toward the entrance. "Jasmine likes everyone, so you don't need to worry about her. And you've already met Dante, and he thought you were great."

"Even though I wanted to mess with you about my tile choices?"

"Pretty sure that's *why* he likes you so much." I hold open the door. "Come on. Let's go make them uncomfortable with insufferable PDA."

She laughs as she walks inside, brushing up against me as she does. On purpose, I'm sure, based on the little smirk tugging at her mouth. "You sure we wouldn't be making *you* uncomfortable?"

I pull her toward me, tucking her under my arm as I glance around for Dante. He waves from a table near the back. His grin tells me he knows exactly why we were late. "Nah. I think Frank desensitized me with his TikToks. All of Oakley has already seen us kissing anyway. Might as well expand our reach."

Dante and Jasmine greet us with hugs, and Merritt scoots her chair closer to mine as we sit down, gripping my hand under the table. It's challenging to flip through a menu one-handed, but I don't mind.

"I heard you tried to prank this guy," Jasmine says to Merritt. "Something about Versailles tile?"

I groan. "Am I ever going to hear the end of this?"

"No," Dante and Jasmine say at the same time.

Beside me, Merritt laughs and releases her grip on my hand, just a little. "You're so fun to mess with," she says, ruffling my hair.

I pretend to be annoyed, but I don't think I'm fooling anyone.

The longer we're there, the more Merritt relaxes, talking naturally with Jasmine, laughing at Dante's bad jokes. I was mostly joking about the PDA, but I find myself wanting to touch her anyway. Not just holding her hand but tracing her palm with my fingertips, curving my hand around her knee, skimming my fingers across her bare shoulders, pressing my lips against her temple. Each time, she leans into my touch like she's hungry for it, like it's as much a revelation for her as it is for me.

We were meant for this. For each other.

"We're going to the bathroom," Jasmine says, then points a stern finger at Dante. "And don't even consider making a comment about ladies always going together."

Dante holds up both hands, and I find myself wanting to

do the same. Jasmine is sweet but not *soft*. Reminds me a little bit of Merritt in that way.

"I would never," Dante says. But the second they're out of earshot, he leans across the table. "They do always go in packs though, right?"

"I'm not saying a word."

He laughs. "You shaved."

"I trimmed." I took scissors and then a razor to my beard today, and am still getting used to the feel of it. Merritt hasn't once complained about my overgrown beard, but I saw the chapped skin on her cheeks and neck last week—a byproduct of making out like teenagers. I hope this shorter trim will result in less beard burn on her pretty skin.

Do I plan to test this out tonight? Absolutely I do.

Dante kicks me under the table, his grin wide. "So, things have gone from zero to trimming your mountain man beard for her. From sabotaging your tile to making out in the parking lot."

I glare, and when Dante points to the window with a perfect view of my truck, I huff out a breath.

"Jas and I had bets going on how fogged up the windows would get."

"Shut up. Not like you and Jasmine are any better."

Dante's grin is one hundred percent smug. "Oh, we're much worse. But back to you. This seems to be moving fast for a man who hasn't been on a date since his divorce."

I shrug, but I can't really deny it. "I already loved her once. Call it muscle memory."

"You were sixteen," Dante says. "It's not exactly the same thing. You think you loved her back then?"

He looks doubtful. I'm not. No, it wasn't the same as now. But it was more than I ever felt for Cass. I slid right back into these feelings the minute I stopped resisting.

Which makes me wonder if I ever stopped loving Merritt at all. Only now, what I feel is deeper, brighter, more solid.

I only wish I knew if it's the same for her.

"I'm just saying, I already know her. It feels fast, but we didn't start from scratch. And we're still moving slow in a lot of ways."

Like only kissing. And never talking about the future.

The first is just fine—I'm a patient man and there's something about prolonging that I really like. But the second ... well, I just don't want it to come back to bite me.

"So, she's staying then?" Dante asks. When my shoulders drop the tiniest bit, Dante's expression shifts to something more like pity. "Aw, man. You don't know, do you? Are you going to talk about it?"

"Of course," I snap, and I'm glad the women return when they do.

I watch Merritt cross the restaurant, laughing at something Jasmine says. Merritt's eyes spark with more life than they did when she first arrived on Oakley. That day on the beach when she twisted her ankle, she was a different woman.

Surely that means she'll want to stay.

I want to believe that she will. But Dante's right. We still haven't talked about it. We've danced around the subject plenty. Hinted at a future that includes us both—a future I'm assuming would be here on Oakley. I won't leave Isabelle, which means my life is unequivocally here. But until Merritt says something concrete, I'll be a man clinging to hope like a castaway holding onto a piece of wreckage while the waves roll by.

A part of me worries this is all wishful thinking. That not addressing this head-on is just a way to keep the fantasy alive a little bit longer. But what I'm really, really good at is not talking. Avoiding. Bottling things up and shutting down when the emotions get too intense.

"Miss me?" Merritt asks, bending for a quick kiss before taking her seat.

I nod, suddenly choked up at the thought of missing her for real if she goes. "Always."

"I want to be this woman when I grow up," Jasmine says, nudging Dante. "Did you know she's the one who picks those giant images in Times Square?"

I glance Merritt's way. *I* didn't know that.

"Yeah?" Dante asks.

"It's not a big deal. I just broker the contracts," Merritt says, and when Jasmine raises one eyebrow slowly, Merritt sighs. "Fine. It's kind of a big deal. Literally big, I mean. Some of those things are like ten stories high. Pick the wrong campaign image, and you've got half a building's worth of a mistake."

Merritt pulls out her phone, turning it to show us some of the ad campaigns she helped bring to life. Dante and Jasmine seem fascinated and impressed. I am too.

I'm also hit square in the chest with all my fears about not being enough, about Oakley not being enough. I mean, Merritt helps make skyscraper-high ad campaigns. The largest structure on Oakley is four stories because the preservation society has strict building codes.

These images feel like a very literal representation of the two paths set before Merritt. I can see from the glances Dante shoots my way that he sees it too.

Me and Oakley: small life.

New York: big life.

When my phone buzzes, and I see Cassidy calling, I'm relieved. I've been making a point to keep my interactions with Cassidy to a minimum now that Merritt is a part of my life. I remember my mom's tone when I cut out on dinner early, and I do have *some* sense, even if I'm rusty at this whole dating thing. But I need a minute away. I need to breathe. And with Cass being pregnant, it's an easy excuse.

"I should take this," I tell Merritt, showing her the screen. "Could be baby news."

"Of course."

I slip outside, taking a deep breath of warm night air as I answer. "Cass, are you okay? What's going on?"

"Geez, why does everyone respond that way whenever I call?" Cassidy asks. "I'm fine. Everything is fine." She sniffs and then sniffs again.

"You don't sound fine."

"I mean, *physically* everything is fine. The baby is still staying put. Do you have a second to talk?"

I look back toward the restaurant, hesitating.

"It will only take a minute. And it has to do with Isabelle," Cassidy says quickly, laying down the trump card she knows she can always play.

I sigh and drop onto a bench in front of the restaurant. "Fine."

"Your parents just brought Isabelle by the hospital. We had a nice visit."

"Okay. I'm glad."

Cassidy is quiet for a long moment. "Hunter, Izzy told me she's been spending a lot of time with Merritt. She said you're on a date right now, actually."

I'm on instant alert. Cassidy knows a lot of what went on between Merritt and me as kids. Not all, but enough to inspire definite feelings about Mer. Not the good kind.

I haven't brought up Merritt lately, mostly because Cass and I do a pretty good job of staying out of each other's personal lives aside from Isabelle. Plus, I figured she'd hear it from the town anyway. Or Frank.

"Yeah, which is why I only have a few minutes. And she's spent some time with Isabelle. But I wouldn't say a *lot*. They're together a few afternoons a week after school. My parents aren't always available and neither are yours. I have to work," I remind her.

I'm not trying to make Cassidy feel bad. It's not like she wants to be on bed rest. But being a full-time single dad while working isn't the easiest thing in terms of logistics.

"That's not how Isabelle made it sound."

Now I'm wishing I stayed inside the restaurant. I definitely don't want to have this conversation right now. "Isabelle is only eight years old. She also thinks Bigfoot might actually exist."

"Hunter, are you and Merritt dating seriously?"

"Yeah," I say simply. "We are."

Another long pause. "I guess I'm feeling like maybe you should have talked to me before letting our daughter spend so much time with someone else."

"Cass, you and Adam were practically engaged before you let me know how serious things were. This thing with Merritt is still pretty new."

"But not so new that she hasn't spent time with my daughter?"

"*Our* daughter."

Cassidy is a reasonable, level-headed person, and nothing about this conversation, from her tone to the way she's talking in circles, feels reasonable. It reminds me a lot of the talks we had right before the divorce. I'd really love to not relive that time in my life right now. One emotional minefield at a time is about as much as I can handle.

"Look, Cass. When Isabelle is with Merritt, I'm there too.

We're all spending time together. I don't know why this is a problem."

"See, that's not what Isabelle said either. She said she and Merritt have secrets. *Secrets,* Hunter. You know the rules on that."

I do. One of Cassidy's big things she learned in some baby book or blog was that we should teach Isabelle not to have secrets with other kids or adults. Surprises—yes. Secrets—no.

"I trust Merritt. And I'm sure she didn't realize. She doesn't have kids yet, so this is new to her."

"That's the other thing," Cassidy says, and I can almost feel her winding up for a big pitch. "Isabelle said Merritt told her she didn't ever want to have kids."

I expected a fastball but got a curveball instead. I literally have no words to respond to this statement.

Merritt doesn't want kids?

The thing is—I know Merritt wants kids. *Wanted kids,* a voice reminds me. We last talked about that when we were starry-eyed kids ourselves. But she's been great with Isabelle. More than great, to be honest. This is like the game of telephone, but the grown-up edition. Cass tells me something Izzy told her that Merritt told her. Something clearly got lost in translation.

Didn't it?

Because I am a package deal. I can't imagine Merritt not knowing that. Maybe she doesn't want to have kids of her *own?* Which would be ... maybe disappointing. But fine, I guess. I wasn't even thinking about that kind of future yet. Right now, I just want Merritt to stay.

And now ... Cass has put my head in a weird place.

"I'm sure that's not exactly what she meant," I say, really

hoping that's the case. "I mean, we're getting Isabelle's version of the conversation."

"I don't know how you misunderstand something like that."

"I'll figure it out, but it's not your concern. Isabelle is safe with me and with Merritt. Is there anything else you need?"

My voice is sharper than I intend, and when I hear a muffled sound on the other end of the phone, I know it's a sob. I'd feel bad about it, but I'm already feeling enough other things.

"I'm being irrational and petty, aren't I?" Her voice is watery.

"No," I say, even if she is. A little bit, anyway. "You're a concerned mom."

"I'm also a concerned *ex*. I worry about you, Hunter."

"Well, you can stop," I say, standing as I see Dante and Jasmine exit the restaurant, Merritt following right behind. "I need to go. Call me if you need anything. But Merritt isn't up for discussion."

So stay out of my dating life.

"Everything okay, man?" Dante asks as I'm sliding my phone back into my pocket.

"Baby news?" Merritt slips her arm through mine, her expression hopeful. And, maybe slightly jealous?

Little does she know, there is absolutely zero to be jealous about.

But she's right to be concerned because it feels like Cassidy just dropped a bomb in my lap. It's a mess of different colored wires and a countdown clock, and my arms are duct-taped behind my back. Though duct tape or not, it's not like I'd have the first idea how to diffuse the thing anyway.

"Nah. She just had some questions about Isabelle. It's fine."

"You're good?" Merritt asks, her eyes narrowing the slightest bit as she studies me.

"So good." I lean down and kiss her, crossing my fingers that the distraction will keep her from seeing right through my lie.

TWENTY

Merritt

"THE BIGGEST THING," Sadie is saying, with the kind of authority she in NO way deserves as the sister most averse to relationships, "is that you make the decision to stay on *your* terms. Because of *you*, not because of a man."

"That's actually good advice."

I wish it weren't good advice, because then I could give Sadie a hard time, maybe tease her about not having the experience to back up her words. I also wish Eloise had stayed on the three-way video call long enough to weigh in. But the moment I mentioned needing relationship advice, she suddenly had research she needed to do at the library. *Urgent* research.

Research being another way of saying she can't handle talking about relationships, because Eloise is still avoiding her feelings for a certain grumpy lawyer who lives next to me.

But I'll count this call as a win. It's the first three-way video chat we've had in I don't know how long. All spurred on by Isabelle asking me if I was close with my sisters and me realizing that no—I'm not. But I *want* to be.

This call was a less than auspicious start, what with Eloise hanging up rather than opening up to us, but it's a *start*.

"Don't sound so surprised," Sadie says. "I've probably dated more than both you and Lo put together."

"*First* dates, maybe. How about *relationships*? That's where a man and woman make a commitment to—"

Sadie pretends to sneeze loudly. "Sorry. Must be allergic to something you said."

I shake my head and prop the phone up on the dresser, angled in such a way that Sadie can't see what I'm doing. Which is: running my hands over the paintbrushes Hunter bought me.

I've been treating these art supplies like a twelve-step program. The first few days, I just stared at the box in the corner from a distance. Next, I got close and actually looked at everything.

Hunter did *good*. He picked out the nice kind of synthetic brushes where the bristles don't fall out as you're painting. The kind of paint with higher quality pigment for vibrant colors and better mixing. Even the canvases are the heavy-duty kind I used to use.

Did he remember? Or did he just Google it or ask an employee for help?

Probably the second, but I prefer thinking it was the first.

A memory washes over me. I'm standing at my easel on Gran's sun porch, paintbrush in hand. Hunter is standing behind me, his arms wrapped around my waist and his head resting on my shoulder.

"Go bolder," he says softly, his breath tickling my cheek, making me think about anything but paint. "Add more red."

"Red? When have you ever seen a red sky?"

"It won't look red when it blends with the other colors. Just trust me."

"But I want it to look real."

His grip tightens, his lips moving close to my ear. "Do you want it to look real? Or feel *real?"*

I shake myself back into the moment, where Sadie is still on the phone, and I'm still staring at this box of supplies.

After looking closely, the next step was talking to them. Yeah—I know it's ridiculous. I don't even care. Oakley Merritt embraces talking to inanimate objects. If research shows that plants grow better with human words, maybe talking to my supplies will help me create better. Whenever I get to that step.

Fine. I'll admit it. Talking to tubes of paint and brushes is not a thing. But it hasn't stopped me from murmuring sweet nothings to them.

Today is the first time I moved on to actual physical contact—touching the bristles of each brush, holding every tube of paint in my hands and feeling the familiar weight. I even put one canvas on the easel Hunter brought. It's ready and waiting *just in case*. My fingers are practically twitching with the need to put a brush in my hands and fill the blank canvas with color.

They're also twitching with the need to touch Hunter, who has been suddenly and intensely busy the last few days. He still has Isabelle, which means carpool lines and activities. There's also some issue I didn't understand with insulation in the crawl space under the house. That is about the only place I won't follow Hunter while he works—because of spiders and snakes and who knows what else that might be creepy crawling under there. Between Isabelle and the insulation, I haven't seen much of him in a few days.

The timing actually couldn't be better for a breather. Things with Hunter went from awkward, because of all the past stuff hanging between us, to making up for lost time with our mouths. But we've had very little discussion about our current reality, much less about what the future might hold. It's been nice in some ways. But we can't ignore the elephant in the room forever.

Then we had that double date.

Dinner itself was fine. Great, actually. I never liked Simon's friends so it was refreshing to enjoy Dante and Jasmine. Conversation flowed. I enjoyed Hunter beside me, always touching me or glancing my way.

Things were perfect right up until Cassidy called. I don't think Hunter and Cassidy still harbor romantic feelings for each other, but their pasts are tangled up enough to carry over into the present. Maybe too much? I can't tell if I'm being irrational or if maybe they need to shore up some firmer boundaries. Rational or not, it doesn't stop the uncomfortable and insistent whine of jealousy.

I get it—they were married. They share Isabelle, who is an amazing human. There's a whole history there, one that badly hurt me, even if Hunter still doesn't know *how* badly. It's itchy and uncomfortable and something I'll absolutely have to bring up at some point. Or just get over.

Because it's not going away. The past has been written.

But did Hunter *really* have to spend ten minutes on the phone with his ex in the middle of our date? I mean, she wasn't popping out a baby that *minute* or anything. I saw Dante and Jasmine exchange a look, so I know I wasn't the only one who thought it was odd.

Okay, and maybe slightly rude.

On the ride home, before Hunter dropped me off, he seemed distracted and a little distant. Not cold. Not even cool. Just not fully present.

I've seen this with him before, his need to pull away when he has a lot on his mind, so I figure the space this week is probably good for us both. If we're really doing this relationship—and more and more, I REALLY want to do this—I have to make some decisions.

"Are you still with me?" Sadie asks, squinting at the phone screen. "What are you messing with?"

"Nothing." I snatch the phone off the dresser and move to the living area, holding the camera close enough to my face she can probably see my every pore—but not the art supplies behind me.

"Anyway," I say brightly, flopping down on the couch. "Any suggestions for sorting out my emotions? Like, how do I separate wanting to stay for me and wanting to stay for Hunter? *Me* isn't very trustworthy right now. Because *me* wants Hunter."

"Like Cookie Monster wants cookies?"

I snort. "Maybe a little more than that."

Sadie shoots me a shocked expression. "Really? Because Cookie Monster really, *really* wants cookies."

And I really, REALLY want Hunter. Enough that I'm considering moving permanently to this small island I never thought I'd set foot on again in my life.

But is Hunter the whole reason I want to stay? *That* is the question.

"What are you going to do about Cassidy?" Sadie asks.

That's a quick way to sour my mood. "Ugh. I don't know. I think I'm just being overly jealous and immature. I mean, they're co-parenting, so I'll have to get over it. Or get along. Or at least, not feel weird and possessive."

"Yeah," Sadie says, sounding unconvinced. "But it sounds to me like maybe they need to also revisit how much she relies on Hunter."

"You think?" I ask, feeling validated to hear Sadie echo my concern. I don't have the first clue how to know what's normal for divorced couples. And the last thing I want to do is act like a jealous teenager.

"I do. Just broach the topic. Share what seems off or makes you uncomfortable. It'll be fine."

I hope so. But thinking about Cassidy adds one more tiny doubt or worry adding to a growing pile in my mind. "Is this stupid? I mean, leaving New York City for Oakley Island—that's so ... I don't know. Backwards?"

"There's not some hierarchy of places to live. You weren't happy in New York," Sadie says. "Were you?"

I'm quiet for a moment, letting my mind play back memories of the years I spent in the city. I remember my excitement at first. The magic of New York, the energy of the city. I had a great job and everything was lining up to accomplish all my goals.

Except, now that I'm thinking about it, all my goals were solely career-related. And that's mostly what I remember after the first few months in New York: work. Well, work and Simon. Turns out he wasn't much of a draw after all.

"I thought I was happy," I tell Sadie. "But now I'm not sure."

"So, go back," she says. "Didn't you leave all your stuff in storage? Tie up the loose ends. Sell your stuff or move it down. But see how the city feels now that you've had a taste of something different. You've got to deal with your stuff in storage at some point anyway, unless you want to hemorrhage money for no reason."

"You really think I should go back?"

"I do. You'll either realize the city is your true home, or you'll realize you miss island life more."

I'll miss Hunter if I go. THAT I already know.

But maybe it would help to see the city again. I could handle the things I didn't when I practically ran down here. Maybe being there will give me clarity. I already suspect this will be more of a goodbye tour, but at least going, I'll know for sure. Even thinking about the idea now, a weight lifts off my chest.

"Am I allowed? Like, with the conditions of Gran's estate—can I leave temporarily or does one of us have to be here all the time?"

"I don't know," Sadie says, her eyes going to something off-screen. She frowns, then chuckles. "But I gotta go. Some newb thinks he can get past my firewall. Ask Jake about the will stuff. Bye!"

And then she's gone. Sadie has always been an abrupt hanger-upper, but I've never gotten used to it.

Jake isn't next door—not surprising as it's the middle of a workday. But as I'm walking away from his door, Naomi pulls into the front drive, practically leaping out of her car. She drops her keys and then her purse when she bends to pick them up.

A boy who must be Liam climbs out of the back. If I had to guess, I'd say he's around Isabelle's age, maybe a little younger. He pats his mother's hand, a sweet gesture. Then I catch him rolling his eyes.

I bite back a smile. Not so sweet, then.

"Is Jake not here?" Naomi calls as I approach. When I shake my head, she makes a frustrated growl, staring down at her phone. "I know his car is gone but sometimes he walks home for lunch. Gah!"

"Can I help?" I'll happily return the favor after she helped me pick out clothes for my date.

"He's supposed to watch Liam for me, but I'm running late and need to go."

"I'm headed to his office, actually. If you're comfortable with it, I could walk Liam there. I mean, I know I don't know you that well or anything but—"

"You're Lo's sister," Liam says, like this fact answers all potential questions. "That makes you fine."

Oh, for the world to be so simple.

"Are you sure?" Naomi says, but she's already backing toward her car. "I mean, I normally wouldn't foist him on someone like this, but I knew your grandmother, and I love Lo, and—"

I hold up a hand. "It's fine."

"I appreciate it so much! Thank you!" Naomi practically peels out, oyster shells from the driveway spinning under her tires as she goes.

Liam adjusts his backpack, which isn't a normal kid's backpack but more like one of Sadie's computer bags. "Which sister are you—the oldest or the middle?"

"Oldest. I'm Merritt." I start walking toward the row of businesses on Main Street where Jake's office is located in a small, updated cottage.

"Cool."

Liam isn't chatty or bubbly like Isabelle and I find myself panicking a little about what to say. "Does your uncle Jake watch you a lot?"

"Yes. But he usually doesn't forget. He's been forgetting a lot of things lately." Liam wrinkles his nose. "I'm never falling in love. It makes a mess of your life."

"I can't argue with your logic there."

We walk a few blocks in a silence that starts to feel

comfortable. A stirring somewhere in my midsection fills me with unexpected warmth.

I'm enjoying this. I could do this.

This being a parental-type figure. My feelings have been shifting for a while now, new possibilities rising up and poking through my consciousness. I mean, it's impossible to be with Hunter without thinking about what it would be like to help Hunter with Isabelle. Even to *have kids* with Hunter.

But this sensation is different. This isn't about changing my plans just to make them match Hunter's. This is only about me. About deciding what I want with or without Hunter.

I could be a mom. I could be a great mom.

Not like I know what I'm doing or am, in ANY way, practically equipped right now, but I feel like I've passed some entry-level exam of even wanting to be a parent. I will read the parenting books and listen to the podcasts and do all the things to fill in the gaps of years spent not even considering the idea. And I'll probably screw up. A lot.

But now ... it seems possible. Even like something I *want*.

I hook a hand around Liam's backpack strap, tugging him away from the curb as a car zips past. As soon as it's safe, I let him go, and we cross the intersection together.

I could have this life. Walk these streets with my own kids. With Hunter.

I could. And I don't even need to go back to New York to know I not only *could*, but I *want* to.

I'm so distracted, I almost miss someone calling my name.

"Merritt Markham."

Benedict King saunters toward us, all confidence and easy charm in worn boat shoes and a brand-name polo that screams, *I just stepped off a yacht!* Which, given that Ben owns Oakley Island, might actually be true.

"How's my main man, Liam?" Ben asks as soon as we're close enough. He tousles Liam's hair.

Liam gives him a look that could dry up a succulent, and I fight the urge to laugh.

"I'm good," Liam says, smoothing back his hair. "Uncle Jake forgot me again, so Merritt is walking me to his office."

Ben's eyes lift to mine, offering a smile. "I suspect the forgetfulness won't get better until your sister comes back. The man's got a real bad case."

"A bad case of what?" Liam asks. "Is Uncle Jake sick?"

"In a way," Ben says, chuckling.

I give Ben a look, then turn my attention to Liam. "He means that your uncle Jake is *love*sick. It's an expression."

Liam scratches his arm, and it really looks like the wheels are turning. "That makes sense. Uncle Jake is writing Eloise letters. Maybe that will help him not be so lovesick."

"Letters, huh?" Ben says.

"I even wrote one," Liam says. "I bet it's her favorite."

Ben's smile grows wider. "You're probably right." He runs a hand over his jaw, looking thoughtful. "Old fashioned love letters. That's very . . ."

"Eloise," I say, suddenly realizing exactly how romantic Jake's letter writing truly is. He's speaking Lo's language. "It's *very* Eloise," I repeat.

Like Hunter bringing me art supplies.

He didn't need any words to tell me how he felt when he handed over a box full of things he knew I would love. He may not be a man full of easy words, but he *is* a man of action.

A new idea comes alive, buzzing with fresh energy, the way new ideas do.

Oakley has a pretty thriving downtown, as far as tiny islands go. Harriett's deli and Frank's barber shop. The Big Tuna. A bakery that makes the best almond croissant I've ever eaten. A used bookshop. A touristy store full of seashell necklaces and t-shirts with slogans like *Being Southern Is a State of Mind*.

But there isn't an art gallery or a place to buy upscale furnishings and decor. Nothing for the clients building and renovating homes here, the ones like Hunter's nightmare client with the Versailles tile that Dante told me about. People like that are always looking for high-end decor to match their high-end renovations. They'd probably also love touting their one-of-a-kind things are locally sourced from artists and artisans living on Oakley or in nearby Savannah.

Things like Hunter's tables.

Like my paintings.

Well. Maybe my paintings, if I ever work up the courage to paint again. But absolutely for sure—Hunter's tables. Assuming he'd agree, even if just to clear space in his full workshop to make more tables.

Best of all, this idea would solve my problem of what to do for work. Running a gallery … it's different. Not similar to my old job, at least not on the surface. But I do have an idea of what's going to make people tick. I know marketing. And I know art. Marrying the two together feels very … *me*.

"Ben, you own Oakley Island, right?"

"You own this whole island?" Liam practically shouts.

"Yes." I didn't think Benedict King could look uncomfortable, but as he shifts from one expensive boat shoe to the other, he actually looks a bit embarrassed. "My mom passed full ownership on to me five years ago."

His neck flushes pink. Definitely embarrassed—which is kind of endearing.

"How can a person own an island?" Liam still looks flabbergasted. "Does that make you our landlord? Mom hates our landlord and says he's a—" Abruptly, Liam stops, then whispers, "I'm not supposed to repeat the word."

Ben grins, returning to his easy, playboy charm. "I guess I'm sort of like the landlord—hopefully not one your mom would call names you're not supposed to repeat. People own their land, but there is a yearly maintenance fee and the historic preservation society—this is all very boring stuff."

"I'm actually *very* interested," I say. "Specifically in any open retail spaces. Is that something you handle?"

Understanding lights his green eyes. "It is. And it's funny you should ask. The dog grooming place at the other end of Main Street just let me know they're relocating to Savannah. It's a hard space to fill though. Double the size of most of the places on Main Street."

"That sounds perfect, actually." I think of the size of the tabletops hanging in Hunter's workshop.

My eyes drop to Liam. Knowing how much he's already told *me* about the other adults in his life, I don't really want to ask any follow-up questions while he's listening. There aren't enough degrees of separation between Liam and Hunter for me to trust my questions wouldn't get back to him. And there are too many loose ends for me to iron out before I even let *myself* get excited about this idea, much less get Hunter excited about it.

Back then, we dreamed of ways to work together on the island. We talked about building a future. This would be one way to do that—even if Hunter doesn't want to sell his tables, this could work. This could be *my* work.

For the first time since I quit my job, I'm actually excited about something work-related.

"Can I email or call you?" I ask Ben. "Maybe at a better time?"

He nods knowingly, glancing at Liam. "Sure thing. Jake knows how to reach me. And let me know next time your other sister is in town. We didn't finish our argument last time she was here."

I get the very distinct sense he's not just interested in finishing an *argument*. But whatever. Sadie is the sister I don't need to worry about. She'd eat Ben for breakfast and then spit out his bones by lunch. Probably end up owning half the island in the process.

As Liam and I finally make it to Jake's, I find myself smiling, wondering if maybe, in the end, all three of us—Eloise, Sadie, and me—will end up calling Oakley home.

TWENTY-ONE

Hunter

I'M A HUMBLE MAN. A man with simple wants. Simple needs. Simple life.

But when it comes to feelings—having them, having to talk about them—I am an absolute *king*. The king of avoidance, that is.

Deciding to do practical but not fully necessary updates underneath Genevieve's house this week helped me avoid dealing with my current emotional turmoil. No way was Merritt going to wiggle under there with me.

Conveniently, when I'm not at work, Isabelle's constant presence makes it impossible for me to think too hard or have a conversation alone with Merritt. And as long as we aren't having any conversations—will she stay, does she want me, will she ever want a family—I can muddle along in blissful ignorance.

So why don't I feel blissful?

I heave my ax overhead and swing it down onto the waiting log like it's personal. *Okay.* Maybe *not-so-blissful* ignorance.

As for Merritt, at this exact moment, she seems determined to sit on my porch, waiting out both Isabelle's bedtime *and* my avoidance.

It's why I'm chopping firewood—a task I won't technically need to do for at least another month or two. It means I don't need to talk. I can just grunt.

And if doing it shirtless means Merritt gets an eyeful, well, that can't exactly hurt my cause. It's not like I think my muscles are enough to make her stay.

But they certainly won't *hurt*.

Isabelle has been explaining some school drama for what seems like an hour. "And then she said I took her stickers, but she's just jealous because hers don't glow in the dark."

"Wow. I had no idea stickers were so complicated," Merritt says, but she sounds like she's hardly paying attention to her own words.

Thwack! I split another log, picking up the pieces and tossing them toward the growing pile. Glancing over as I wipe sweat off my forehead, I feel a thrill at Merritt's expression.

Oh, yeah. She's *definitely* into the shirtless lumberjack thing.

But are you sure you want her to be into it? What if she plans to leave as soon as the house is done? Or before it's even done, like Lo did. Has Merritt given you any guarantee or even a hint she's going to stay on Oakley?

"Shut up, brain," I murmur as I grab another log.

Talking to myself is usually something I reserve for when

I'm alone or with the animals. It's how I process, especially when I'm loaded down with worried—and loud—thoughts like I am now.

Thwack!

Another big log splits. Two more for the pile.

Why would Merritt stay? What's here for her now? The woman puts ads up on whole buildings in Times Square. She dates white-collar men like Simon. There's nothing for her here.

"Except me. I'm here."

Yeah ... but that wasn't enough back then. Why would it be enough now?

Sweat drips into my eyes, and I wipe it away before lining up one more log.

Thwack!

This is stupid. I'm an adult, acting like a kid. Worrying without talking to Merritt. Making assumptions without asking her what she thinks or how she feels. I watched enough Hallmark movies to last a lifetime while married to Cass—enough to know what I'm doing is the kiss of death to a relationship.

"Talk to her. Stop avoiding, dummy."

Thwack!

My arms are aching, and my back twinges a little as I toss the latest pieces on the stack. I blink a few times, taking in the pile of logs as Banjo skitters over the top, pressing his nose into the freshly cut wood to smell.

"I didn't think winters got that cold here."

I jump a little at Merritt's voice. I didn't even see her walking over. I give her a brief glance before turning back to the large pile of logs.

"It doesn't," I say. "I'll give most of this away."

"Is that something you do every year?" she asks.

Nope. "Only when I have a lot of extra."

Like when I'm taking out my frustrations and worries on innocent, dead wood instead of having a conversation like a mature adult.

Merritt runs a hand over the log pile, tilting her head like she's about to ask another question. Or maybe she's about to call BS on my whole log-chopping thing. She's no dummy. But Banjo clambers over, a perfect distraction. He stands up on his hind legs, nuzzling into her.

Thanks, nosy raccoon. I owe you one.

"He's so cute," she says, petting his back.

"Most raccoons are terrors, so don't think this is normal."

"You're not a terror, are you?" Merritt says in the most ridiculous babytalk voice I've ever heard. "You're just a cute, sweet little bandit, aren't you?"

Banjo chooses that moment to stuff his entire little raccoon face down the front of Merritt's v-neck shirt.

"Aah!" She half screams as Banjo manages to wiggle his whole rotund body into Merritt's shirt. "He's in my—ow! Banjo!"

I stand there like a dope, waving my hands ineffectually because I don't know how to help remove Banjo without copping a feel in the process. I'm not about to get to second base during a raccoon extraction, especially not with my daughter twenty feet away. "Banjo!"

Now Isabelle's here too, laughing and grabbing at Merritt, who now looks like she's pregnant with a large, wiggling racoon baby. She throws her head back, laughing while Isabelle is holding her stomach and the dogs are dancing around her feet. For a moment, time stops.

This is it.
This is the love of my life.
This is my future.

My whole world.

Right here.

Maybe ... without the raccoon in the shirt.

I'm going to fly in the face of all my doubts, tell Merritt what I really want and hope she wants the same. I'll show her the inside of my house, and she'll understand why I didn't before.

She'll understand everything.

Banjo pops his head back out of Merritt's collar, looking totally unrepentant, of course. Merritt untucks her shirt from her jeans with a yank, and the raccoon tumbles down to the dirt with a thud. Chittering, he gives Merritt a look that I swear is more of a glare before he scurries back to the house, followed by Vroom.

"They say there's a first time for everything," Merritt says, a blush lighting her cheeks. Paired with her gorgeous smile, it makes my heart start thumping. Even more when she pulls her shirt away from her body and glances down. "I think he scratched me a little."

"Need me to take a look?"

Did that come out sounding like an offer to check her out or an offer to *check her out?*

"It's fine. But do I need to worry about rabies?"

"He's up to date on all his shots," Isabelle says, reminding me she's *right here* and I need to get my head in the right place. But I don't feel like anything will actually be *right* until Merritt and I have a conversation. Alone.

Preferably now.

"Is it time for bed?" I ask, and Isabelle squints at me.

"We haven't had dinner yet. Silly Daddy."

"Oh, right."

"Are you okay?" Merritt asks.

Not really. Not yet. Maybe I will be in a few hours. First, I have to get through dinner. Tucking Isabelle in. Hoping Isabelle won't want me to make up twelve stories tonight.

This whole dating with a kid thing ... how in the world did Cassidy manage? I don't think I'd be good at dating anyway, but add in Isabelle, and I don't know how to do any of this.

"Hunter?" Merritt asks, touching my arm.

"Yeah. Sorry. I'm just—"

"Grammy and Pops!" Isabelle cries. The dogs begin barking and running in circles through the yard as my parents' sedan bumps along the driveway toward the house.

Just what I need—more people to deal with.

But after greeting Isabelle and Merritt both with hugs, my mom says, "We thought we'd take Isabelle out to dinner and give you a little time."

She winks, and I have to wonder if I sent out some kind of cosmic bat signal that only my parents could see. I'll take it.

"Yes, please! I want ice cream!" Isabelle says.

"For dessert!" My dad calls after her. "Not for dinner."

"Go find your shoes," Mom urges, and Isabelle runs off to the house.

"Are you sure?" I ask Mom. "That would be amazing. I mean, if Merritt wants to—"

"Yes," Merritt says quickly, and I don't miss the way her eyes dip quickly to my bare chest and then away. "I want to."

Mom grins, and Dad, still standing by the car but close enough to interject himself in the conversation, says, "It's a date!"

"Matchmaking by my parents," I say with a chuckle. "Not embarrassing at all."

Merritt smirks. "Your parents always did love me."

They're not the only ones.

I move the ax out of the way and pick my shirt up off the ground where I left it earlier. Twisting the fabric in my hands, I'm suddenly struck with nerves. "I should probably shower."

Merritt's gaze trails over my chest and down to my abs before coming back up. "Yeah, you're dirty," she says, and her words *sound* dirty.

Filthy, really.

I grin, tugging the shirt over my head. Over by the car, my dad coughs loudly into his hand, obviously able to hear everything.

Merritt shakes her head, her eyes wide. "I meant, *literally* dirty. Like from all the wood chopping and—"

"I know what you meant," Dad calls, winking.

Mom materializes from the house. Her grin is so smug, that I know I'll never live any of this down. But I don't even care.

Not when Merritt bites her lip, looking more than happy at the idea of time alone.

"I'll help Isabelle pack her school things," Mom says, sauntering off toward the house.

"And I'll just cool off in the car," my dad says, waving before getting in.

It should be awkward, given the last few minutes, but Merritt and I are grinning at each other like fools.

"Don't get any ideas," I say.

Her brows lift. "Ideas? Why Hunter, whatever do you mean?"

"We need to *talk*," I tell her, needing the reminder myself.

"Talking is good. I have some things to say too."

That would usually sound ominous, but she looks happy.

Relieved. Like this is going to be good talking, not bad talking. Then maybe we can have some time ... *not* talking?

"So, talk first. Then ..." I trail off, very aware my parents are unabashedly still trying to listen to every word.

"Talk, then dinner. I'm *starving*," Merritt says, somehow conveying a literal and suggestive meaning in the same breath.

So am I.

As Isabelle emerges from the house, my phone rings. Cassidy's ring. Merritt must recognize it too, because her face falls, her eyes suddenly unsure.

One more thing we need to talk about.

I'm not planning to answer—not now—but Isabelle also recognizes the ringtone and grabs my phone, answering before I can stop her. "Mommy! Grammy and Pops are taking me to dinner and—"

Isabelle stops mid-sentence, and I know what's coming even before she shrieks loud enough to make Sunbeam howl.

"She's having the baby!" Isabelle screams, thrusting the phone at me. I take it, holding it to my chest as Izzy hugs me, then hugs Mom, then Merritt, who is starting to back away, her eyes down.

"Mom wants to talk to you," Isabelle says, still dancing around the yard, kicking up little clouds of dirt.

Sighing, I put the phone to my ear, giving Merritt a pleading look. *Don't go.*

She pauses, but her lips are pressed in a tight line. All the joy has been washed from her face, like it was never there at all. She hugs her arms around herself, and I hate the vulnerability this phone call is causing.

"Cass?" I say.

Her words come through the line in a desperate rush. "It's

time and Adam's in surgery across town and the doula went to the wrong hospital and I'm *all alone.*"

The last part goes from fast talking to a groan. I don't know what a doula is, but it's clear what Cassidy wants from me right now. She curses quietly and then gives a small sob.

"I don't know that I can be there," I say.

"Hunter, please. I know it shouldn't be you, but I need someone. I don't want to be by myself."

She needs Adam, but I can hardly fault the guy for being a surgeon. Or fault Cassidy for wanting someone to be with her.

"What about your parents?"

She laughs. "You think my mom and dad would be helpful right now?"

No—they absolutely wouldn't. Her parents are germophobes. I doubt they'll even go to the hospital to meet the baby. They'll just wait until Cassidy is home.

"I wasn't helpful the first time," I tell her, dragging a hand over my beard.

"I need *someone*," Cassidy pleads, and even though I want to kill her for this, I also know I can't leave her alone.

"I want to go to the hospital, Daddy," Izzy says. "I want to meet the baby."

Vroom starts barking as Mom wraps an arm around Izzy and leads her away a few steps. "Honey, your mom needs to focus on the baby right now. You come with us just like we planned. Dinner and ice cream, remember? Then you can meet the baby tomorrow or the next day."

Cassidy lets out another groan, only slightly louder than Vroom and Banjo who are chasing each other in circles around the yard. My stress level ratchets up a little higher. Merritt is still standing a little ways off, waiting.

Isabelle shrugs out of Mom's arms. "But I want to see Mommy *now*. She's having the baby *now*."

Mom reaches for Izzy again, but she lunges away and makes a beeline for me, grabbing me around the waist before bursting into tears. "Daddy, what if Mommy loves the baby more than me? And what if I hate the baby or the baby hates me?" she bawls. "I'm s-s-s-scared."

"Please," Cassidy begs in my ear. "You know I would only ask this in an emergency ... ahhhhh."

Her pleading words move into another long groan, telling me she's pretty far along in this process. So far that if I don't go now, I may not make it at all.

I am slowly sinking into what feels like emotional quicksand. Pulled deeper by my ex-wife's voice in my ear and my daughter's small hands clutching the back of my jeans as she sobs.

Glancing up at Merritt, I know she's already as good as gone. Giving me a quick nod and a wave, she calls, "It's fine. She's having a baby. What can you do?"

Her shrug looks like an admission of defeat, and it's only Isabelle glued to my body that keeps me from chasing Merritt to her car, giving her a kiss she won't forget and a promise to reschedule our date.

It takes a minute after Merritt's car starts for me to realize Cassidy hung up. My mom clucks her tongue as I lower the phone. Her look is pure disapproval. My parents have long been telling me I do too much for Cass, especially now that she's married, and I didn't realize until Merritt how right they are.

But is the time to deal with that really right this second as Cassidy has a baby?

Maybe if I realized this before or handled it earlier, Cass wouldn't even think of asking me to come to the hospital.

But now, I'm kind of stuck. Surely, Merritt and I can push off our talk for a day. Or two? I watch her tail lights, a sinking sensation settling in the pit of my stomach.

"Come here, Izzy," Dad says as he tugs her arms from around my waist and lifts her into his arms. "Let's take Vroom and the rest of the animals inside." Isabelle is almost too big to be held like this and would usually shimmy away in protest, but right now, she buries her head in Dad's shoulder and wraps her limbs around him like a baby monkey.

"Funny," Mom says as she watches them move away. "Something about this situation feels familiar. It was at dinner, right? That you left Merritt and ran off to do another woman's bidding?"

It was. And then it happened again on the double date, which mom doesn't even know about. She's so, so right.

"What do you expect me to do right now?" I hiss, running a hand through my hair. "You're right. But Adam is in surgery across town—"

"And that is *not* your problem," Mom says, cutting me off. "You need to set up some boundaries before you lose the woman you've loved your whole life. Again."

I sort of thought parental wisdom came with the territory. Like I'd suddenly be able to offer advice and make logical choices after having a kid. But so far, I'm only made aware over and over of how little I know. Meanwhile, my mom just keeps getting smarter.

"You're right," I tell her. "I'll fix it."

"Good," she says with a curt nod. "When?"

"Tomorrow. And I might need help with ..." My gaze shifts to Isabelle who is on the front porch with Dad, luring Banjo into his enclosure with fruit loops.

"Anything you need," Mom says, then pokes me in the

chest with a perfectly manicured fingernail. "But whatever you do, don't let Merritt go."

I don't plan to.

But when I reach the hospital and see the text that came in during the drive, I wonder if I'm already too late.

Merritt: *I hope everything goes well for Cass. Heading to New York in the morning. Hopefully we can talk soon.*

TWENTY-TWO

Merritt

NEW YORK SUCKS. And I couldn't be happier about it. The familiar smell of exhaust plus whatever food is sold in that block—pizza, falafel, pretzels, hot dogs, curry—makes me smile with nostalgia, but that's it.

Fine. And it also makes me get a giant pretzel I eat while walking through the city that somehow, after all these years, feels like a familiar stranger.

New York is like the blond guy who got on the train the stop after mine every Monday through Friday. I could pick his blond curls out in a crowd, and sometimes we made awkward eye contact, but we never spoke. We didn't learn each other's names. He won't miss me.

"You won't miss *anything*. Really?" The sarcasm drips from Jana's words.

To her point, I'm almost ready to lick the butter masala

sauce off my plate. If the waitress doesn't bring me the extra naan I ordered, I might.

"I'll miss *you*. Obviously."

I roll my eyes to emphasize the point, even though I'm quite certain Jana is a work-only friend, whose memory will fade a little slower than subway guy. Maybe we'll call and text a little, but since we hardly did over the past month, I doubt it.

Sad, but a testament to the life I built here, which was, as it turns out upon closer examination, thin. Insubstantial. Almost—and this was a rough realization—*inconsequential*.

As a literal testament to this, I braved the Times Square tourists only to discover my latest campaign has already been replaced by a Kardashian. Or a Kardashian look-alike. They're pumping out new ones so fast, I can't tell anymore.

"And the food," I say, glancing around for the waitress. "Oakley Island does *not* have curry."

"Not *good* curry?" Jana asks hopefully.

"No curry at all."

"How will you survive?" Jana asks drily.

"No idea."

I drag my finger across my plate, then lick off the sauce. Her expression shifts to horror. Jana, of the sleek, dark hair and perfect winged eyeliner does not condone such behavior.

Initially, her sarcasm drew me to her as a sort of pseudo-Sadie I could relate to. But I didn't realize how much her uptightness fed that part of me too. Together, we were tough New York women, surviving the city and a male-dominated workplace together. Somewhere along the way, my *strong* became *hard*. Not in a way I particularly like.

Now, as I'm embarrassing her with my uncouth dining manners, the gulf between us has widened.

"You've changed. Already."

Her words sound like an accusation. But they land like praise.

Good. I'm glad I'm not who I was when I left. But I can't say that out loud, so I file it away for later.

I try to make it funny so this conversation will stop feeling so painful. "What? I wouldn't have licked delicious sauce from my fingers before?"

"You know you wouldn't have."

Well, that's a shame. I probably missed out on some good sauce.

But I don't say that. Because Jana, my oldest and best New York friend, clearly disapproves. Not just of my manners, but of the whole idea of me not returning to New York.

"Oh, you've got—" Jana pauses, her hand reaching toward my forearm. "What is that?"

I glance down at my arm and see a smudge of blue paint just above my wrist. "Oh. It's paint." I must have missed it when I was cleaning up.

Cleaning up, because I *painted*. And it felt amazing.

"You paint?" Jana asks. Her tone isn't judgy so much as it's disbelieving.

I smile, a sense of peace blooming in my heart. "Yeah. I do." I don't offer her any other explanation. One, because it isn't going to matter. And two, I'm throwing all my energy toward keeping things light, and discussing my painting history is not that. This has already been one of those dinners where polite conversation feels one step away from devolving into an intervention I don't actually need.

Which I realize is probably what ninety-nine percent of people being interventioned (is that a word?) would say. But in my case, it's true. Every minute I spend in the city makes my longing to go back home—yep, *home*—to Oakley more clear.

To Hunter, I mentally correct. But my chest tightens at the thought of him. After the weird way we left things, I'm in a rush to get back and have that conversation we put off because of Cassidy.

Which ... he and I also need to discuss. Later.

"The office isn't the same without you," Jana says.

"You're just saying that because now you have to be the kitchen police."

She smirks. "Turns out, interns can be scared into cleaning out the fridge and washing the crusty plates Nelson leaves in the sink. It's much more effective than passive-aggressive notes."

I'm grateful Jana is steering our ship back to the safer waters of work talk. Though I'm not interested at *all* in office gossip, even from the source of the best gossip herself.

Until she has to go and mention the ex-who-should-not-be-named.

"Merritt, honestly. Yes, Simon sucks. As a human, but also as the head of the department. But you can't let him derail your whole life."

"That's not what I'm doing."

Her face says she doesn't believe me. Understandable. Jana only knows me as her veritable twin. She knows New York Merritt. Not FULL Merritt, who isn't just New York or Oakley, but *me*. I haven't changed so much as I've stopped putting on the very well-fitting mask I wore for so long that it molded to my features.

"Are you sure?"

More now than I was before coming up here. I need to send Sadie a candy—or, no! A *coffee*—bouquet. "Positive."

Jana leans over and drops her voice to a whisper, as

though someone at a neighboring table might be a corporate spy. "Because word is, they're already discussing moving Simon to the Philly office."

"He's screwed up that much *already*?"

We all consider the Philly office to be like the airplane seats next to the lavatory. No offense to the city—it's more about the staff in our branch there. Maybe I shouldn't take glee in the idea of Simon being transferred to our worst branch. But I do. It fits him.

She sits back, crossing her arms and giving me a smug look. Jana is the patent holder of smug looks. "It was evident almost immediately that he is lost without your help."

When I say Simon stole my promotion, I don't mean *literally*. Nothing so dramatic as the movies. Nothing nefarious or legally incriminating. But I didn't realize how much my help actually helped him until I was watching his face after the announcement that he got the promotion the whole office assumed was mine.

While my brain slowly processed the horror and humiliation and disappointment, there was hand-clapping and back-slapping from the execs (which also served as a reminder of how completely male and white our office is) and even a photo taken for the corporate newsletter. Not once did Simon glance my way.

It was then I remembered with painful clarity the way he would ask for one more set of eyes on his proposals. How I usually pointed out some significant changes he needed to make or gaps he'd overlooked. Sometimes—and even now I feel nauseated remembering—I'd even rewrite things for him.

So, no—I'm not at all shocked he can't handle the new position without me offering up my help for free behind the scenes. Getting sent to Philly though ... Simon is more incompetent than I thought.

"Your name came up," Jana says casually, her smugness dialing it up a notch.

"Seriously?"

"If it wasn't clear they made a mistake before, it's painfully obvious now. Expect a generous offer in the next few days."

In this precise moment, I'm more aware of how much has changed in the last month. Part of me is preening over the idea of being chosen. Getting my due. Seeing all my hard work pay off.

While this new, improved, finger-licking version of myself is not even a little tempted by the offer. I feel a distant sort of pride about finally being recognized for my work, the way I might about a friend's nephew graduating college with honors. I have zero desire to think about putting on a dark suit and being brilliant in a board room where it's obvious most men appreciate the eye candy more than the ideas.

"I hope they can find a good replacement," I say.

An expression crosses Jana's face I've never seen before. It's more than a little murderous. I'm honestly grateful for the arrival of extra naan because the server's well-timed distraction might have just saved me from being stabbed in the eye with a fork.

"Could I get the check, please?" I ask.

"I can't believe this," Jana says. "Did you get brainwashed down there? Fall in with a cult?" Her perceptive eyes narrow, and she gasps. "Oh my gosh. You met a man."

"I didn't meet a man, and that's not really what—"

"You're really letting a man change your career goals? All because of Simon and a stupid promotion?" Jana shakes her head. Disapproval. Disappointment. And ... is that disgust?

"My decision isn't because of a man. It's me." I pull out my wallet while I talk, leaving enough cash on the table to cover us both. No way am I sticking around to wait on them to run my credit card. "For the first time in years, I'm actually taking a hard look at my life. Who I am. What I want. Who I want to become."

"How very woo-woo of you."

I shrug, then stand. "Jana, I wish you the best. I enjoyed working with you."

I stop short of saying I enjoyed dinner because the only part I enjoyed was the food.

Back on the sidewalk, after stilted goodbyes and no hug or kiss on the cheek, I shiver. It's legitimately becoming fall here, whereas Oakley still feels like a slowly fading summer. I sense the pulse of the city beating around me, but it's separate from me now. I'm on the outside, an observer.

But inside, my heart's rhythm is thudding out a name. *Hunter. Hunter. Hunter.*

I'm still nervous about how we left things. I haven't spoken to Hunter since that last text I sent after leaving his house. He never responded, not then, or the next day, not even to acknowledge the gift I left on his front porch before flying out. He hasn't even given me an update on the whole Cassidy-baby situation.

I don't fault him. He's probably busy. Consumed with Isabelle as she transitions into big sisterhood. And my text to him was short—intentionally so—because I was feeling a little testy when our plans were ruined by his ex-wife. *Again.*

I worried I'd wake him up when I drove out to his place right before my flight. Or at least the dogs. I parked down the drive and walked the last fifty yards or so for that reason. Luckily, the predawn hours worked to my advantage and I managed to prop the canvas against the rocking chair to the left of Hunter's front door without anyone inside the house making a peep.

I can't think too hard about how Hunter responded when he saw it. About *why* he hasn't mentioned it to me. Or texted at all. But I do know with absolute certainty that I won't find the answers in New York. The only thing the city has assured me of is that my chapter here is done.

No matter what tomorrow brings—whether my future is with or without Hunter—it's time to go home.

TWENTY-THREE

Hunter

FOR THREE DAYS, I stared at the painting Merritt left on my porch. Stared and stewed, which sounds like the kind of word my mom would use. But I can't find a better one.

When I finally got home from the hospital, after Adam arrived and Isabelle calmed down and Cassidy had her new baby, Evelyn, the painting wasn't here. But the next morning, there it was, leaning against the chair. A surprise. A gift.

Hopefully, not a parting one, but I'll be honest—I'm freaking out.

Since the last text Merritt sent while I was on the way to the hospital, there's been no contact.

Which is entirely on me. Have I reached out to ask why she went to New York? No. I haven't.

I've practically written a dissertation's worth of messages before deleting them all. Because what do I even say?

Come back.

I miss you.
Sorry I ditched you to help Cassidy.
I want you to stay. Forever.
When will you come home? Why did you go?
Why didn't you tell me you were going?

Everything sounds cheesy or stupid. And I can't stop picturing the last look I saw on her face, which was deep disappointment. Maybe hurt. Probably both.

Which matches how I felt when I got her text that she was going to New York. No reasons why. No telling me when she'll come back. It's like we're in a fight, but one without words.

And ... I'm not sure what exactly we're fighting about. Only that things have an uncertain feel to them.

A gnawing restlessness has been rising up in me. An energy I don't know how to dispel. It doesn't help that Cassidy is home from the hospital, which means Isabelle is with her now. So I'm not just restless, I'm *alone* and restless.

Even more so when I allow myself to consider that it might not be a *when* but an *if* Merritt comes back.

"My family is leaving. I'm leaving."

I squeeze my eyes closed, remembering.

Her eyes are bright but cold. The expression doesn't suit her, and I can't understand it. I don't understand her words either. It's only July. She and her sisters always stay until August. It already felt like the end was too close. This summer, we finally became more than friends. Officially. And I've been dreading the time she leaves every day since.

But leaving now?

"I don't understand."

"Plans changed."

"Talk to me," I plead.

This makes no sense.

Merritt shakes her head, then takes down her hair only to tie her ponytail tighter. Higher. Every loose strand accounted for.

"This will be my last time on Oakley Island," she says.

"Until next summer."

I make it a statement, not a question. Because she always comes back. And for the last few years especially, the time in between has felt painfully long and pointless.

I live for summers. Only this year, I realized what I'm really living for is Merritt.

"No."

Her single word is like a blade to my gut.

"I won't be back," she continues.

I lick my suddenly dry lips, trying to slow my thoughts enough to locate a rational one. "But ... our plans."

She doesn't need to answer. The tightness in her mouth says it all.

Stupid. I was so stupid to count on promises we'd made. I know we're young. Too young to feel this way, too young to plan for a future. Not like it made much sense, anyway. Just some vague thoughts about her painting and me figuring out what I want to do, then doing it together.

Forever.

Here.

My heart clenches. No other guys my age are talking about a future with their girlfriends. When I mentioned things being serious with one of my football friends, he laughed and made a rude comment about taking some things to the next level.

I punched him for the suggestive comment and the look on his face. But I should have known better than to tell him.

No. I should have known better than to think Merritt and I were something special.

"This place is too small," she says. "Your life is too small, Hunter. And if you never leave Oakley, it always will be."

I guess it's too late now to take back all the times I talked about wanting to live on Oakley forever, how I saw this as the perfect place to build a life.

Because what really matters is Merritt, not Oakley, but I can see from her face, she's already gone.

I shove away the memory, one that has haunted me ever since. More than normal this week.

"Your life is too small."

No. I refuse to let my doubts and words she already apologized for rule me now. It was a long time ago. More than a decade.

But if Merritt still feels the same way ...

I glance at the painting, trying to shove the past back where it belongs.

If Merritt makes the same choice again, so be it. I would have regretted not trying. The same way I regret not going after her years ago.

There's still hope, and this painting gives me more reason. At least, I *think* it does.

Unless it *is* a goodbye gift. Which I'm trying my hardest not to think about.

Stylistically, I can see Merritt in the bold colors. I can close my eyes and picture her standing in front of the easel, her arm sweeping the brush across with wild, controlled strokes. Merritt is the only woman I've met who seems to be both equally: wild and utterly controlled.

When she first arrived here this month, all I could see was tightly wound control. It was slipping, and she was panicking, but now ... it seems like she's given in, letting herself be more free. More of herself.

Aside from the recognizable style of the painting, the subject matter is completely different. She used to paint skies and the ocean or abstracts focused on color. But this painting is different. This painting is me.

Merritt painted *me*.

I mean, I'm pretty sure it's me. I'm gonna feel really stupid if it's some other bearded guy staring off over my marsh.

Her style is ... well, I don't know how to talk about art in a formal way. But her style isn't realistic. Not like a photo. Impressionist? But maybe that's the one with dots.

Anyway, there are purples and pinks in his—*my?*—hair and beard, and other colors in the clouds that don't make sense. Up close, it's a riot of color in some vaguely recognizable shapes. But back up even a few feet, and it's clear. All those colors somehow come together perfectly to look like ... well, *me*.

I can't help it. The painting looks like hope.

There's a tug on my pant leg and I glance down to see Banjo on his hind legs, his dark paws waving as he reaches for me. I scoop him up, letting him settle against my chest. He wastes no time putting his nose and paws all over my face and neck.

"You've got no boundaries," I tell him, and he makes a little chuffing sound.

I keep staring at the painting, which really needs to come inside off the porch. I've been covering it with a tarp when I'm not staring at it, but until I know what's going on with Merritt, I don't know if I can make room for it inside.

"What do you think?" I ask Banjo. His advice consists of sticking his wet nose in my ear.

"I draw the line at wet willies," I tell him, gently lowering him back to the ground.

He scurries off toward the dogs, who are suddenly barking and running toward the driveway. I didn't even hear a car approaching, and when I see that it's Merritt, my heart suddenly decides to lodge itself in my throat.

I amble over, much slower and much less enthusiastically than the dogs. I consider and discard different greetings, just like I did while overthinking my unsent texts.

What I want more than anything is to throw myself at her moving vehicle and yank her out and into my arms. Instead, I keep my hands balled into fists in my pockets as she steps out of the car.

She casts a quick glance my way before dropping down to pet all the dogs and Banjo, who weaves between them all like a cat. Is it bad to be jealous of the animals?

It's so simple for them—they missed her. She's back. Give her all the love. The end.

Where I'm over here giving off I don't know what kind of vibes because I missed Merritt like crazy, but I also feel so uncertain.

She stands, brushing off her hands on her jeans. "Hey."

Like an idiot, I pull one hand out of my pocket and wave. "Hey."

Her lips twitch, but she doesn't smile. Instead, she leans back against her car, her expression not telling me anything at all.

"So, you went to New York."

She nods. "I did. I wanted to tell you before I left but …"

I don't need her to finish saying what's on her mind to know she's upset with me about Cass. Rightly so. "Can you walk and talk? Or walk and fight, if that's what we're doing?"

Now she does smile. "Is this to make up for the date we missed?"

Her smile and teasing tone settle some of the worry pinching my chest. "Is that the norm for dating now—walking and fighting?"

"You forgot swiping. First, there's usually swiping on some app. Then walking and fighting."

"Glad we skipped the swiping part."

I incline my head toward the path, and we start off, side by side. Banjo opts for a nap on the hood of Merritt's car, while the dogs run after us, oblivious to the mood between us.

Which is ... tense. It reminds me of how things were between us when she first got here six weeks ago. Not quite so much ugly between us. But definitely air that needs clearing.

"We should—" I start, just as she says, "I want you to know—"

We both stop and glance at each other. Then away. I chuckle. "You first or me? I'll let you choose."

Merritt sucks in a breath, then pauses to take the stick from Sunbeam's mouth where he's nudging it toward her hand. Merritt gives it a big throw, and Sunbeam bolts after it.

"I went to New York to take care of loose ends. Said goodbye to my work friend, got rid of the stuff in my storage unit, all that. I'm done there."

Hope rises like a bird out of a thicket, wings thrashing, desperate for the clear skies above.

"Yeah?"

"A man of one word." Merritt gives me a smile before tossing the stick again for Sunbeam.

"He won't leave you alone now. He's going to bring you that stick forever."

"I hope so," she says, and again, I feel that thrashing in my chest.

Maybe it's not hope but my heart.

"So ... does that mean you're staying?"

Those words are hard to get out. My voice is rough and uneven.

"I want to stay," Merritt says, and it's all I can do to keep walking in a straight line. "For you, for us, but also for *me*."

I nod, processing her words and telling myself to *be cool*. As much as my ego wants to hear Merritt say she's staying for me, for us—I think hearing her say it's for *her* is more assurance than any other words could give.

"I'm sorry for what happened the night before you left. We made a date, even if it was last minute, and I broke it."

Merritt makes a sound somewhere between a growl and a groan. "Look. You need to know I'm jealous of Cassidy. Of what you had with her but also of what you have with her right now. That said, she was having a baby. Kind of extenuating circumstances. Being angry or jealous makes me feel small and insecure. I can't exist as that person. It's not ... healthy."

"Can I—"

Merritt stops and presses a finger to my lips. I freeze too, turning to face her. For a moment, we stand here, my heart thumping at the feel of her finger grazing my lips and the look in her eyes. Her lips part, and I think she's about to move her hand and kiss me, and I'm about to forget the importance of this conversation and kiss her back.

But she draws in a breath as she takes a step away. Her gaze moves from my mouth to my eyes.

"Me first. Okay?"

I nod. When she turns back to the house, I follow. The dogs race ahead of us as we continue to walk in silence. Whatever she has to say next, they're hard words. I'm trying not to stare, but it's hard to keep my eyes off her. She's blinking a lot, her mouth opening and closing.

Taking what feels like a risk, I reach for her hand, relieved when she holds on like my grip is the only thing keeping her from falling down some deep gorge.

"I need to tell you something about the past," she says. "It's hard. I probably should have told you sooner."

I squeeze her fingers. "Take your time."

She's still taking her time when we reach the cabin, and we sit down on the steps. Banjo gives up his napping spot in favor of Merritt's lap, nudging her free hand until she smiles and scratches his belly.

"Shameless," I say.

"As long as he stays out of my shirt," Merritt says. Then, with a deep but shaky breath, she says, "I was here the day you got married."

The air seems to leave my lungs like I've been punched. Or like I've taken a battering ram or boulder to the chest. That's how it feels.

Merritt was here?

Merritt was HERE.

I squeeze my eyes closed as I feel heat traveling up my neck to my cheeks and my ears. Your wedding day is supposed to be the happiest of your life.

Mine was ... not that.

From the moment Cassidy tearfully told me she was pregnant, panic making her look like a scared deer, everything changed. A heaviness fell over me like the weighted blanket Isabelle uses sometimes. Cass bought it for her to help with nightmares, but for me, that weight was the nightmare.

I couldn't—or wouldn't—let Cassidy go through it alone. We made a baby together; we'd face it together.

No matter how much my parents and her parents tried to encourage us to consider adoption, the one thing Cass insisted on was having the baby. So we made the choice to get married.

Okay, so I let Cassidy choose. And she chose marriage.

She chose *me*. As wrong as it felt from the start, I gave her what she wanted. It felt like the least I could do.

The guilt I felt for all of it was immeasurable. For being careless in the first place. For trying to force myself to feel for Cass a fraction of what I felt for Merritt.

I think Cass knew all along that she couldn't live up to a ghost, but she hoped.

I try to imagine Merritt there that day, while I was dying inside, fighting the urge to run. Knowing already at some point we would fail, wishing so hard I deserved the hope and excitement in Cassidy's eyes.

"I didn't see you."

"I didn't let myself be seen," she says. "And I didn't stay long once I realized what was happening. Gran tried to tell me not to come that weekend, but she never gave me the reason. So, I came."

"Why?"

"Why didn't she tell me?"

I shake my head. "Why did you come?"

The pause feels endless. Like whole lifetimes pass in this moment. Birth, death, everything in between.

"I came back for you. I knew I'd screwed up, and I hoped … I hoped maybe for another chance to tell you I loved you."

Her hand crushes mine, and when I open my eyes, I see that she's crying. Delicately removing my hand from her grip, I pull her toward me, dislodging Banjo, who gives us both a withering look so intense, we both manage to laugh.

"Mer, I'm so sorry."

"You can't be sorry. You made the choices you felt you needed to make. I said I wouldn't come back. I hurt you. I pushed you away—on purpose. So you can't apologize for marrying Cass."

Even knowing what I know, I still think I'd make the

same choice again. I don't know how I couldn't. But I hate that I hurt Merritt in doing so.

"I can say I'm sorry for how much that must have hurt. I know if I'd walked in on your wedding day, I'd have—"

I stop. Because there's no need to detail the kind of violence I'd inflict. Not on a person. But I could envision trashing hotel rooms. Shattering glass. Punching holes in walls until my knuckles bled.

Merritt snuggles closer against me. "Is it bad that I like thinking of you getting jealous?"

"Not if I love it. And I do."

I love you, I almost say. But it doesn't feel right. Not when we're talking about marrying other people.

"I say all this because I still struggle with Cass. I want to be a bigger person. To be mature and handle this with grace. But when you took the phone call on our date, when you left me for her—even if she really did have the most legitimate reason—it takes me back to that day. To watching you choose her over me."

I'm gutted at her words. I know why she's saying them. What I *don't* know is how to tell her they're untrue.

"Mer ..."

"I couldn't help but notice my painting is still outside," Merritt says, her voice painfully small. "Do you not like it?"

I grab her hand before I can overthink it, my pulse like an alarm bell in my ears. I can't find the words, but I can show her.

"Come with me," I tell her.

When she sees me walking toward the screen door, her eyes go wide. "Bluebeard's secret room," she says. She laughs a little when I glare.

"You and your Bluebeard obsession," I say, chuckling.

"There are no other women in here, dead or alive. You'll see."

And when I walk her into my house for the first time, she does see.

Merritt stops right inside the door and gasps.

Heat floods my face again as I watch her look around my house. But I'm not embarrassed I'm ... I don't even know. Terrified? A jumbled hot mess of emotions is more like it.

"You kept them," she whispers.

"*All* of them. I hung up my favorites, but the rest are in a closet in the spare room. Go. Look." I nudge her into the house, and as she looks at everything, I look at her.

Half the walls in my home are filled with paintings. Merritt's paintings.

Gallery, shrine—I don't know what you'd call it. Both, maybe?

I let Merritt be as nosy as she wants, looking in every room, touching some of the canvases with a look of wonder. When she finally opens my closed bedroom door at the end of the hall, I hang back.

Now, maybe I *am* a little embarrassed.

Merritt comes back out a moment later. She's still crying, but she's laughing a little now too, her cheeks pink.

"My self-portrait is in the *closet?*"

I don't point out that this means she went into my closet. "I didn't feel right hanging it above my bed."

The self-portrait is the only painting I'd never seen until Genevieve brought it over with the rest of them. Merritt must have done it years after I last saw her. I don't know how old Merritt is in the painting, twenty or so, maybe, but she's definitely grown up. In the painting, Merritt is turned to the side, only her profile visible. She's laughing, her hair in a long tangle down her back. Behind her, there's only sky, and, like the painting she did of me, it's a mix of colors that look like they shouldn't work up close.

She looks beautiful. And happy.

I liked seeing it so I could imagine that she was living her life with this kind of laughter, this kind of happiness. As much as I ached when I thought about her, about us, about what I wish had been, I hoped this was a picture of her life. When she got to Oakley, though, there was none of this joy in her.

I see it now, though.

"It's the only thing I painted after I left," Merritt says. "And only because Gran insisted." She faces me. "How did you get it?"

I push my hands into my pockets. "She brought it to me. Said she wanted me to have it."

"But when?" Merritt asks, like she can't quite make sense of how her self-portrait made its way to my bedroom. "How?"

I think back. "It's been a while, I guess. A few years. I ran into Genevieve over at Gators—actually, I remember I'd just signed my divorce papers, so I was in a terrible mood. But your grandmother had a way of making people feel better, and sure enough ... anyway, I asked about you. Asked if you were still painting. I tried to keep my interest casual, but she must have seen right through me because a couple of months later, she was pulling up to my apartment with a car full of canvases."

"Which was when? Do you remember the month?" She props her hands on her hips like the answer is very important.

I run a hand through my hair. "June, I think? June six years ago."

Merritt lets out a little laugh. "So you got divorced in

June. And my grandmother, probably not so coincidentally, called me and *begged* me for a self-portrait, also in June. I remember because it was right before my twentieth birthday. If she gave it to you a couple of months after you saw her—Hunter, she didn't even keep it a month before she gave it to you."

I grin. "What's your theory?"

"My theory is that my grandmother was a sneaky little matchmaker." She sniffs and wipes away a tear. "That woman. She tried to tell me these things have a way of working themselves out. Guess she didn't want to leave it to chance."

"I was in a pretty dark place, Mer," I say softly. "Your paintings were a lifeline I didn't know I needed until Genevieve showed up with them."

She walks slowly toward me, placing her hands on my hips, yanking me closer by my belt. I swallow, my gaze snagging on her small smile.

"Think we can hang my self-portrait on an actual wall? If we hang it side by side with yours, they'll look like a matched set."

"I don't know how I feel about having my own portrait hanging in my bedroom."

She bites her lip. "What if it's *our* bedroom?" Her voice is low, sultry, and it sends a wave of heat coursing through me. "I mean, not right now," she says quickly. "But just ..." She shrugs. "You know. Eventually. If that's something you want, too."

I lift my hands to her face, brushing away her tears with my thumbs. "As you might be able to tell, you've had a place in my life, in my heart, for years. Even if you weren't here. But"—I glide my thumbs down her cheeks until I'm cupping her face—"to make it perfectly clear—I want you here. I want you to stay. I want the forever we talked about back then."

She blinks and smiles. "Yeah?"

"Yeah. And I talked to Cass at the hospital." I grimace. "I didn't mean to have the conversation right then, but she kind of brought it up. I told her I need more boundaries. That I want to continue to have a peaceful relationship as we co-parent Isabelle, but nothing else. I won't be at her beck and call anymore. I never should have been. And if Adam isn't stepping up like he needs to, that's between them. It's not my job."

I pause, searching Merritt's face. She's so beautiful, even with red eyes and her lashes clumped together with tears. I definitely see relief and hope in her expression now.

"Is she ... okay with that?"

I nod. "She apologized. I think she knew. And I realized I've been doing this because I feel guilty—still—about everything. Especially about not really ever loving her. Merritt—it's only ever been you. You, Mer. And I know it hasn't been long since you came back, but I feel like I've waited my whole life for you to be here with me."

"This is really what you want?"

"*You* are what I want." I want to kiss her right now. To finish this conversation and begin another kind altogether. But there are still a few things I want—no, *need*—to know. "Are you really okay with leaving the city behind? Are you okay being here? I mean, if I had to, I could probably relocate to Savannah and still be involved with Isabelle—"

"I want to stay here." She grins. "I want all of it. You, Isabelle. Even Banjo."

I chuckle. "He'll be happy to know he made the list."

"Oh! I almost forgot!" She pulls a worn slip of paper out

of her back pocket and hands it over. "Just so you know exactly what my expectations are."

I slowly unfold the paper. It's soft and thin, like it's been unfolded and refolded dozens of times. I recognize the swirly handwriting the moment I see it. It's Merritt's handwriting. A game of MASH we played when we were kids. My smile grows as I read.

"A garbage truck driver, huh? I might have to disappoint you on that one."

She waves a hand dismissively. "But sometimes you *haul* trash with your truck, right? It totally counts."

"But a mansion?"

She rolls her eyes. "There's no *actual* square footage requirement, is there? They say a man's house is his castle, so ... yeah. It counts."

I swallow, my eye catching on the one thing I'm afraid to say out loud. But I'm too far in now. If I don't bring it up, Merritt will realize I skipped it.

"Two kids?" I say, hoping she doesn't notice the catch in my voice.

I've already given it a lot of thought after Cassidy told me what Isabelle told her. If any of that was true and Merritt doesn't want any kids of her own, I'll find a way to be on board. I have Isabelle. She's enough. I'd love to have more children—ones with Merritt's ocean eyes and her smile and her brains. But if that's what she wants, I've made peace with that because more than anything, I want *her*.

"Or three," Merritt says a little shyly. "Maybe four? But not yet. I'd like you all to myself—well, to myself and also with Isabelle—for a while. Okay?"

"Okay." I can't help my smile as tension leaves my chest. "I can't believe you saved this." I fold up the faded sheet and hand it back, watching as she carefully tucks it back into her pocket.

"Says the guy who has all of my paintings hanging in his house?"

"Not *all* of them. There's a few that were really awful. I left those in the closet."

She smacks my arm and lets out an indignant scoff. "I painted most of these when I wasn't even out of high school. Give me some credit!"

I catch her hand and pull it back to me, wanting the feel of it flat against my chest. "You deserve all the credit. The fact that you were this good when you were just a kid ..." I press a kiss to her temple. "I'm glad you started painting again, Mer. Are you going to do it full time?"

"Um, sort of? Not really. But I have a plan."

"Of course you have a plan. Want to tell me about it?"

"Very much. But not quite as much as I want to kiss you right now."

"Is that so?"

Merritt looks like she's going to answer, but instead, she lifts up on her toes and presses her mouth to mine.

Her lips are soft and slightly salty from her tears. Her hands slide from my hips up my chest, resting right over where my heart is doing its best to break free from my chest. I keep one hand on her jaw, angling her head exactly where I want it, and slide my other hand through her hair.

When she pulls back, we're both breathing hard, both smiling. "I hope you mean this," she says. "Because I just signed a contract with Benedict King to lease a property on Main Street."

"You don't want to live in the carriage house anymore?"

What I really want is for her to live here, but that's a big step—and one I'd prefer to make once she's wearing my ring.

"Not to live," she says, suddenly looking shy again. "For a gallery."

"To sell your paintings?"

"Maybe, eventually. I need to get back in my groove. But I want to sell art, especially local art. For the high-end clients who are moving onto the island and want unique pieces for their homes. I'm hoping"—her look turns devious—"I could sell some one-of-a-kind tables there."

It takes me a minute to catch on, probably because I'm still caught up in the reality of finally feeling secure about having her in my life, of seeing my future the way it always should have been. And also, her kisses are very good at making me forget everything else.

"*My* tables?"

"Your tables. I mean, if you want to. But I'm going to make sure I convince you that you do want to."

I process for a moment, then meet her gaze. "It might take convincing."

She leans closer, kissing my neck, just under my ear. "I'm told I can be very persuasive."

"And I'm told I'm very stubborn."

"Mm. Guess I'll have to do my very best persuading, then." Another kiss, this one ending in a little nibble on my earlobe. My hand tightens a little in her hair, and she grins at me.

"I love you, Mer. It was true then, it's been true since, and it's true now. It'll be true forever."

She sighs and slides her hands around my back, pulling me close, her head resting on my chest. Right over my heart where her hands just were, where she always is, always has been.

"I love you, too, Hunter. I never stopped."

The words fill me near to bursting. I've wanted to hear

them for years, not that I thought I ever would. Now that I have, it feels like everything in my life has changed, is changing.

Or maybe a better word is *settling*. It feels like my life is finally settling into what it was always meant to be.

I know better than to think it will always be easy. That Merritt and I will always be on the same page. That life won't be messy and complicated and hard.

But if life is going to be hard, at least we'll be facing it together. Side by side. Hand in hand. Not exactly like our MASH game, but close enough and even better than what we dreamed of so many years ago.

EPILOGUE

Merritt

FASTENING a bow tie when the wearer does not want said bow tie is not for the faint of heart. Full-contact bow-tying is also not what I imagined doing on my wedding day.

"Hold still," I tell him, but he ignores me. "Stop your wiggling."

He doesn't. And then, like magic, Sadie appears next to me on Hunter's porch with a handful of Fruit Loops. "Here you go," she croons.

And suddenly, all resistance is gone.

"Those aren't good for you," I scold as Banjo shovels them into his mouth.

"But it allowed you to tie the bow tie," Sadie says. "That's why they pay me the big bucks."

"Again—you aren't getting paid. Being a maid of honor is a free gig. Also? These will make his poop green. It's the color additives."

"Ew! Gross. Why do you know about his—never mind. You know, one change I don't love since you moved here is how you've become positively ..." Sadie pauses, searching for a word.

"Uncouth?" I offer.

"No, but that works too." And then Sadie is throwing her arms around me in a tight hug. "I love you. I've always loved you. But you're a lot easier to *like* now, Merritt."

"Gee, thanks?"

"You're welcome. Now—let's get this wedding started! Where's the champagne?"

Eloise materializes, as though she could scent trouble on the wind. "No champagne until after the ceremony."

"Boo! We don't need a new no-fun sister," Sadie says.

"Hey!" both Lo and I say at the same time. Then we share a smile.

It's not all bliss and rainbows with my sisters. But things between us are markedly better. Before Gran died, we were almost strangers. Or maybe more like work friends, where you share some things in common that stop short of reaching your personal life.

I can't help but wonder if this was part of Gran's grand plan. (And I *do* believe she had a grand plan.) Eloise confessed she thinks Gran wanted to set her up with Jake—and thankfully, things with the two of them are very much back on. Add in the way she gave my paintings to Hunter mere months after his divorce? She had to have an ulterior motive. But more than matchmaking, the stipulations in her will brought my sisters and me back to Oakley, back to each other.

Mom appears from around the corner of the porch, Vroom following behind. *He* doesn't seem to mind wearing a bow tie at all.

"I know I said it earlier, but you're beautiful," Mom says.

"Thank you," Sadie says. "I wasn't sure you'd like my hair."

Since the last time I saw her, Sadie chopped off her long, dark hair in favor of a platinum pixie cut. On me or Lo, this style would make us look ridiculous. Somehow on Sadie, the extreme cut makes her look like a forest elf or sprite—adorable but also maybe deadly.

"I do like it," Mom says, smiling, "but I meant Merritt is beautiful, since *she's* the one getting married today."

"The dress is okay?" I smooth my hand down the front.

My choice is an unlikely wedding dress. I pulled it off a rack when Naomi was dress shopping with me. The simple ivory satin looked like a nightgown next to the beaded and lace dresses Naomi and the sales associate picked. I'm honestly not sure this is even a wedding dress. Maybe a bridesmaid dress? Mother of the bride? Decidedly *not* a wedding gown.

But once I slipped the fabric over my head, I could *feel* the rightness of it. Naomi blinked rapidly when I walked out, her mouth falling open in surprise, and the sales associate sighed, knowing her commission would be much smaller.

"It's perfect," Naomi said. "It's too simple—it shouldn't work on you, but it does. Absolutely. This is the one."

Naomi also requested to try it on in case it was a *Sisterhood of the Traveling Pants* situation where the dress magically looked good on everyone. Instead, it made her look like an apparition—all ghostly pale and lost in the loose white fabric.

"The dress is subtle and classic." Mom cups my cheek. "But it's your happiness shining through that makes it."

I manage a smile that feels like the precursor to a sob. "Thanks."

"No crying!" Sadie warns, shoving a ball of tissues at me.

"It's a wedding day," Lo says. "We're all supposed to cry. That's why we bought waterproof mascara."

In a sudden move, Mom grabs all three of our hands and pulls them together in both of hers. "Just let me say one more thing."

She draws in a breath, and I realize that this is one of those Important Moments. The ones that *matter*. A few months ago, before coming to Oakley, I might have rolled my eyes or snatched back my hand. I would have thought that Mom gave up the right to be all sentimental like this.

But now—I appreciate it. I'm grateful and only a little sad about the years when it wasn't like this.

"I owe the three of you an apology," Mom says. "I should never have stopped you from visiting here, from seeing your grandmother. Being here now—I realize how wrong I was."

I suck in a breath, briefly meeting Eloise's and Sadie's eyes. Lo's expression I think mirrors mine—soft and sad. Sadie's eyes—more gray-blue than either of ours—look hard and unyielding.

"Whatever happened between your father and me shouldn't have ended with you losing your connection to your grandmother. To this island. Seeing all the love people have for the three of you, watching you blossom…"

I don't miss Sadie's eye roll. Neither does Lo, who kicks her.

"I'm just sorry I took this away from you," Mom finishes, sniffling. "I'm sorry, and I'm so grateful you've come back here to connect however you can."

Sadie wrestles her hand away, supplying us all with tissues as she mutters something about not needing to test the limits of waterproof mascara. "I'm going to track down Banjo and make sure he's not eating the cake," she says, and then she disappears around the corner of the house.

Clearly, *someone* hasn't caught the sentimental moment bug.

Mom dabs her eyes. "Are you sure you want a raccoon as your ring bearer? Jake's nephew, Liam, looks much more responsible than that ... rodent."

"Liam would be a fine choice," I tell her. "But Banjo is *our* choice. Also? He's not a rodent, and he looks adorable in a bow tie."

OF COURSE, I'm regretting this choice an hour later when Hunter has to wrestle the rings from Banjo. He walked—waddled—down the aisle just fine, but then decided he didn't want to give up the rings.

"We talked about this," Hunter grumbles, fighting to keep Banjo from bolting.

The rings are attached to the back of his bow tie, but with the raccoon tucking into a ball and attempting to squirm away, it's impossible to reach. Hunter looks caught somewhere between irritated and amused as our small group of guests laugh.

Sadie leans forward. "Check your bouquet."

I do, and I'm not sure how I missed the tiny baggie of Fruit Loops hidden below the blooms. "You're a lifesaver," I whisper back, and within ten seconds, I've plied Banjo with cereal and Hunter procures the rings.

"Sorry," he says quietly, giving me a chagrined smile.

"I wouldn't have it any other way."

And it's true. I hadn't ever spent a lot of time imagining a wedding. I was too busy manifesting corporate success. But this small backyard wedding at the edge of Hunter's marsh with two dozen guests and a raccoon ring bearer is somehow magically perfect.

Even the weather cooperates. There are heat lamps Dante managed to find, but we may not need them on this unseasonably warm December day. Though I guess it depends on how long the party goes into the night.

Personally—I *will* be dancing.

The ceremony is intentionally brief, and when Frank—who got his officiant's license just for this—tells Hunter he may kiss his bride, I step closer first, kissing my groom.

The world falls away a bit as Hunter's hands find my waist, tugging me closer still. His mouth tastes of mint and feels like warm affection against mine. It's only when our guests start to cheer, startling the dogs into barking, that we break apart, smiling against each other's mouths.

"Later," Hunter promises, and the gleam in his eye makes me shiver.

I'll be looking forward to *later* for the rest of the night.

I'M STILL THINKING about *later* and shooting Hunter *later* eyes across the yard lit with fairy lights when a hand touches my arm. I'm in no way sad about anyone interrupting Virginia Hopkins from a story about some new neighbors who had the audacity to get solar panels. But when I see that it's Cassidy, I'd rather keep discussing how tacky the panels are.

"I'm about to take Isabelle home," Cassidy says, and I watch with regret as Virginia slips away, probably to grumble about something else or to enlist a new member of her Panty Melters book club.

"Thanks for coming," I say, wishing it weren't so obvious from my voice how awkward this is—being greeted on your wedding day by the woman who married your husband first.

Yay.

If Isabelle hadn't insisted and begged and cried to me about her mom coming with her, believe me—Cassidy wouldn't be here. Things have been fine since Hunter talked to Cassidy. Or maybe she's just been too busy with a baby to call Hunter for every little thing. But it doesn't mean this moment isn't incredibly uncomfortable.

Sadie catches my eye from across the yard where Benedict King is trying and failing to win her over. She raises her brows, checking to see if I need backup. Actually, her look says more, *let me know if I need to drop-kick her behind out of here.* I give a slight shake of my head. *Give me a minute,* I hope my look says.

Cassidy draws up her shoulders until she's ramrod straight. "I just want to say, officially, that I'm sorry for overstepping with Hunter. Adam has worked out some things with his schedule so he'll be around more. But even if not, it wasn't right for me to ask Hunter for so much. I see that now, and I'm sorry."

Man—next time I need people to apologize, I'll just have another wedding. Something must be in the air. Or the champagne.

I almost tell her it's fine, but instead, I say, "Thank you. I'm glad you came."

The words are *mostly* true, even if it's primarily for Izzy's sake. Though for the first time, I can feel a bit of tension leaving the air between us.

Cassidy smiles, looking relieved. She glances over to the house, where Hunter is watching us from the porch, Lilith and Vroom by his side. He lifts his glass in a silent toast. We both wave, and it should still be super awkward—maybe it is for him; I'll have to ask later—but this moment of peace feels like a truce. A start to something new. Not like I want to be friends—but because of Isabelle, I don't want there to be friction between her mother and me.

"It was always you, you know," Cassidy says, a note of wistfulness in her voice.

"What?" I ask. I got caught up staring at Hunter's handsome jaw underneath his neatly trimmed beard.

"Hunter always loved you," Cassidy says. "I knew it, even when he didn't. And I thought maybe our friendship was enough of a foundation or that, over time, once we had Izzy, that might change. I was naive." She shakes her head, then smiles. "You have always owned Hunter's heart."

I have no response to that, but I'm saved from it when Cassidy gasps. Her arms come up, hovering over her chest.

"Oh no. My milk just let down. Guess I've been gone a little too long from Evelyn."

"Here." I pull off the light shawl around my shoulders.

She hesitates, but dark circles are already appearing on her green dress. "Are you sure?"

"Yep."

Isabelle appears, as though she already sensed that it was time to go. She hands Cassidy her purse, and her mom gives us both a grateful smile. "Thank you."

"I love you," Isabelle says, throwing herself at me in a hug. "I'm glad you're my special mom."

We decided on *special mom* as my title because there are too many fairy tales with evil stepmothers. "Me too, Izzy."

When the two of them have gone, I turn back to find Hunter, but he's no longer on the porch. I glance to the clearing under the lights, where Jake and Eloise are swaying and Dante and Jasmine are doing what looks like the shag—a complicated and beachy dance a lot of Oakley residents seem to know. I'm about to head into the house to see if Hunter has disappeared to get a break from the guests when familiar arms wrap around my waist and warm breath finds my ear.

"Shall we dance, or shall we get out of here?" he murmurs in the kind of low voice that activates every nerve in my body.

"Hm. Considering we're honeymooning right here tonight, I think dancing."

"I was kind of hoping you'd choose door number two," he says, dragging his lips up the side of my neck.

"You really want to head inside with all these guests out here? Frank would probably be taking a video from outside, and Virginia Hopkins would be peeking in the windows."

Hunter sighs. "You're right. I guess dancing will have to do."

Since the only dancing Hunter can do is the slow kind, we join the small group of dancers and start to sway. I tuck my head into the crook of his neck, breathing in his musky scent.

"I always dreamed of this day," Hunter says after a moment.

"Yeah? Is it living up to your expectations?"

"Better," he says, pulling back so our eyes meet. "You are the woman of my dreams, Merritt Markham, and the woman who has given me more than I could ever dream of."

I smile. "Why, Hunter, that's an awful lot of words for you."

"I'm happy to show you how I feel *without* words," he says, cocking an eyebrow.

And as I lean forward to press my mouth to his, I know I've never looked forward to anything quite so much.

THE END

ABOUT EMMA

Emma St. Clair is a *USA Today* bestselling author of over twenty books. She loves sweet love stories and characters with a lot of sass. Her stories range from rom-com to women's fiction and all will have humor, heart, and nothing that's going to make you need to hide your Kindle from the kids. ;)

She lives in Houston with her husband, five kids, two covid-decision cats, and a Great Dane who does not make a very good babysitter. She earned her MFA in fiction at University of North Carolina at Greensboro writing literary fiction, but for now is focused on LOLs and HEAs.

Let's connect!

Newsletter signup: http://emmastclair.com/romcomemail

Instagram: https://instagram.com/kikimojo

Facebook Reader Group: https://www.facebook.com/groups/emmastclair/

Facebook Page: https://www.facebook.com/thesaintemma

BookBub: https://www.bookbub.com/authors/emma-st-clair

Website: http://emmastclair.com

ABOUT JENNY

Jenny Proctor grew up in the mountains of North Carolina, a place she still believes is one of the loveliest on earth. She lives a few hours south of the mountains now, in the Lowcountry of South Carolina. Mild winters and of course, the beach, are lovely compromises for having had to leave the mountains.

Ages ago, she studied English at Brigham Young University. She works full time as an author and as an editor, specializing in romance, through Midnight Owl Editors.

Jenny and her husband, Josh, have six children, and almost as many pets. They love to hike and camp as a family and take long walks through the neighborhood. But Jenny also loves curling up with a good book, watching movies, and eating food that, when she's lucky, she didn't have to cook herself. You can learn more about Jenny and her books at www.jennyproctor.com.

Let's connect!

Newsletter Sign Up: https://subscribepage.io/S933oF

Instagram: www.instagram.com/jennyproctorbooks

Facebook: www.facebook.com/jennyproctorbooks

Facebook Fan Group: www.facebook.com/groups/jennyproctorbooks

Bookbub: https://www.bookbub.com/authors/jenny-proctor

Website: www.jennyproctor.com

A NOTE FROM THE AUTHORS

Hey, you! Reader! It's Emma. And I'm so grateful you picked up this book! Jenny and I had so much fun writing Eloise, and maybe more fun (if possible) writing Merritt.

If only you could see our notes to each other in the margins…

I love a good childhood romance turned real thing. Even if the guy I thought I'd marry as a kid promised to marry me if I'd give him my after-school snack, then ate it and laughed, telling me he was lying.

I learned a big lesson that day.

Thankfully, that's not how Merritt and Hunter's story ended. :)

It's a true joy to write books people actually read and enjoy, and we really hope you love this one. We've loved writing the different sisters' stories, and are amped up about rounding out the series with Sadie and (you guessed it) Benedict.

Thanks so much for all the support and for sticking with us on this book journey.

Jenny here! Another Oakley Island Romcom is in the books! Friends, we had so much fun working on this book together.

We honed our process a little, got a little faster, but the one thing that didn't change? How much we LAUGH while we're working.

You know what else is fun? Finally sharing the book with all of YOU. Thank you for reading, for cheering us on, for caring about the world we've created. We hope you love Oakley Island as much as we do.

Also, a special thanks to our beta readers who, when asked if they could read a book in a ridiculously short amount of time, replied with enthusiasm and then gave us excellent feedback that helped give the book just a little extra polish. Until next time!

ACKNOWLEDGMENTS

A giant thank you to Teresa, Jordan, Ali, Rita, Laramee, Cindy, and Lori for the early reads and the great eyes catching all the stupid typos.

Thanks to Rebel Ann for sharing all the rescue animal deets. Miss skating with you, lady.

Also, we're just SO grateful to all the readers and fans and bookstagrammers and silent lurkers (we see you—not really, but we know you're there!) who read and buy and borrow in KU and tell friends. Y'all are the best.

Also, does anyone else feel like they REALLY need a good tomato sandwich now?

Made in United States
North Haven, CT
25 February 2023